To. Jenni

We have time, And not thanks for Keeping me looking young with awesome hair LOL!! Happy Reading and thank you for your Support.

FLESH and DESIRE

A Chloe Pierson series

Christine Cofer

This novel is entirely a work of fiction. The names, characters and incidents portrayed in it are the work of the author's imagination. Any resemblance to actual persons, living or dead, events or localities is entirely coincidental.

First edition

ISBN: 9781698113005

DEDICATION

To my loving husband who has stuck by me since the beginning of this long journey. You are my rock, my conscious, and my anchor. You have given me the strength and courage to follow my dream and made me believe in myself. With you by my side, anything is possible.

To my son. With your creative mind, you will achieve many goals in life. There isn't anything you can't do. I'm so proud of you and all of your accomplishments you have made.

ACKNOWLEDGMENTS

Special thanks to KH Koehler for editing and beautiful book cover

CHAPTER 1

The words *Rising Flame*—written in red—hung above the double glass door on the three-story red brick building. People stood in line along the side of the building, dressed in different styles of gothic and industrial clothing ranging from black mesh shirts, vinyl pants or jeans with chains, colorful corsets or strapless tops with short black or checkered skirts, fishnet stockings, and boots.

"I should've arrived sooner," I mumbled.

The bouncer at the door whistled and motioned for me to step forward. A hint of ink on his right arm peeked out from under the shirt's sleeve as he unclasped a red rope.

People cursed at him for letting me cut to the front of the line. He looked over the top of his sunglasses, which was a little odd for nighttime, and bared a hint of fang as he hissed. Those in front gasped, taking a step back.

The bouncer chuckled and clasped the rope back onto the iron bar.

My eyes widened as I leaned in for a closer look. This was the first time I'd encountered anyone with fangs. "Are those real?"

The man shrugged. "Maybe." He gave a slight nod toward my hand. "Whatcha got there?"

I handed him the invitation. As he read the card, he bobbed his head a couple of times and paused. He glanced back and forth between the card and me several times before asking for my ID.

I pulled my license from my small purse and handed it to him.

He crooked his head to the side as he looked at it, and then stared at me once again.

"What is it now?" I crossed my arms.

"Are you *sure* this invitation is for you?"

"It has my name on it." I stared at him while tapping my foot.

"Do you know anything about this club?"

"No."

He grasped my upper arm and moved us away from the crowd. He shoved the invitation in my face. "You have this and you don't know?"

I flinched, blinked a couple of times, and then repeatedly shook my head. "I don't even know who sent it."

He turned his back on the line of people and took off his sunglasses. His irises blended with the whites of his eyes. The only things noticeable were the small black dots at the center of both eyes—the pupils.

"Nice contacts."

He leaned in closer. "Try again."

As I studied his eyes, I realized he wasn't wearing any contacts. "You were born this way?"

"Depends on what you mean by born, Miss Pierson." He sighed and pointed at the door. "In there you will find the unexplainable. Beings whose existence is unknown to mankind."

He stepped closer, leaned in, and said in a deep, rumbling voice, "Once you step inside, you'll experience erotic pleasure. You'll be pushed to limits you didn't know were possible. It is intense and not for everyone. Most will never get the chance to go inside. Do you think you can handle it?"

"We can!"

The bouncer and I glanced over his shoulder.

Five women had their hands up.

Suddenly, the small hairs on my arms stood on end as if someone had rubbed a balloon against my skin. I'd had no idea a vampire role-playing club even existed in this area. He sure played the vampire part well. I nibbled on my bottom lip and shook my legs back and forth. "I'm sure I can handle whatever's inside."

The man raised his left eyebrow as he gave me a closed-lipped smile. Finally, he placed his sunglasses back on his nose. He swept his hand to the side. "Then, please. Go on in. Give the invitation to the girl at the window." He handed it back along with my ID.

I entered a hallway painted black and decorated with claw marks and splattered red paint that was supposed to look like blood on the walls. Mirrors on the ceiling reflected the burgundy carpet.

At the end of the hall, a girl behind a small window flipped through a magazine while blowing pink bubbles through the wad of bubblegum stuffed in her mouth.

I placed the invitation next to the slot under the window. "I'm supposed to give this to you."

The girl glanced at me just like the man outside had. She scooted to the edge of the chair and opened her mouth to say something when the phone rang. She answered on the second ring.

"Yes." She paused, still staring at me. "But,

why? She isn't…" The girl relaxed her tight posture and her shoulders sagged. "Yes, of course. Not a problem."

The girl hung up and grabbed a small, round stamp. "May I see your hand?"

I slipped my hand under the window and she stamped the back, leaving a red VIP imprint.

"What does the VIP get me?"

The girl gave me a sideways grin. "You'll find out soon enough. Enjoy your evening."

"Thanks."

When I touched the double glass doors that led to the club, the pulsing techno music from the other side vibrated in my fingertips, continued down my arms, and then passed through my body. The loud music deafened me as I pulled the door open.

The club's seductive ambiance made me feel as if I was in a strip club. Red strobe lights from the ceiling crisscrossed with the white lights on the dance floor. Cages, placed randomly on the floor, contained male and or female dancers. Large movie screens displayed the images of flickering flames along the walls.

My stomach quivered, and the static sensation I'd felt outside became stronger as it swept through me. I tried to ignore the tightness in my belly as I searched for an empty table, but it was a full house.

I squeezed my way through the mob to the bar and ordered a chocolate martini. The girl behind the counter smiled.

A man slapped the counter with the palm of his hand, making me jump at the sudden noise. "Hey, Riley, I need a cold one real quick."

I had been so focused on the bartender's eyes—a red-orange hue with small, pepper-like specks—that I never notice the man slipping up beside me.

The bartender placed my drink on the bar and handed the man a bottle of water. "You know Cyrus doesn't like us drinking while on the clock."

The man frowned and leaned on the bar. "Seriously?"

"Hey, I'm only obeying the rules."

I rolled my eyes and asked, "How much do I owe?"

Riley, the bartender, licked her bottom lip and took my hand in hers. She tapped the temporary tattoo on the back of my hand. "This will get you whatever you want. Money is no option." She winked and let my hand slip out of her grasp before helping the next girl in line.

The heat from Riley's touch was twice the normal human temperature. I rubbed my palm while I watched her pull two bottles out of the ice cooler, popped the caps off, and make a daiquiri.

The girl next to me pointed at my hand. "How did you get that?"

I shrugged. "I had a special invite."

"Oh! Who did you sleep with?" The girl snickered.

"Excuse me?" The girl was annoying me. It was none of her business how I'd gotten the invite. I even wondered myself.

The man next to me moved to stand in front of the girl, placing his hand on the counter. "I think you should take your drinks and move on. We don't want to cause a scene, now do we?"

The girl ran her finger down the front of his abs and smiled. "Not unless you wish to punish me."

Riley picked up a number of beer bottles and placed them heavily on the counter, making a loud *thunk*.

The girl's smile faded when she looked at Riley. She took her drinks and left the bar.

The guy next to me took a drink of water and turned to me, hand extended. "I'm Drake. One of the entertainers."

I looked into his Arctic blue eyes and nearly melted. "I'm Chloe. Nice to meet you--and thank you for stepping in."

"You're welcome. Chick was out of line. Would you like a private dance?" Drake gulped more water as he stared at me.

Raising my eyebrows, I looked around, but it didn't look like a strip club. Was I missing something?

Drake gave me a slight grin and licked his bottom lip. "You're new here, aren't you?"

"Is it that obvious?"

Drake set the empty bottle on the counter.

My eyes trailed down his belly. His tight abs glistened under the red lights. There was an aching need to have him between my legs. I'd never before reacted like this to a man I didn't know.

Drake placed his finger under my chin, raising my head. "Let me show you."

I found myself pulling away. I wanted more than a dance from him. "I'm good, but thank you."

"If you change your mind, I will be over there. Enjoy your evening, Chloe." He headed for the cage to the left of the dance floor.

Riley put another drink on the counter and placed a stool at the end of the bar. "Here. Have a seat before you fall." She laughed.

"Thanks."

"Are you enjoying the club so far?"

"Yeah, it's…ah…different."

Riley nodded to the right. "You're on someone's radar."

I turned, sipping my drink. A man on the second floor VIP lounge was watching me. His black hair was draped over the left side of his face and cascaded down his shoulder to his pectoral muscles.

"Who is he?"

"His name is Erik. He's one of the dancers here."

Erik and I stared at each other. He stood there like a statue and not once did he move--even when a girl draped her arms over his shoulders. She placed her hand on his cheek, pulling the side of his face to her lips. But, he didn't acknowledge her.

I smiled, looking away. "Is she his girlfriend?"

Riley rested her arms on the counter. "Her name is Josephine. As for being Erik's girlfriend, I'm not sure what they are. But, you need to watch out for her. Don't make a big deal over Erik."

She began wiping the counter. "The way he is focusing on you…" She shook her head. "Josephine picks up on this stuff. She is the jealous type."

"How long has the club been here? I've lived here all of my life and I've never heard of it."

"I'm not sure. I've only been here for about two years." Riley glanced at the other end of the bar and excused herself.

I sipped my drink a few more times until it turned into gulps. Before I knew it, I had an empty glass. I observed the club a bit more. There were many good-looking males here. How could anyone choose only one?

I still couldn't shake the vibrations strumming deep inside of me. Was I nervous? No. Anxiety? Maybe. Whatever it was, it wasn't going away. It was only growing stronger.

I noticed Erik descending the stairs. There was no bounce to his movements. He approached a woman with wavy gold hair and took her by the hand, leading her to the dance floor. He wrapped his arm around her and their hips moved in synchronized motion. She tilted her head as he kissed along her neck. I could see the pleasure on her face as she closed her eyes and parted her mouth before licking her lips.

I wanted to experience the erotic pleasure of dancing with one of them, too. I turned my attention to Drake. Women had gathered around with their hands in the air, trying to touch him. He caught me watching and the corner of his mouth curled up into a grin. The muscles in his arms flexed as he held onto the bars of the cage and pulled himself forward, thrusting his hips to the beat of the music. Each time he moved, his abs contracted tighter.

My heart raced as Drake stared at me. He raised his eyebrows as if waiting for me to come to him. But, I hesitated too long. A redhead caressed Drake's thigh through his tight pants. He looked at her with a smile and opened the door, pulling her in.

She yelped as her hands slid along his chest. She wore a short skirt, and when she brought her leg around Drake, I could see her black thong as she rubbed herself against him like a dog in heat.

I couldn't take my eyes off Drake. The way he rolled his hips revealed what talent he likely had in bed. I could only imagine being trapped under him with the sheets tangled around us. The weight of his body grinding into me. My core burned with a desire to be with him.

This wasn't me. I didn't behave this way.

A tap on my shoulder interrupted my erotic fantasy.

"You like him, don't you?" Riley rested her elbows on the bar.

I swiveled around to face her. "I don't know him well enough to like him."

"The thing is…you don't have to know him. It's all about living in the moment with the sensation of pleasure enveloping you. You should consider having a private dance with him. You won't be disappointed."

"Have you had one?"

"Yes. When I first came here. I saw they needed a bartender, so here I am."

"How was it?"

Riley's cheeks turned a light shade of pink as she rubbed her chin on her shoulder. "How should I put this? He's very…attentive. He takes his time to admire every part of you." She shook her head. "I can't explain it. You would have to see for yourself."

"Are you two a couple?"

Riley smiled. "No, we're not together." She excused herself again and walked away.

I pushed away from the counter and made my way around the club. I saw an orange sign with *Private* over an open doorway. A man stood next to the entrance with his arms crossed, which made his biceps look even bigger in the dark shirt. His light and dark brown hair rested on his shoulders.

I poked my head around the corner. A stairwell, rounding to the left and then down, was lit by a blacklight.

"You're not allowed down there alone."

I gasped, jerking my head to the left, and then stood up straight. "Huh? Oh, sorry. No, I was just…"

"You know what curiosity did to the cat?"

My mouth dropped open.

The guy bent forward, arms still crossed. "I'm kidding."

I managed a smile. "Oh, right. What's down there?"

The guy pointed above his head.

"That could mean anything."

He noticed the red mark on my hand. "Why do you have a VIP stamp?"

I shrugged. "Someone sent an invitation to me. It's my birthday."

"Oh, well, happy birthday."

"Why does everyone keep asking me about this stamp?" I held up my hand.

"Only people like us are marked with it."

"What do you mean like us?"

The guy grinned. "You have no idea, do you?"

I stared into his teal eyes. They had shards of silver that reflected like a mirror. They must have been contacts. They all seemed to have them.

"No idea about what?"

The guy stepped back, licking his lips. "You're not that observant, are you?" He chuckled. "You here alone?"

"Yes. Why?"

"A girl like you shouldn't come here alone."

I tilted my head to the side. "Are you going to tell me what's downstairs?"

He shook his head. "You'll find out soon enough, I'm sure."

"What's that supposed to mean?"

He let out a small laugh. "What's your name?"

"Chloe."

"Well, Chloe, go on and enjoy yourself. Scope out the club. Do your homework or whatever. Don't worry about what's down there…for now."

CHAPTER 2

I forced myself not to look in Drake's direction. Taking the guy's advice, I headed to the dance floor, joining the others as they jumped to the beat. Spinning around, I saw Erik standing across from me. He made his way in my direction gracefully, as if he was sliding on ice. The entire time, he and I couldn't pull our gaze away from each other.

I was drawn to him. I could feel the invisible lasso around my waist as he pulled me in. Before I knew it, he was inches away. I couldn't move. I felt frozen as if time stood still. The air surrounding me felt so powerful and heavy I thought it was going to crush me. The need to touch him gnawed at me, but I held back.

Erik's magnetic attraction was even more intense and inviting than Drake's. He took my hand, bringing it to his lips for a kiss. "I'm Erik."

I didn't know what to say. I knew I had to say something, but nothing came out right away. I felt like an idiot.

Erik raised his eyebrows as if waiting for a response.

Still holding his hand, I cleared my throat. "Uh, Chloe."

"It is a pleasure, Chloe." He glanced at the mark on my hand and his smile widened. "What would you like this evening?"

I didn't have a clue as to what he was referring to. Sex? A drink? Hanging out? Again, no words formed upon my lips.

Erik chuckled. "How about a dance?"

"As long as I don't have to dance in one of those." I pointed to an empty cage.

Erik swooped me into his arms and spun me around. The warmth of his body caressed me. I placed my hands on his upper arms, squeezing lightly as he flexed his muscles. My hands slid to his shoulders and around his neck. I trailed my fingers along his jawline to the gap of his shirt, which exposed his smooth skin. I moved the shirt to the side, laying my hand over his heart. It beat against my palm and seemed to match the rhythm of the music.

Erik slipped behind me, placing my back against his chest. I tilted my head as the other girl had done, anticipating his next move. His breath brushed the tiny hairs on my neck as he nibbled my ear lobe. Goosebumps formed along my arms from his touch. I closed my eyes, visualizing the two of us alone. His hands massaged my shoulders as his lips moved along my collarbone.

I gasped, sucking air between my teeth. He's so erotic. Drake, too. Everything about them screamed sex.

When the music switched to a different tune, Erik kissed my cheek and whispered, "Thank you."

I watched Erik disappear to the second floor, leaving me weak. I placed my hand over my heart, panting. "Oh, my God."

A girl bounced around me, yelling, "Isn't he amazing? Do you know what he is?"

I stared at the girl, blinking. "Huh?"

The girl laughed, playfully hitting the side of my arm. "He's a vampire, silly! Which do you prefer? Vampire or lycan?"

The girl danced and jumped in circles around me. "I can tell you who's who if you want. I'm a regular here. I can't get enough of them."

I pressed my lips together tightly, trying not to laugh. Was this girl on drugs? She believed they were real. I wished they were. "No, thank you."

I glanced at a dark area on the second floor where two glowing red embers caught my attention. I assumed it was the lights hitting someone's eyes, but no one else seemed to have that issue. I wanted to look away, but it appealed to me. A figure was starting to form. Just as I was about to see what was causing the glow, Drake stepped in front of me, blocking the view. With his chest in my face, the orbs of light weren't of interest anymore.

"So, you'll dance with Erik and not me?"

I tried stepping back to give us some room, but my feet wouldn't move. "Well, um, he's not in a cage."

He held his arms out to the side. His shirt dangled in one hand. "I'm not in one now."

"He has on a shirt."

"Is this how you're going to play?" He pulled his shirt over his head, tugging it over his fit body. "Better? Less distracting?"

He stepped near me, whispering in my ear, "Let me guess. Erik drew you in with those hypnotic eyes, yes?" He slowly pulled away. "Dance with me."

His hands rested on my hips. My pulse didn't slow. In fact, the adrenaline had been pumping since I'd arrived. I was still reeling from the dance with Erik--and now Drake was against me.

"Why are you stalling? Do I intimidate you?"

"Are you like this with all the women?"

"No, just you."

"Why?"

"Because the others are willing and eager. You, on the other hand, are hesitant. Which makes me more attracted to you."

God help me. Why did he have to be so damn good looking? Why did they all have to be so attractive?

Drake took my hand, directing me to the private area. The guy guarding the door winked and stepped aside to let us pass without a word.

Drake helped me down the narrow stairwell and into a hall. I got a preview of what was to come as I caught sight of the many occupied rooms. Half-naked dancers performed for their lucky victims.

"Drake? What's going on?"

"This is where we give our private dances."

Not only did my palms begin to sweat again, but beads were also forming on my forehead. My pulse quickened even more as he led me farther down the dark hall and into one of the rooms. A black chair was situated in the corner, and a small bed, covered with a red silk sheet, was pushed against the opposite wall.

Drake stripped off his shirt and began unbuttoning his pants.

I grabbed his hands. "No, don't." I swallowed the lump in my throat and stepped back. "Drake, I don't think I can do this."

"Nothing bad is going to happen."

He stared at me for a moment and then placed his hands on my hips.

"Have you been to a strip club before?"

"Of course I have. It was for a bachelorette party."

"But you were not the guest of honor."

"No. I sat there and watched."

The pulsing sensation in my body had now

spread to between my legs. A few minutes ago, I'd wanted the erotic pleasure of dancing with them and now…I was enjoying this attention. Why was I having such a difficult time with this? Because I wanted to do more with him and it scared me.

I didn't sleep around. I hadn't even been in a relationship for a long time. A few years, at least. I was always busy with work or taking care of my mother. I never had time for myself. My last relationship ended because I couldn't commit. I was hurt, but I wasn't going to get depressed over it. It wasn't meant to be.

Drake kept walking forward, making me back up until my legs hit the bed. "That's too bad. All you have to do is lie down or sit in the chair. Let me do all the work. You can touch me anywhere. Even here."

My eyes widened as he grabbed himself.

Drake kissed the mark on my hand. "Only those with the stamp can touch and, like Riley said, this gives you anything you want."

He placed my hand between his pecs. His muscles twitched as he guided my fingers down the crevice between his abs and to the top of his jeans. I was ready to lie on the bed and let him do whatever he wanted to me. Maybe I would be safer in the chair.

I didn't have time to decide. I found myself on my back as Drake's hands slid up my thighs and pushed my skirt up to my waist. That exposed my lace thong. He placed soft kisses along my inner thigh. His breath tickled and I let out a giggle. His tongue trailed closer to the edge of my thong. He looked up at me and smiled. I knew he could feel the heat escaping from my skin.

He shimmied his way up my body and held my arms above my head, kissing my neck. I felt his erection as he moved his hips into me. My hard nipples strained against the corset. It only caused my core to ignite more. I was close to reaching an orgasm. He was that good.

I closed my eyes, moaning his name. "Oh, Drake."

When he let go of my arms, I managed to caress his back. My nails dug into his shoulders. I was ready for him. I needed him. In the heat of the moment, I began unzipping his jeans, but his voice broke my groove.

"Chloe."

My eyes snapped open. I wasn't sure if he'd said my name to make me aware of what I was doing or if he was in the moment, too. He held himself up with his arms and I looked into his eyes. They were changing to a lighter blue. Almost an ice color. I swear I'd heard a low growl rumble up from his throat.

I pushed him the rest of the way off. "I'm sorry. I didn't mean…I need to go."

I ran out of the room, almost knocking the security guy over as I pushed past, heading to the other side of the club to get as far away as possible. Since the upper section was for VIPs, I knew I had passage.

Even though a man guarding the stairs was busy chatting with a couple of girls, it didn't stop him from grabbing my wrist. He examined the mark and then let go, tilting his head at the stairs.

At the top, a section on the right with tables was roped off. Straight ahead was a dimly lit hall and I headed in that direction. I leaned against the wall, resting my hands on my knees while I tried to calm myself. I should have left the building, but a part of me still wanted to stay.

A low moan at the end of the hall caught my attention. A beam of light streamed across the floor. I crept to the open door and peeked inside. I wasn't prepared for the horror unfolding before me. I stumbled backward and hit the wall, unable to avert my eyes. It wasn't fear as much as it was disbelief.

"No way," I whispered.

Erik had a woman bent over the back of a red leather couch. I realized she was the one Riley had warned me about—Josephine. His teeth were sunk into her neck as he feasted. He licked the wound and gradually raised his head. Blood dribbled from the corner of his mouth to his chin and his fangs were exposed. His eyes were no longer dark. From a distance, he seemed to have empty sockets. His head jerked in my direction. His brow furrowed and his mouth curled, twitching as he let out a hiss.

I gasped. In one swift motion, Erik was inches from me. I swear I didn't even see him move. How the hell had he done that? I could see my reflection in his obsidian eyes. I wasn't afraid. Only curious. The smell of blood flooded my nose. The need to lick his mouth confused me.

Erik inhaled slowly and exhaled with an "Ahhh." He smiled, showing his crimson-stained teeth. "I smell Drake on you. Did you enjoy yourself?"

Before I could answer, a voice behind him called out. "Who do we have here?"

A hand slipped over his shoulder, moved him to the side, and Josephine stepped up next to Erik. "A curious cat, I see. Do you want to play?"

"You mean role play?"

Josephine closed the space between us, glancing at my hand. "You're not one of us. Is this a game to you?"

"No, I assumed…"

"Don't assume anything. For someone who witnessed something they shouldn't have, you don't seem scared."

"Because I'm not."

"You should be."

"Back off!" Erik stepped in front of Josephine,

pushing her back. “Leave her alone.”

“She doesn’t belong up here. If Cyrus were to…”

“Look…” I held up my hands. “I’m sorry for intruding. I was exploring and there wasn’t a sign stating I couldn’t come this way.”

“We will have to change that.” Josephine crossed her arms and stood with slanted hips.

“I’ll go. Don’t worry. I won’t say anything.”

I fled down the stairs to the main floor, shoving away or dodging the people in my way. I could hear Josephine’s cackle of a laugh even above the loud music. The people outside in line jumped back when I burst through the doors.

“What’s wrong, Chloe?” The bouncer yelled.

I ignored him as I ran around the block to my car. I fumbled to get the keys out of my purse. Once safely in the car, I gripped the steering wheel.

“Shit! What the hell just happened? Was it even real?”

I lightly banged my head on the steering wheel. “It can’t be real. They were playing.”

I’d heard of people pretending to be vampires by drinking blood and sharpening their teeth, but I hadn’t seen any fangs on Erik when we danced. Not until I witnessed…well, his feasting. And, his eyes changed color so fast.

The only thing clear to me was my attraction to a blood-drinking fiend. So, what was Drake? A lycan?

I started the car and left behind the most erotic men I had ever encountered. The farther away from the club I drove, the more the static vanished. In its place was a severe headache and stomach cramps. Maybe I needed food? I hadn’t eaten dinner and I did drink in the club. I pulled into a McDonald’s drive-through and ordered a nugget meal with a Diet Dr. Pepper.

I had the meal gone by the time I pulled into the driveway. I sat there for a moment before getting out of the car. My hands were gripping the steering wheel to the point where my knuckles had turned white. I let go and shook off the pain.

My stomach became queasy. I opened the car door and fell to my knees, vomiting in the yard. After a few minutes, I was fine, but the hair on the back of my neck was standing on end. You know the feeling you get when you know someone is watching? I sensed it beyond the trees. I tilted my head, listening.

A swift breeze caressed my skin, yet not a single leaf moved on the trees. I held onto the car door to help me stay on my feet and hurried inside. I locked the door and leaned against it.

Taking two Tylenol from my purse, I went to the kitchen for a glass of water. Standing at the sink, I saw the same two red orbs from the club in the woods. The glass slipped from my trembling hand, shattering in the sink.

I squeezed my eyes shut. “It’s not real. I’m tired and it’s only an animal,” I mumbled.

When I glanced back out the window, it was gone. I closed the blinds and cleaned up the broken glass. One of the shards cut my finger.

“Ouch! Damn it!”

I ran my finger under cold water, and when the blood disappeared, my finger looked fine.

“What the hell?” I examined it but found nothing wrong. “I need sleep.”

I went upstairs to get ready for bed. Grunting and wiggling, I managed my way out of the black and red corset.

“How did I manage to get this thing on? Ugh!”

Finally free of confinement, I put on a t-shirt and climbed into bed, snuggling under the white fluffy comforter. It was going to be one of those nights where it was hard to fall asleep. For a year, it was because of my mother. Now, it was because of the sexual tension building up inside me all evening.

I lay there, staring at the ceiling before turning to look at the window. Then, I turned to the other side to stare at the wall. I fluffed the pillow and lay on my stomach. Rolling onto my back, I moaned and slapped the bed.

I grabbed the TV remote to watch the news, which I never do. Nothing changes. Same old information. Shootings, car crashes, and fires. One brief announcement was about a woman found dead in her apartment near Soulard. That was it. No other information.

I switched to some horror movie on SyFy. I didn't make it halfway through. I finally turned it off.

When I closed my eyes, images of Erik flashed through my mind. At first, it was the beauty of his flawless skin. Next, he was drenched in blood. All of a sudden, I saw Drake naked, beckoning me to come to him. I was trapped between the two. I couldn't decide who I wanted more. Closer and closer, they inched their way to me until it was only Drake standing there. He picked me up, holding me against the wall.

I began massaging my breasts. When I pinched my nipples, my body jolted at the pain. The tension that had been building since I left the club was released. Panting, I rolled over and into a ball. It had been so long since I'd wanted someone sexually.

I mean, yes, I'd fantasized about celebrity men. But, not someone I'd met.

I didn't know what to do. I wanted to go back to the club. I wanted more from Drake. I even wanted Erik. Seeing him with Josephine made me want him to bite me in the same manner. I was curious. What did it feel like?

Was it painful? Was it erotic?

My body became aroused again just thinking about it. I reached down and caressed myself between the thighs. Closing my eyes, I saw Erik's dark eyes and fangs as he hissed. My fingers moved with my hips. I called out his name as I reached my peak, finally erupting into a massive release.

I lay there, panting. My body sated and relaxed, it sent me into nothingness.

CHAPTER 3

I woke the next day with the sun's warm rays illuminating the room. Rubbing my eyes, I glanced at the clock. It was one in the afternoon. I hadn't meant to sleep late, but even after the sleepless night I'd had, I could have slept longer.

A noise from the balcony caught my attention. A shadow behind the sheer curtain transformed into human form. No one could access the balcony unless they climbed the tree next to it or went through my room.

I threw the covers off and grabbed my Bo staff from the closet. I tiptoed to the balcony and moved the curtain aside with my staff. No one was there except a blackbird perched on the rail. It squawked and fluttered its wings when it noticed me. Its beady eyes were not the normal black they should have been. Instead, they were red.

I threw my hand over my mouth, letting the curtain fall into place. I peered again through the curtain. The bird was still there. It tilted its head as I stepped onto the balcony.

Something was different about these red eyes as compared to the ones I'd seen last night. They were not evil looking. They seemed to have compassion. Maybe it was because I was seeing them during the day.

"What do you want? Shoo! Shoo!" I swiped my hand at the bird but it didn't move. "Are you hungry?"

The bird took two hops in my direction.

"Go find a worm."

It ruffled its feathers, shaking its head as if to say, "No."

"Oh, my God! I'm talking to a freaking bird. I have lost my mind."

I shut the balcony door and changed before going outside to check the mail. On the way to the porch, the blackbird landed in front of me. I jumped, tripping over my own feet, and almost fell on my ass.

"What the hell, bird?"

It was standing on the *Riverfront Times* paper. It wasn't there a minute ago. I picked it up and it was only a torn page advertising the Rising Flame club.

"What is going on?" I looked around to see if anyone was watching. Someone had to have put it there. "Is this a joke?"

When I turned back to the porch, the bird was no longer there. I didn't even hear it fly away. I stared at the article, wanting to go back. A part of me needed to see Erik and Drake again. But, I wasn't sure if I could face them after what had happened.

As I reached for the handle on the screen door, a voice from behind called to me.

"Hello, Miss Pierson."

I spun around and gasped. Erik stood at the foot of the steps.

"Are you trying to give me a heart attack? How…?"

He held up his hand, shushing me. "Before you

ask how I knew your last name and where to find you..." He took three slow steps to the porch and held a piece of paper in front of me.

"What is that?"

"Your invitation." He took two more steps, pinning me against the door. "You're a little flush, Miss Pierson. Is the heat getting to you?" He leaned in, whispering next to my ear. "Or is it something else?"

He moved his head to the right, making me look into his eyes. His lips were inches from mine.

I cleared my throat and managed to ask if he wanted to come in.

He moved away, leaning against the post. "No. I can't stay long. I shouldn't even be here."

With him at a distance, I was able to breathe again. But only a little. "Then why are you here?"

Erik stepped to the shaded part of the porch, smiling as he waved a finger. "You piqued my curiosity, my dear. I was too busy to notice at first, but Josephine is right. You're not one of us."

He was messing with me. It was an act. He wasn't a real vampire. How else would he be able to stand here during the day?

"Erik, I don't know who sent me the invite or why I was stamped. I assumed it was a birthday present. But, don't worry, I won't tell anyone what I saw."

"Birthday, huh? If I had known, I would've given you a private show, as well." He smiled with a wink. "I know you won't tell anyone. I'm not worried about that."

"What are you worried about, then?"

"Josephine sees you as a threat. She doesn't like competition. You impressed me last night, standing up to her."

"I'm not afraid of her, and who says I'm competing? I was there having fun like everyone else."

"But, you were the one in a non-secure location." Erik kissed my cheek and slipped on a pair of sunglasses. "See you tonight, Chloe." He spun on his heel and trotted down the steps.

"Who said I was going back?"

"You will. They all do." He disappeared behind some bushes.

I waited for him to reappear, but he never did. I went inside and plopped down in a plush chair, throwing my arm over my eyes. I shouldn't go just to prove him wrong. But, how could I not go back? There was a gnawing sensation eating away at my gut. A need to return. A myriad of questions bombarded my mind about last night and I wanted answers.

Tingling sensations developed along my arms and legs. A sharp pain stabbed me in the stomach, nearly knocking me out of the chair. The pains had been occurring off and on since I went to the club. Food didn't seem to help.

My phone went off in my pocket. It was my friend Hannah from work, texting me to see if we were still working out today. I'd forgotten it was our workout day. I wasn't going to go, but what a better way to work off stress.

Yep. Be there in a few.

I grabbed a pair of shorts and a shirt and shoved them into my gym bag.

When I arrived at the gym, the parking lot was half full. I guessed the partiers from the night before were still sleeping it off—as I should have been.

I entered the reception area where an employee was stocking tanning supplies on the back shelf. She looked over her shoulder with a smile. "Hey, how are ya?"

"I'm good. How about you?" I swiped my membership card through the small machine.

"I'm good. We have a tanning special going on today if you are interested."

"No, thank you. See ya later." I headed to the back of the gym where the locker room was. I liked having a locker in the far back for privacy.

I put my bag next to me on the bench and pulled out my shorts, tank top, and shoes. As I was undressing, I heard laughter echo off the walls as someone entered the room and two locker doors were opened and shut. A few seconds later, two girls walked by with their bags as they headed to the shower area. There was a counter with a huge mirror and four wall outlets for hair dryers or curling irons. They undressed and stepped into a shower stall together, closing the door behind them.

I found myself standing there with my mouth partially opened. Visions of what the two girls were doing made my skin flush with embarrassment and envy. I finished getting dressed, and by the time I put on my shoes, one of the girl's moans had become louder. I put in my earbuds and turned on the music. Hurrying out of the room, I bumped into Hannah.

"Oh! Hey! Sorry."

She laughed. "Are you in that much of a rush to work out? You look a little flushed."

"I'm fine."

"Let me put my stuff in the locker. I'll meet you at the treadmills."

Hannah and I had been friends for about a year. I was the one who trained her when she was hired. We connected right away, but we were like flowers with many layers of petals. One by one, we'd learned a little more about each other. I envied her. She was gorgeous.

We both had long brown hair, but my eyes were green and hers were brown. I wished I could tan as easily as she did. But, I didn't. The only thing the sun did was turn me into a lobster.

I was setting the timer for thirty minutes when Hannah jumped on the treadmill next to me. I began a short warm-up. After five minutes, I cranked it up to speed walking.

The girl to the left of me was jogging, and soon Hannah was jogging, too. Not me. I hated running. Sure, I ran outside while playing as a kid, but I never did it for sport. It was my downfall in high school. I was always the last one to finish in gym class when we had to run track.

I had a steady pace going, matching the beat to the music that was playing in my ear. I ignored the boring TV shows playing on the flat screens above. Instead, I checked out the guys lifting weights. One caught my attention and I lost my footing. I almost tripped over my own feet. Grabbing the sides of the machine, I pulled my feet off to the side rail. Thank God no one noticed--except for Hannah.

She slowed the machine until she came to a stop and then took out her earphones. "You done?"

"Yeah. I'm going to go work on some weights. You coming?"

"I'm going to finish my jog. I'll be there in a few."

I stood for a good five minutes, trying to figure out how to use the equipment. I studied the pictures, but I couldn't seem to comprehend what I was supposed to do.

"You seem confused."

I spun around and saw the security guy from the club—the one near the privacy area—was leaning on one of the machines. Since I could see him better in the light than in the dark club, I noticed he was eye-catching. His hair was pulled into a man bun, which most women find sexy. Some men can't pull it off, but he sure as hell could. I glanced at his biceps and he playfully flexed them.

I looked away, my cheeks burning with embarrassment. “Confused? Yes. This looks like an alien torture chamber. I don’t know how to use any of this stuff. It’s why I’ve never tried.”

He laughed, holding out his hand. “I never properly introduced myself. Name’s Kyle. I can show you how to use this. It’s no problem.” He reached down, setting the weighs on forty-five, and then patted the blue seat. “Put your knees on here and either hold onto the bars at your side or above your head.”

As I put my weight on the seat, it sank down.

“Whoa!” I grabbed onto the side bar and he held onto my waist.

“Now, let yourself slide down and then push yourself back up.”

I did five reps and then stopped to give my arms a rest.

“Now, if you want to do pull-ups, grab onto the bars above your head and pull up. Let your weight guide you back down.”

I did ten reps and stopped. I hadn’t realized how hard these machines were. I did two more reps of ten, resting in between. I climbed off the seat, rubbing my arms.

“That wasn’t so bad.” I lied.

“You want to learn a few more?”

I would have loved nothing more than to watch him lift weights, but every time I looked at him, I felt all giggly inside. “Bring it on.”

Kyle nodded. “Okay, then.” He went to the next machine and set the weight. He reached up with one hand and pulled down. “Come here.”

Kyle stood behind me. “Put your legs at shoulder width and grab the handle with both hands.”

I laughed. My dirty mind had me grabbing

something else.

"Sorry." I took the handle as instructed.

"Now, pull down only using the elbows and not the whole arm. Try and do ten reps, and breathe out as you pull down."

"Hey, Chloe. Who's your friend?" Hannah strolled up behind me.

I finished my ten and carefully let the weight go. "This is Kyle. Kyle, meet Hannah."

She batted her long lashes as she always does and smiled. "Nice to meet you. I was heading over to the café. You two want to join me?"

I glanced at the small café near the entrance where they sold salads, wraps, water, energy drinks, and energy bars. "Yeah. I could eat."

Kyle followed us to a table and offered to buy us lunch. I ordered a water and a chicken wrap. Hannah chose a salad.

I watched Kyle as he swayed side to side while waiting in line. The back of his dark blue tank curved inward, exposing his back shoulder muscles. My eyes trailed down to the roundness of his ass and then ended on his thick calves.

I turned my attention to the window to calm my nerves. I'd already had sexual thoughts about Drake and Erik. I didn't need another. I smiled at the thought, wiggling in my seat.

"My God, Chloe. Where did you meet him? He's hot."

"He works security at the club I went to last night."

"Wow! I still feel bad that I couldn't join you last night."

"Don't worry about it. It's not your fault you had a bridal shower to go to."

"I just wished I could've gone with you instead,

but as maid of honor, I had to report for duty. So, how was the club?"

"It was different."

"Different…how?"

I shrugged. "It's not like any other club."

"Did you figure out who sent the invitation?"

"No, but I got VIP treatment."

Hannah scooted her chair closer. "Spill. What happened?"

I shook my head. "Don't want to talk about it right now."

"Are all the guys there as hot as he is? You need to see if he's single. You want me to ask?"

"No. Don't you dare."

Hannah laughed. "Fine, but you need to get some action and soon. You're too uptight these days."

"What are you smiling at?" Kyle asked as he placed the food and drinks on the table.

"Huh?" I snapped my head around. "Oh, it's nothing."

"Are you sure?"

I quickly shoved my mouth full of food and, with a nod, said, "Mmm-hmm."

"By the way, what happened last night? You practically knocked me over when you left the privacy area."

With my sandwich wrap in my hands and my mouth full, I froze. What was I going to say now? Hannah glared at me, her eyebrows raised.

"Privacy area? What kind of club is this?"

Kyle's eyes met mine. I tilted my head to the side a little, trying to send a message to him not to talk about the club in front of her. I think he realized his mistake and saved the situation.

Kyle smiled. "It's nothing. She just wandered off into a part of the club that was for employees only.

So, what's your story, Chloe? What do you do?"

I washed down the food with a gulp of water and dabbed my mouth with a napkin. "We work for a cosmetic surgeon."

"You say that like it's a bad thing. Do you not like your job?"

"I do, but it's not what I want to do. My passion is writing. It gives me the freedom to escape into another world. I have this saying…'Freedom of imagination is creation.'"

Kyle sat back in his chair. "Wow! That's deep. What do you write about?"

Hannah laid her hand on my shoulder. "She writes about sex. It's hot."

"Hannah! Really?" I rolled my eyes. "I write many things. Novels and short stories. Suspense, erotica, and the paranormal. Also, poetry and songs."

"Most of which has sex." Hannah laughed.

"Nothing wrong with that," Kyle said. "Are you going to publish anything?"

"Someday. What I am working on isn't ready for the public eye. What about you?" I tossed the last of the wrap in my mouth.

"Well, you already know I work at the club, but I also take classes and work part-time with my step-dad."

"What are you going to school for?" Hannah asked.

"Right now, I am majoring in English Literature. Not sure what I want to do at this point." Kyle glanced down at his watch. "I need to get going. I have to work tonight. Hope to see you again soon." He winked.

Hannah and I watched him walk out the door and to his car.

"If you don't hook up with him, I sure as hell will." Hannah licked her lips.

"You never cease to amaze me, Hannah. I need to go, as well."

"Oh, come on. Really? I thought we could hit the mall or something. I need some new outfits."

"Hannah, you have enough clothes to start your own shop."

"You can never have enough. Who likes to wear the same thing twice?"

I got up and threw my trash away. "Clearly, you don't."

We went to the locker room to get our things and then said our goodbyes. I did need a new outfit for the club, but I wasn't going to get it with Hannah there. I knew of a store I could go to called GOTh IT. Yes, that is how it's spelled on the store. The capital letters spell GOT IT. They had all kinds of industrial, rock, and metal attire and accessories.

It took me two hours to complete a look, and then I headed home to get ready for the evening.

CHAPTER 4

The same bouncer was outside the club, and he smiled when he saw me walking toward him.

He unhooked the rope. "Well, I didn't expect to see you again. Why did you hurry out last night? Thought you said you could handle it."

"I didn't take it seriously."

"And now?"

"Even more intrigued." We both smiled

"I'm Devin, by the way," the bouncer said.

"Good to know."

Someone had called my name from the line of people. A hand popped up overhead, waving. Hannah stepped out of line and came over to me.

"What are you doing here?" I asked.

"You got me curious about the place."

I wanted to tell her she shouldn't be here, but then she would say, "Well you are," and I didn't want to argue. Nothing I said would make her change her mind. I looked at Devin, the security guy, thinking he would restrict her. If he did, I wouldn't be able to go in. I would feel bad about leaving her alone. To my shock, he let her pass.

"Go ahead. Enter at your own risk." He opened

the door and we stepped in.

"I love your outfit, Chloe. It's sexy. I wished I had something else on."

"Thanks, but you look amazing, as always."

Hannah's eyes widened when she saw the wall of photos. "Oh…my…God." She examined each and every one. "This one is cute. His name is Luke. Where is Kyle?"

"These are the entertainers. He's not here."

"Entertainers?" Hannah clapped her hands, bouncing up and down. "Is this a strip club?"

"Sort of. You'll see soon enough. Please be careful in there, and don't wander off like I did."

The same girl sat at the window and, this time, she was polite. "Good evening, Chloe." She reached for the stamp, waiting for me to put my hand on the counter.

I tried to get by without it, but the girl wouldn't let me.

"You can't go in unless your hand is stamped."

"I thought you did that yesterday because of the invite?"

"I'm only obeying orders." She held the stamp closer to the window. "Please."

"Orders from who?" I didn't mind getting free drinks, but what I didn't want was the attention. Who was I kidding? Of course I wanted their attention. It was why I was here. Plus, I had to find out more about the club.

"I'm not entitled to say. Just doing my job."

I slipped my right hand through the slot. The pressure from the stamp left a red wet mark. When I stepped away, Hannah slipped her hand through without a second thought.

The girl behind the window shook her head. "Afraid not, sweetie."

"Why?"

"I have rules to follow. And you having a stamp is not one of them."

I took Hannah by the wrist. "Be thankful. Come on."

When I opened the doors, I began scanning the room for Drake. He was in his cage, dancing with a girl. The sight of him made my pulse beat rapidly against my neck. My mouth watered as I licked my lips. I wanted to turn around and leave, but my gut was pulling me farther inside. I wanted to be here. I needed to be here. The craving was gnawing at my insides. My body vibrated and tingled the same way it had last night.

"This is badass. Did you dance with anyone last night?"

I pointed to Drake, and then I saw Erik and pointed to him.

"Since you have claimed them, I will stay away." She laughed.

I pulled her over to the bar and Riley waved with a smile. "Hey! How are ya?"

"I'm great." I kept my eyes on Drake. The urge to go to him was unbearable. I gripped the edge of the bar, watching him intensely.

"Did you get a dance from him yet?" Riley placed a drink on the counter for me.

"Sort of. Can you get a drink for my friend? I'll pay for hers."

"No need. What would you like?"

"Dry martini with extra olives."

Riley nodded and began mixing the drink.

Hannah leaned into me so I could hear her. "She's exotic. I love her eyes."

"Take it all in, Hannah. You would be surprised by their eyes."

Riley tapped Hannah on the arm and handed her the drink. While Hannah observed the club, Riley and I continued our conversation.

"So, what did you mean when you said you sort of got a dance from Drake?"

"Well, I ran."

Riley laughed. "You don't know what you are missing."

I didn't sip my drink this time. I chugged the whole thing down. I needed the buzz to calm my nerves.

Riley placed another drink on the counter. "Erik is staring at you again. I saw you dance with him last night, too. Maybe you should get a private dance with Erik and Drake at the same time. I'm sure it would rock your world."

I turned my attention to Erik. I locked eyes with him as he danced with a girl with long blue hair. She shook her ass as she raised her arms above her head, wrapping them around his head. He held her against him while kissing her neck up to her ear, all the while watching me for a few seconds.

I don't know why, but a rage of jealousy flooded my veins. I gulped the drink and stomped over to Erik, tapping the girl on the shoulder.

The girl raised her hand to my face. "Wait your turn, sweetheart."

Erik stepped around the girl, smiling. "I told you that you'd be back." He examined my stamped hand. "Are you anxious to be with me?"

The girl looked over Erik's shoulder. "I never got a stamp. What does it mean?"

"It means I'm entitled to whatever I want and, right now, I need another drink." Now that I'd interrupted Erik's show, I spun around and headed back to the bar. Riley had another drink waiting for me.

"You are bold," Riley said.

I guzzled the beverage until it was gone and wiped my mouth with a small cocktail napkin.

"Wow! Third one gone in a matter of minutes. Do you want another?"

"Yeah. Give me something else. I don't care what."

Hannah put her empty glass on the counter and patted my shoulder. "I'm going to go see if Luke wants to dance."

"Have fun. I'm sure I won't see you for a while." I laughed.

Riley tossed a towel over her shoulder. "What is going on with you? You seem…I don't know…agitated? What happened last night?"

Once Hannah was out of hearing range, I blurted out how I'd seen Erik consume Josephine's blood. I threw my hand over my mouth.

Riley raised her eyebrows. "Really?" She flung the towel to the counter. "And still you come back?"

"I take it he isn't supposed to do that?"

"It depends on where he did it. How did you see?"

"I explored the second floor. It was an accident."

"You're lucky Josephine didn't rip your throat out." Riley placed another drink on the bar. "This is a screwdriver."

I took a sip and gave her two thumbs up. "Can I ask a silly question? Is Erik…I mean, is he…you know?"

Riley leaned on the counter with her arms. "You mean are *they* the real deal?"

I nodded as I took a sip.

Riley smiled. "You don't have a clue, do you?"

"Why can't I get a straight answer from anyone?"

Riley opened her mouth to say something when there was a tap on my shoulder. Drake stood there, smiling. "Would you mind if I stole you away for a few minutes?" He took my hand, leading us to the VIP section on the second floor.

Josephine stood by the rail. She half smirked when she saw me. She placed one hand on her hip and the other on the rail as she glared at me through narrow eyes. Her hips slanted to one side as she put all her weight on her left leg.

"Back again so soon, I see." She glanced at Drake. "This time escorted on the arm of a dog."

"Screw you, Josephine."

"Whatever. I don't have time for this." Josephine turned up her nose and, with a prissy attitude, stomped down the stairs, disappearing into the crowd.

Drake clenched his jaw. "What the hell was that all about?"

"I…uh…caught Erik drinking her blood last night."

"Jesus, Chloe! How…?" He shook his head. "Did she threaten you?"

"Not in so many words. Erik told her to back off."

"Oh…" Drake threw his hands in the air. "Even better."

I followed him to one of the empty tables.

He held out a chair for me. "Do you need another drink?"

"No. I'm fine."

Drake sat across from me and leaned back in the chair, crossing his leg.

A waitress strolled up to the table and set a soda down in front of Drake. He took a swig and wiped his mouth with the back of his hand. "We need to talk about what you saw last night."

"Yes, we do."

"Were you not the least bit scared?"

"I'm intrigued and want to know what the hell is

going on here."

Drake sighed, shaking his head. "We all have secrets live, Chloe. We are trying to fit in amongst society."

"Well, that didn't answer my question."

A man distracted me as he came up the stairs. He stopped to speak with a man dressed in a security uniform.

"Who is he?"

Drake turned around to look. "Who? The security guy or the man in the red tie?"

"The one in the red tie."

"That's Cyrus. He owns the joint. Why do you ask?"

"I'm curious."

"What exactly are you into, Chloe?"

We starred at each other until Drake leaned on the table. He spoke in a low, raspy tone. "Do you want to try us all?"

I shied away, trying to hide my smile. "That's not it at all. I'm just trying to figure out who sent my invitation. Do you think he did since he owns the club?"

"Doubt it. He doesn't send out personal invites that I know of."

I looked over at Cyrus, and, before he turned to go down the hall, he glanced at me and offered a nod as if to say hello.

"All right, Drake. Enough dancing around the issue. Am I living in a fantasy or is this all real. What are you?"

Drake sat back in his chair and laughed. "Take a guess."

I concentrated on the different types of feelings I'd had around him and Erik. His eyes were not as hypnotic. I decided to blurt out the obvious and hoped I didn't look like a fool.

"Lycan?"

Drake smiled. "Very good."

My eyes widened. "Are you serious? I was only kidding. How did you become one?"

"I was born." He laughed and moved his chair next to me. "Are you okay after what happened between us last night?"

"Yeah. It was my first time doing something like that. I'm sorry if I was too forward. Ya know…with trying to take off your jeans. I thought I was in trouble with the way you said my name."

Drake stood. "I said you were entitled to anything and I meant it. Come with me. I won't take no for an answer."

I didn't know what he had in mind, but I didn't want to go to the private room again. I followed him to his cage and he helped me inside. He shut the door and stripped off his shirt, tossing it to the floor.

I held onto the cage for safety as I admired Drake. My body quickly responded to the sight of him. My breasts became taut and felt constricted inside the black vinyl top. That, in turn, made my core ignite. My grip tightened around the bars, and I fought the urge to touch him as he moved his hips in my direction.

Maybe I could touch him with one hand. I let my right hand slide down the bar to his shoulder and bicep. It flexed and I squeezed his arm. The heat pouring from his body enveloped me. Before I knew it, my other hand made contact with his left pec.

My libido was rising. Ever since last night, my desire for him and Erik had grown stronger. I was drawn to them as if magnetic energy was surrounding me—beckoning me closer. I closed my eyes, swallowed hard, and tried to concentrate on my breathing. My stomach tightened when Drake's hand slowly traced my arm to my neck. I didn't want to look into his eyes but did so anyway. They changed from their Arctic blue to a crystal color with shards of white rays. I knew it was his real eye color. They weren't contacts, after all. I caressed his face with my hand.

"Wow! Your eyes are changing again. Is it…?"

"My wolf? Yes."

Drake's hand slithered down my back to my thigh. Bringing my leg up around him, he pushed me against the bars. My skirt rose past my thighs, putting my sensitive area against him. He was erect and waiting. The sensation of warmth spread between my burning thighs and beads of sweat formed on my skin.

"Drake," I whispered.

"Yes."

"I…feel you."

It was his turn to push me away. "I'm so sorry." He leaned against the other side of the cage. "I don't get this way with others. Only you." He was holding onto the bar as he stared at me. His chest was heaving with each breath.

"Chloe, you need to get out. Please."

I didn't argue with him. I knew he needed help, and the only person I could think of who might be able to do that was Cyrus. I flung the cage door open and ran upstairs, bursting into the office.

I didn't see Cyrus anywhere.

Visions of the last time I looked into this room flooded my mind. I glanced around the office to take in its beauty. Two of the office walls were black, and the other two were red with abstract paintings. The floor was dark wood and a large oak desk with a black leather chair sat near the far wall. To the left was a bar filled with all kinds of drinks. On the right were a couple of doors.

"You lost?" Cyrus appeared from the balcony.

"Sorry. I don't mean to intrude but I think Drake

needs help."

"What is wrong?" Cyrus stepped farther into the room.

"I'm not sure, really. I was with him in his cage and…"

Cyrus held up his hand. "Say no more. I'm sure he is fine, but I will check up on things.

"Where is the restroom?"

He pointed to one of the doors on the right. "You may use the one over there."

"Thank you. I will only be a moment."

I ducked into the bathroom and flipped on the switch. I splashed water on my face and looked around for a towel. I noticed a narrow door across from the toilet and found a small closet that contained red and black towels all perfectly folded from small to large. I used a small hand towel to dab my face.

Feeling a bit lightheaded, I sat on a small bench by the door. There was a light tap on the door and a woman's voice called from the other side. "Are you all right in there?"

"I'm fine. Thank You."

"May I come in?"

The door opened and Josephine stepped in. The aroma of cinnamon filled the room.

"I saw you hurry in here." She leaned against the door. "What's the matter? Can't handle Drake?"

"I can handle him just fine." I kept my head down and focused on the towel in my lap as I neatly folded it. "I'm having a difficult time figuring things out."

"Maybe I can help. What's the problem?"

I didn't want Josephine to know about my feelings for Erik and Drake. But, she probably already knew. In no way did I trust her. The air became thick and heavy as Josephine sat beside me. I didn't want her anywhere near me.

"Are you trying to decide whether or not we truly exist?"

I gradually raised my head, meeting Josephine's eyes. She leaned in and whispered, "We do."

There was a knock at the door and I jumped at the sudden noise.

Drake poked his head in. He looked surprised to see Josephine. He glared at Josephine and she stared back. "Chloe, Erik is looking for you."

He stepped to the side, letting us pass.

"Is everything all right with you now?" I asked.

He smiled and caressed the side of my face with the back of his hand. "Yes, all is good."

As I started to walk away, I caught a glimpse of a smoke-like figure moving past me so fast that I didn't know what it was until I saw Josephine standing next to Drake. She licked the side of his neck.

Drake's mouth partially opened and his eyes closed for a brief moment before he grabbed her by the arms to push her away. "Knock it off!"

Josephine hissed, baring her teeth. "Oh, come on, Drake. I'm just trying to have some fun. I get bored sitting around here. You know how it is. To want something so bad that you can almost taste it, or to want something you are forbidden to have."

She leaned in to kiss him, but he turned his head and stepped away.

"Your loss." Josephine stormed out of the office.

Drake shook his head and rolled his eyes. "She annoys the hell out of me. Anyway, I hope I didn't scare you too much in the cage. I've just never had that happen before."

"I understand. You can't control certain things."

"No, you don't understand and, yes, I should be able to control myself but…"

The tapping of fingers on a desk turned my attention to Cyrus. He leaned back in his chair and propped his feet up.

I don't know what made me go to him, but I was curious about what he was. I didn't sense that he was either a vampire or a lycan. I wanted to introduce myself. It was the least I could do since I had burst into his office.

"Hi! I'm Chloe."

Cyrus flopped his feet to the floor and stood, offering his hand. The weirdest thing happened when I shook it. He shut his eyes tight as if a light was blinding him before quickly letting go. He held onto the desk for a brief moment, then straightened his tie.

"Nice to meet you. Please excuse me." He walked around the desk and disappeared onto the balcony.

"Is he all right?"

Drake waved his hand. "It's nothing. Happens all the time."

"What happens? What is he?"

Drake shook his head. "That is for Cyrus to speak of--not me. Come on. Let's get back downstairs."

As we walked down the hall, Drake said, "I can't believe you ran to tell Cyrus I was in trouble."

"Was I wrong in doing so? I didn't know what was happening, and I was concerned."

Drake smiled. "It's fine. No one's in trouble."

Erik was waiting by the rail when we arrived. "You had me worried. I thought you left."

"I had other engagements to try and deal with."

Erik looked over my shoulder at Drake. "Is that so?" He took my hand, leading me to the dance floor. "It is your turn, my dear."

Erik drew me against him, his arms around my waist. He moved his hips against me and I felt his erection. He spun me around, putting my back against him. He grabbed a handful of my hair, yanking my head to the side. His teeth nibbled my neck.

I gasped at his forceful domination. Aching for his bite, my body burned with desire. I wanted him right there. I didn't care if people were watching.

Drake approached my side, staring at me. I felt some force of nature pulling me even as the smell of musk filled my nose. It was a tug of war between Erik and Drake.

Erik's arms tighten around me as he whispered, "Do you want to dance with him?"

I shivered. His voice strummed every nerve in my body. I couldn't move as I looked into Drake's eyes.

"The ball is in your court, Chloe. Anything you want. You can have us both. Or, will that be too much?"

Was he serious? Of course I wanted them both. I could only imagine what would happen if I were alone with them. Shit. What was wrong with me? I didn't do things like this. But, I couldn't fight them. I don't want to. I felt my temperature rise.

I managed to whisper, "I…I already danced with…"

"Fair enough." Erik lifted me off the floor, carrying me over his shoulder.

Drake grabbed Erik by the arm. "Whoa! Where are you taking her?"

"My bedroom."

"I don't think so! You're not allowed to."

"Watch me."

Drake jumped in front of Erik. "Put her down now!"

"Or what?"

I lifted my head to look behind me and saw Erik staring at Drake, waiting for him to make a move in front of everyone.

The vein in Drake's forehead pulsed while a crease formed between his brows. His lip slowly twitched as he snarled at Erik.

"You better tame that animal before it does something bad." He pushed Drake aside. "Out of my way!"

"No! You're the one who needs to be tamed. Especially after what she saw you do last night. Either you take her to the private area or I will get Cyrus."

"You think that taking her to the private area will change what I do to her?"

"What the hell are you planning to do?"

Erik put me down, still holding me tight against him. "None of your business. I don't interfere with your dances." He poked Drake in the chest. "Don't interrupt mine."

Erik stormed off to the private area with me snug under his arm.

CHAPTER 5

Kyle reached out and took Erik by the arm, stopping him abruptly. Erik glanced down at the hand and then looked directly into Kyle's eyes. They exchanged no words. Kyle let go and stepped to the side as Erik pushed past, pulling me down the steps and to the last room on the left.

I spotted a four-poster bed draped with a sheer black canopy. The matching silk sheets were accented with two large red pillows. To the right was a black leather chair.

"On the bed," Erik ordered.

I obeyed, kneeling in the middle.

Erik glared at me through pieces of hair that had fallen around his face. His mouth opened enough to show his extended teeth. He crawled on the bed like an animal. His muscles flexed, making them look larger.

Erik's power swirled around the room as he crept up behind me. It felt like a weight pressing against me. When Erik pierced the side of my neck with his fangs, a rush of heat caressed my skin, sending pleasure deep into my core. Orgasms swept through me one right after another. To have this experience without intercourse overwhelmed me. I heard his heart beating as he drank and the sound became hypnotic. I was drowning in his power. Losing all self-control.

Erik's right arm held me against him and he wrapped his left hand around my throat. The electricity between us was powerful and the need for release built inside me once more.

My moment with Erik was rudely interrupted when Josephine burst into the room. Erik raised his head, hissing, blood dripping from his mouth. He pantomimed swinging his arm, using his power to fling Josephine against the wall.

Erik turned his attention back on me, finishing his desire by running his tongue along my neck and then kissing me.

The metallic taste of my own blood on his lips and tongue excited me. Heat flared between my thighs and I ached to have him quench the yearning that rose within me. I became dizzy and the room seemed to spin, making me nauseous.

Drake stumbled into the room. When he saw what Erik had done, he rolled his fingers into tight fists. "Let go of her!" He took one step forward and stopped when a strange sensation filled the room. He couldn't go any farther.

Erik carefully slipped off the bed, licking the small drops of blood from his hand. He smacked his lips as if tasting something a little unusual.

I was left on the bed, trying to regain my composure. The weight I felt had shifted to the other side of the room.

Josephine darted toward me, but Erik hastily clenched her arm. "Don't you dare touch her!"

She jerked away from his grasp and raised her hand to slap Erik, but he caught her hand.

He stepped forward, inches from her face. "Do

not piss me off tonight, Josephine."

Drake jumped on the bed, wrapping his arms around me as if to protect me. He was a little late for that.

I leaned against Drake and inhaled his scent.

Drake looked at Erik. "What the hell are you doing? Are you out of your freaking mind?"

"Obviously, she knows what we are, Drake."

"No thanks to you. Still doesn't give you the right!"

"I can't help it that she caught me feeding last night. That wasn't my fault."

"I want you to leave her alone."

Erik shook his head. "I can't do that. I want her. She's not like the others."

"What do you want to do? Turn her? Well, I've got news for you. You can't have her."

Erik's eyes darkened as he fixed his gaze on Drake. A growl rumbled from his throat. "You have no claim on her." He brought his hand to his mouth, smelling the blood that lingered on his skin. "I've never tasted such sweetness."

Drake's veins pulsed in his neck and forehead. His arms twitched as if he was waiting to lash out. He jumped off the bed and got in Erik's face. "You will stay away from her or so help me--"

"And if I don't?"

"I will let Cyrus know what you are doing."

Erik laughed and turned away. "I don't care if he knows. I've done nothing wrong here."

"Yes, you have. You broke the rules and fed on someone not of our kind!"

Erik spun around. Wrinkles formed between his eyes. "She has a stamp, Drake. Anything goes."

"She isn't one of us, Erik!"

"Hello?" I waved my hand in the air. "Stop

talking about me like I'm not here."

Drake pulled me off the bed and carried me out of the room. He stopped at the bottom of the stairs and sat me down. "Are you okay? Can you stand?" He moved the hair away from my face.

"I think so."

"I'm taking you home. Let's go."

"But, I don't want to leave." I fought every step of the way. He pulled in one direction and I pulled in the other.

Drake stopped and turned around, placing his hands on the side of my face. "You have to trust me, Chloe. Please. Erik has you under a spell. That's what vampires do, and I know what he has planned." He glanced at my neck, rubbing his thumb along the vein. "Did he bite you? I know he did. I saw it. But your skin…it's…it's like it was never touched."

I pulled away, covering my neck with my hand. "Ever since I was a little girl, I've loved the paranormal world. It doesn't scare me. I mean, I didn't think you existed."

"So you know we are real. That's great. But, Erik is someone you don't want to get close to. First of all, Josephine won't let you, and neither will I. Promise me you won't be alone with him again."

I couldn't make that kind of promise. Not with the way I was feeling inside. I had to learn more about Erik and Drake. I wanted to keep them close.

There was a moment of silence before Drake laid his hands on my waist, leaning in as if to kiss me. "Be careful, Chloe. It's all I ask."

I nodded, ignoring his eyes.

Drake put his arm around me and guided me up the stairs. He tapped Kyle on the shoulder for him to move.

Kyle took one look at me and seized my arm.

"Chloe, you're pale. What the hell did Erik do?"

Drake pulled me away from Kyle. "Don't worry about it. I'm taking her home."

"You're not supposed to leave the club with customers."

Drake turned, shoving his finger in Kyle's face. "This is a serious matter. She's in no condition to drive and I'm not tossing her into a cab. If you have a problem, then go to Cyrus."

I pushed away from Drake, almost falling to the floor. "I can drive myself."

I stumbled across the club, bumping into people. The room was moving on me and I was trying to follow the floor. Drake came after me, shouting over the music.

"Chloe! Chloe, stop! I can't go out this way!"

I screamed back at him over my shoulder. "Sucks for you!" I managed to make it outside and fell into Devin the bouncer.

"Whoa! Did we have too much to drink?" He helped me to my feet and I noticed he didn't have on his sunglasses. I stared into his blanked-out eyes.

"You should be more careful." He gave me a crooked grin.

Drake pushed his way through the door. Girls in line began calling out to him, waving, and taking pictures with their phones.

Drake ignored them and yanked me from Devin's hand. "I'm taking you home and you're not going to stop me. You can't even stand, much less drive."

I pulled away, straightening my skirt. "Fine, but no monkey business." I tossed him my keys and headed for the car.

"I will keep my hands to myself. I promise. No monkey business. You, on the other hand…"

I whirled around to find him smiling. "What

about me?"

"Come on. You know you want me." Drake unlocked the door and I slid in.

I couldn't argue the fact. He was right.

"Just shut up and drive before I change my mind."

Drake laughed and started the car. "Am I getting under your skin?"

I pulled the seatbelt over me and locked it in place. "More of an annoyance than anything."

Drake arched his eyebrows. "I annoy you? Really? Then why did you come back to the club?"

I narrowed my eyes and flared my nostrils a little. If I could breathe fire, I would.

"First of all, I didn't come back because of you. Second, I'm trying to get away, but you keep following me like a lost puppy."

We were silent for a second, and then we both started to laugh.

"So, you came back because of Erik, then?"

I didn't answer and looked out the window for a second before turning my head to look at him.

He smiled. "Just admit it. You came back for both of us, didn't you?"

I crossed my arms and looked straight ahead.

"Have it your way."

I suddenly realized I'd forgotten about Hannah. "Shit! We have to go back. I left my friend back there."

"Did you drive together?"

"No. But she will be looking for me."

"Chloe, in this day and age, there is such a thing as texting. Send her a message."

I slapped him in the arm and took out my phone.

Hey, sorry, but I had to leave. I wasn't feeling well. You should find Kyle. Stay close to him and behave. Call me when you get home to let me know you are safe.

I hit Send. I didn't expect to hear from her right away. I knew it was hard to feel your phone go off in a bass-thumping club. I wished I had Kyle's number to let him know to look for her.

"You need to get some food in you. What would you like? Taco Bell, White Castle, or Steak 'n Shake?"

"Ooh, you're a big spender."

"Well, there isn't much open this late at night. Otherwise, I would be taking you to a five-star restaurant. But you would have to change."

I managed a smile. "White Castle."

Drake pulled onto 55 South to Lindbergh. He turned on Sirius radio and Metallica's song "Enter Sandman" was playing.

"I love this song!" I strummed on my imaginary guitar and played drums while singing along.

Drake bobbed his head to the beat and soon belted out a few notes at the end. "I never pegged you for a metal girl."

"I love different kinds of music. Heavy metal, rock, techno, and industrial."

Drake switched over to the far right lane and turned onto Lindbergh. "It's such a beautiful night out. It gives me an idea."

"Oh, no." I laid my palm on my forehead, shaking my head. "I can only imagine."

Drake turned left into the White Castle parking lot and headed to the drive-through.

"We're not eating here?"

"You honestly want to go in looking like that?"

I looked down. "What's wrong with the way I look? Are you embarrassed to be with me?"

"Not at all. What do you want?"

"Two cheeseburgers, fries, and a chocolate

shake."

Drake arched an eyebrow. "Only two?"

"Yep."

Drake pulled next to the intercom and ordered two bags of burgers, fries, and shakes.

"Are you challenging me by ordering twenty burgers?"

"No. I'm hungry."

"How do you stay fit by eating so much?"

Drake turned with a smile. "You really want to know?"

"Nope."

Drake paid, handed me the drink, and placed the two bags between us. He turned right on Lindbergh until he approached Bohrer Park Road. Houses with privacy fences lined the left side of the road. A field for two baseball games and tennis courts were on the right. There were no light posts. The only illumination came from our headlights.

"Uh, Drake? I believe it is way past play hours."

"Yeah. I know a spot where I can park, though. It's hard to see black vehicles in the dark there."

"If you give me a criminal record, I will never speak to you again."

Drake chuckled and reached over to massage my shoulder. "Don't worry. You'll be fine."

He didn't pull into the parking area. Instead, he slowed and turned left onto a short driveway where a small utility shed was located. A sign posted at the entrance read *Park Service Vehicles Only.*

"My car isn't considered a service vehicle."

"Will you chill out? And, yes, it can be of service."

I rolled my eyes, smiling as he veered to the right, carefully rolling onto the grass and inching his way up a small slope. Pulling to the left, he parked behind a set of bushes. Massive acorn and cedar trees stretched high toward the sky, shielding us from the neighbors nearby.

"Here we are." Drake grabbed the bags and headed over to one of the picnic tables.

"As long as I've lived here, I'd had no idea this place existed. How did you find it?" I took one of the bags and placed six burgers in front of me.

"Thought you only wanted two?" Drake winked.

"I'm hungry." I grinned.

"Uh-huh. Well, I researched the parks around this area and found it. I came here one evening after work for some serenity."

"How many other girls have you brought here?"

Drake shoved an entire burger in his mouth and washed it down with his shake. "You're the first."

"I feel so lucky."

"You should."

I turned sideways, facing Drake. My leg rested on the bench. "I hate to admit it, but when I first came to the club, I thought it was for pretend and people went there to role play."

"I figured, but no." He placed his hand on my knee. "We are real. When their fangs are exposed, people think they are fake. We are careful with who we expose ourselves to. That is why we have the stamp. I am still trying to figure out how you have one."

"It's because of the stupid invitation." I got up and walked to a large oak tree, leaning against it. "I just wished I knew who sent it."

Drake stood and stretched his arms behind his back. "Well, good luck with that."

He tossed the trash in a can and stood in front of me. "Are you feeling better now since you've eaten?" He rubbed my arm.

"Yes. Thank you."

"Come with me. I want to show you something." He took my hand, leading us across the grassy area. We passed a pavilion and headed toward a small pond. A wooden platform encircled half of it. The other half was walled in with rocks. We sat on the platform, looking at the stars. Drake pointed out all the constellations that he could find.

I was impressed by his knowledge and asked him how he knew them all.

"I took a few courses in Astronomy. It was interesting." Drake squeezed my hand. "Sometimes, it's good to get out of the club scene for a while, ya know."

"Yeah, I'm sure. All those women pawing at you like you're a steak."

I made the mistake of looking into his eyes. Uh-oh. Those feelings again. I didn't want to be alone with him right now. I didn't trust myself right now, after what had happened. I shifted my eyes to the sky. "What do you look like as a wolf? Are you animal-like?"

"Do you mean are we on all fours like a dog?"

"Uh-huh."

"No. We are two-legged creatures. We still have human features. Do you want to see?"

At first, I wasn't sure, but I was also curious. "Can you shift on command?"

Drake smiled. "It takes me a few seconds to get in the mindset, but yes. Depends on why I'm doing it." He caressed my cheek. "Can you handle it?"

"Um, sure. I guess so." The last time I'd said that, things had gotten a little heated at the club.

He sat on his knees to pull his shirt off, but I quickly grabbed his wrist. "Wait. What are you doing?"

"What I need to do to make myself shift."

"Don't. I changed my mind."

Drake tilted his head, a grin forming across his face. "Scared of what will happen?"

I knew exactly what would happen if I let this continue. But, I didn't have time to answer before Drake jumped to his feet, growling.

I stood, holding onto his hand. "What is it?"

"We're not alone. We need to go. Now."

We sprinted back to the car. As we were leaving, I glanced in the mirror and thought I saw two red dots in the distance. I shut my eyes and didn't open them again until we had pulled onto Lindbergh.

"How are you going to get back to the club?"

"I'll call for a ride in the morning."

"Morning?"

"Yep. I'm not leaving you alone after what happened with Erik and Josephine. Face it, baby. You're stuck with me tonight."

Great. That was just what I needed. A sexy lycan spending the night in my home to try to protect me from an irresistible vampire. How did I get so lucky?

CHAPTER 6

I tried not to look at Drake on the way home. I used the reflection in the window to see him. He stretched out his arm, rubbing his thumb along my cheek. I jumped, for his movement was sudden, and then scooted closer to the door.

Drake laughed. "What's wrong with you? You had a smudge of dirt on your face."

"Oh." I looked out the window, embarrassed. His slightest touch made my body tingle. Ever since I'd left the club, I'd been a bit aroused. Drake wasn't making this easy. I could have refused to allow him to spend the night, but I wanted him to.

"Drake, what would have happened to you had I not left the cage?"

I saw his hands tighten around the steering wheel. His jaw clenched and the nerve in the side of his neck became visible.

"I can contain my animal, Chloe. I have to in this line of business. It's easy to get turned on, but with you…I had to step back. If you had stayed…" He shook his head. "I don't know. I may have become a bit aggressive."

I almost let him miss our turn because of the

distraction. "Make a left here. At the fourth stop sign, go right." I was silent for a while and then asked, "What about Erik? What would have happened had he not been interrupted?"

"Are you serious? What do you think?"

I didn't reply for I knew the answer all too well. I would've made love to Erik and possibly shared blood. Leaning my head back, I closed my eyes. Visions of the brief moment came to mind. The blood. The kiss. The orgasms. Blood upon my lips. My blood.

I flung my eyes open and noticed Drake constantly glancing in the mirror.

"What's wrong?"

"We're being followed. The same car has been behind us since we left the park."

"Who do you think it is?"

"Not sure."

"My driveway is here on the right."

Drake slowed, pulling into the driveway. The car behind us sped past. I caught a glimpse of the vehicle, but I didn't recognize it. It could have been someone going home.

My house was a small, white, two-story with a garage and pool. White rose bushes that my mother planted when I was a child lined the porch. Tall oak, pine and maple trees outlined the property and created privacy. The nearest neighbor was a half-mile both ways and no one lived across the road. It was all wooded area.

"Gee, Chloe. You live in the middle of nowhere."

"Yeah, I like it that way. No nosey neighbors and I can be as loud as I want."

"Loud…how?"

"I mean when I have a party."

"Do you really have parties, Chloe? You seem like the reclusive type since you live way out here. I bet you don't really go out much, do you?"

"No, I don't. And, no, I don't have parties."

I unlocked the door and flipped the light on, quickly giving Drake a tour of the house. The living room was my sitting room. It had a hardwood floor, a blue couch in the middle, and two chairs directly opposite. An oval glass table sat between them with some magazines, a photo album, and a small plant. The cream-colored walls held pictures of my family.

To the left was another room with a hardwood floor. A large, tan carpet lay in the middle of the room with a blue couch and television.

The hardwood floor continued into the modern, spacious kitchen with its white walls and black cabinets. The countertops were white marble with a gray swirl design that ran the circumference of the room. An island dominated the center. A sliding glass door led to the patio and pool. The dining room was off to the left of the kitchen.

I took Drake to the second floor.

"You can stay in the guest room. It's the first door on the left. Mine is the second door on the right."

"Would it be all right if I showered?" Drake asked.

"Help yourself. There are extra towels here in the linen closet and you have your own bathroom."

He smiled and took a towel from the shelf. "Before I shower, I'm going to take a look around outside. I want to make sure whoever followed us isn't roaming around out there."

"Okay. I will be in my room if you need anything."

I started a bubble bath and slipped into the hot water. My tense muscles relaxed. I placed the washcloth over my eyes and laid back. I felt the bubbles popping against my skin. I began rubbing my thighs and belly and thinking of Erik's hands on my body. I visualized him on his knees between my legs. His hands moving up my thighs to the center. I felt Drake against my back as I leaned against him. His hands massaging my breasts.

I gasped at the knock on the door. My body jolted, spilling water over the side and onto the floor.

At first, I had trouble finding my voice. When I did, it was shaky. "Yes?"

"I'm going to bed now," Drake said.

"Sweet dreams." I lay there for a moment to get my bearings. *What does he wear to bed? Anything at all?* I couldn't help but fantasize about it.

I let the water out and dried off, putting on a black silk top with spaghetti straps and matching bottoms. I dabbed a little perfume on and stared in the mirror. Why am I making myself look good? I'm only going to bed, for Pete's sake.

My phone dinged with a message from Hannah.

All is good. Don't worry about me. I've been hanging with Luke and Kyle. Riley is nice too. Hope you feel better.

I climbed into bed, ready to fall asleep, but I couldn't. I tossed and turned, trying to get comfortable, but the only things going through my mind were thoughts of Erik. The way he held me close, his lips on my skin as he drank my blood, and the way he kissed me. Now, Drake was lying in the next room…alone.

I threw the covers off and headed to the guest room. I stood for a brief moment, hesitant to knock when he called out.

"You may come in, Chloe. I know you're there."

I opened the door and stepped in. My mouth dropped open as I saw Drake laying there. The top of his black boxers peeked out of the top of the white sheets.

Drake leaned on his elbow and a beam of moonlight shone across his eyes like he was wearing a white mask. “Is something wrong?”

I was embarrassed. I felt ridiculous standing there, gawking at him. “No, nothing is wrong. Just, um…seeing if you need anything before I go to bed.”

Drake grinned, flinging the covers back. “Do you want to lay with me?”

My heart was pounding and butterflies fluttered in my belly. Here this gorgeous man was lying in bed all alone. I wanted to fling myself on him—just like I had wanted Erik hours ago. He was as tempting as Erik, and I wanted to taste him as Erik had tasted me. I took a step back, hitting the doorjamb.

Drake laughed, putting the sheets back into place. “I forgot. No monkey business.”

“I don’t think Erik or Josephine are going to show up.”

“You want me to leave?”

“No. It’s late. Good night.”

I hurried back to my bedroom, throwing the covers over my head, trying to catch my breath.

I fantasized again about him and Erik. The thought of being with the two of them aroused me in ways I’d never imagined. What would’ve happened if I’d had them both in the private room?

I rolled over, closing my eyes. Visions of Erik played over and over in my mind. I pulled one of my big pillows close, wrapping my arms around it. I swear I heard Erik whisper my name as I drifted off to sleep.

CHAPTER 7

A voice woke me. I rolled over, listening. It was faint.

I threw the covers off and pulled on my robe. The next thing I knew, I was outside, looking around. I didn't remember going out the door.

Erik stood in the distance, motioning for me to come closer. He looked like a ghostly figure. I saw right through him. The thick, pointy grass poked the bottoms of my feet as I crossed the yard. My pace quickened and the closer I got the more solid the figure became. I fell into his arms, burying my face in his masculine chest.

When I pulled away, I wasn't outside amongst the woods, but in a room with low lights. Black leather chairs and couches were randomly arranged around the room, with a pole in the middle for dancing. At the far back, a large, round bed with a black velvet bedspread and pillows to match was positioned under a ceiling of mirrors. People were scattered around the room, talking, having sex, or feeding off each other.

My eyes widened. "Where the hell am I? How did I get here?"

"We're in the basement of the club, my dear.

This is our private room. Not for the customers."

From across the room, Josephine was dancing for someone. She swayed back and forth, her arms raised above her head as her hips made circular motions. When she went behind the chair, I saw Drake sitting there, wearing a pair of unzipped leather pants.

I watched in disbelief as Josephine ran her hands along his bare skin. She leaned in, licking his neck as Drake held onto the back of her head. Josephine glanced in my direction and smiled before sinking her teeth into his flesh. Drake shifted in his seat, adjusting himself.

I averted my eyes and forced myself to look at the floor. "Why am I here?"

Erik took my hand, kissing the palm. "I want to show you what we are all about." He gestured toward the scene behind me. "Look at them. See the pleasure they receive? I sense your need to want to join them. Do you not?"

I did have an urge that I couldn't explain. But, I couldn't watch him and Josephine together. "You're all about sex? Is that what you want?"

Erik fell silent. His right eye twitched as he ogled me up and down. "I know it's what you want, Chloe."

I sensed someone behind me and turned to gaze into Josephine's black marble eyes. I felt as if I could see into her soul—or lack thereof.

She smiled, exposing her crimson-stained teeth, and licked her moist lips.

Josephine pulled me against her. Her lips met mine and I tasted the metallic liquid on her tongue. Something within me awakened as if it recognized the lycan's blood.

She pushed me away, laughing as she wiped her mouth with the back of her hand.

"He tastes wonderful, does he not?" She tilted her head.

"You want Drake, don't you?"

I couldn't answer. I didn't have to.

"You want him like you want Erik." Smiling, Josephine sucked on her own finger, moving her mouth and tongue in ways I knew she would explore a man's erection. "Drake is such a good lay, too."

"Josephine! Enough! Now go!" He pointed toward the door.

She spun on her heel and went to the back of the room instead.

Erik's power radiated off him and stung my body. It seemed to caress me inside and out. I backed away, eyes closed, to try to retreat from the urge burning within me.

I whipped around abruptly, bumping into Cyrus. His black dress shirt lay open, exposing his torso. He closed the gap between us and leaned in, whispering, "Drink from me, Chloe. I know you want to."

A vein twitched in his neck. It was so close to my mouth. I don't know what came over me, but I licked along his pulse before sinking my teeth into Cyrus. The warm fluid from his artery oozed into my mouth. His heartbeat drummed loudly in my ears. His voice echoed in my head, sending me a warning. *Careful of betrayal.*

Erik pried me off him before I could find out more. "Back off! You know she belongs with me."

Cyrus grinned. "Why not let her decide who she wants to be with?"

"She already has."

"With your persuasion. She has much potential, my friend."

"Yes, I know."

I coughed and gagged. I was choking on the blood lingering in my throat. I wiped my mouth with the back of my hand and gradually regained my composure. I glanced at Cyrus, shuffling over to him. "Who are you?

What are you?"

There was something of a mystery to him. I raised my hand to touch him, but Erik grabbed my arm, pulling me back.

Erik smiled and cleaned the blood off my face. But, I couldn't take my eyes off Cyrus. I knew he'd been trying to tell me something before Erik distracted us.

Moaning sounds from across the room caught my attention. Over Cyrus's shoulder, I saw Drake making love to someone. I watched as he drove into her, her legs wrapped around his waist, pulling him in deeper. I wanted to look away but there was something familiar about the girl.

"You do want him, don't you?" Erik said behind me.

There was no denying it. There was no hiding it. I wanted them both. I couldn't help the attraction I felt that was developing for both Erik and Drake.

I watched Drake roll the woman over. His hands helped guide her up and down. The girl leaned forward and sank her teeth into Drake's neck. He howled as he gave into release deep inside her.

I couldn't handle the torture any longer and ran to the girl, yanking her to the floor by the hair. When the girl looked up, I gasped. I saw myself staring back with silver, glowing eyes tinted with shards of green. My mouth was wide open, exposing my fangs.

CHAPTER 8

I bolted up in my bed, panic-stricken. My body was shaking and the bed was soaked from my sweat. The heaviness in my chest made it hard to breathe. I leaned against the headboard, pushing the blanket down with my feet.

I couldn't shake the uneasiness inside. The dream played over and over in my head. I had several questions I needed answers to. What was Cyrus trying to tell me? Why was I a vampire? Was there such a place hidden inside the club?

One thing was for sure. I had more research to do, but I had to be careful.

Licking my dry lips, I could taste metallic blood. It made me queasy. I needed some fresh air, so I went to the balcony. Glancing over the rail, I saw birds fluttering their wings in the fountain, trying to cool off. It was already ninety degrees.

I went in and put on a pair of jean shorts and a blue t-shirt. Before going downstairs, I checked to see if Hannah texted me after she got home. From the time stamp on the text, it was 3:00 a.m. There was a long babble of what all happened. She was sad that Luke had a girlfriend but his private dances were seductive. I texted back, letting her know I was feeling better and I would see her in a week.

I was glad I was on vacation. I didn't think I'd be able to concentrate on work right now.

I opened the bedroom door and stepped out, following the aroma of food and coffee to the kitchen.

"Mm, what smells so delicious?" I hopped onto the barstool at the breakfast nook and Drake set a plate down in front of me.

His eyes immediately went to my breasts, and his eyebrows rose slightly before he turned away, shaking his head. "I hope you don't mind. I made us breakfast. It's my mother's special recipe for French toast."

He sat next to me and watched as I took the first bite.

The taste of powdered sugar and syrup coated my mouth, but something else had been added to make it even sweeter. I didn't recognize the ingredient. "What's in this?"

Drake smiled and pointed the fork at me. "The secret ingredient is love."

I pushed him in the arm, smiling. "I'm serious, Drake. Do share."

"I'll never tell. It's why it's called a secret." He tapped my nose with the tip of his finger.

"You mean you never plan to tell your wife?"

"Of course I would, and my kids, too." Drake cut a piece of his toast and swirled it in syrup. After a few bites, he pushed his plate aside. "More coffee?"

"Yes, please."

Drake scooted off the seat and collected the dirty dishes. He put them in the sink and came back with the coffee pot. He took my cup, pouring coffee halfway.

"Drake, about last night…" I kept drawing

circles on the table with my finger. “I don’t think Erik would intentionally hurt me.”

He sighed, put the pot on the warmer, and then headed to the refrigerator. He opened the door and took the orange juice off the bottom shelf. “Let me tell ya something, Chloe. I’ve known Erik long enough to know when he is interested in someone. Right now, that someone is you. Josephine doesn’t like competition. She is very possessive when it comes to Erik.”

Drake poured a glass of juice. “I think you should stay away from him. He may become upset when you turn him down, but he gets over things quicker than Josephine. He will eventually move on. He always does.”

He put the lid on the bottle and placed it back in the fridge.

I didn’t know what to do about Erik. The feelings I had for him didn’t bother me until I was around him. I did want to be cautious because of Josephine. If they were together, I didn’t want to be the one to break them up. I wasn’t that type of person. According to Riley, she didn’t even know what they were to each other.

“Are you just saying that so you don’t have to compete for my affection?”

“Baby, I don’t need to compete for anyone’s affection.”

I knew that to be true. All the women in the club fought for his attention. Not the other way around.

Drake gulped the juice and started to clean the dishes. “I noticed your pictures in the living room. Is that your mother and father?”

I slid off the chair to help Drake. “Yes. I grew up here.”

“Where are they now?”

“My dad died when I was fourteen. He was a

firefighter. My mom passed a year ago from cancer."

Drake rinsed off the plates and handed them to me to put in the dishwasher. "Jeez, I'm sorry to hear that."

I finished my cup of coffee before placing it on the dish rack. The ringing of the doorbell echoed through the house.

"That must be my ride." Drake dried his hands and followed me to the sitting room.

When I opened the door, it was Kyle.

"Oh, great." Drake threw his arms up. "I didn't know Cyrus would send you, of all people."

I stepped aside to let Kyle in.

"I volunteered when he asked. I wanted to make sure Chloe was okay."

"Of coursc shc's finc. Why wouldn't she be?"

Another conversation about me when I was standing right there. Was I invisible to these people? I laid my hand on Kyle's shoulder, turning him to face me. "Did Hannah behave herself last night?"

"To a point, yes." Kyle took me by the arm, guiding me to the kitchen. "I can't believe you let him spend the night."

"He wanted to make sure I was safe."

He looked over his shoulder at the sitting room, lowering his voice to a mumble. "I'm sure that's not all he wanted."

"Nothing happened, Kyle. Why is this bothering you so much?" I stood there for a minute until I realized something. Could he have feelings for me?

Drake leaned in the doorway to the kitchen, arms and legs crossed. "He's jealous. Are you tired of Riley already?"

Kyle whirled around. "This is a private conversation."

I laid my hand on Kyle's shoulder. "What does

Riley have to do with this?"

Kyle sighed. The corner of his eye twitched. "She is my girlfriend."

That was something I didn't see coming. I guess I should have been upset because he never told me, but, then again, when would it have slipped into a conversation? We had only just met and knew very little about each other. But, if his intentions were to get with me behind Riley's back, I had news for him. It wasn't going to happen.

"Let me just state one thing," I said. "I happen to like Riley and I'm not…"

Kyle held up his hands, stepping back. "Whoa! Don't get the wrong idea. I just wanted us to be friends."

"I'm sorry, I just thought…" I felt the heat rise in my cheeks.

"It's okay, Chloe." Kyle looked over at Drake. "You're a dumbass."

"Why? For exposing you?"

"No, for even thinking I would cheat on Riley. So stop hoping to hook up with her again."

Drake pushed himself away from the wall, fists clenched.

"Oh, I'm sorry, Drake. Did I spill your secret?"

"You mother--"

"Okay! Okay! That's enough!" I placed my fingers at my temples, feeling the pulse in my head. I took a deep breath and the scent of Kyle's aftershave and a hint of cedar hit me. It was then I realized he was a lycan, too.

I stepped closer and caressed the side of his face as I concentrated on his eyes. My touch alone caused his eyes to shift to a deeper shade of teal. Now I knew why his eyes were so vibrant.

"Those aren't contacts, are they?"

Kyle shook his head. "No, Chloe. They are my

real color."

"You are a lycan, too?"

He slowly nodded. "Yes."

I let my hand fall as I stepped away. Drake and Kyle stared at me. Their eyes shifted color and their animal-like scent filled the room. It was too much for me. I excused myself and went upstairs to lie down. I heard the front door close and then a car door, but the car didn't leave. A few minutes later, there was a knock and Drake stepped into the room.

"Kyle's waiting in the car for me. Are you okay?"

I lay on my stomach, my head resting on my arms. I rolled onto my back. "I'm fine."

Drake sat on the chaise next to the French doors. "I don't believe you."

"I'm fine, really. Between your and Kyle's animal swirling around the room, I needed some space." I propped myself up on my elbows. "You used to date Riley?"

"Hardly. We hooked up once. I didn't even get a chance after she met Kyle."

"Oh. Sorry to hear."

The car horn went off a couple of times.

"He's so impatient," I said. "You know, I could've taken you back to the club."

Drake stood and leaped on top of me. I squealed, then let out a light giggle. He took my wrists and held my arms above my head. "Is this your way of asking me to stay longer?"

His breath smelled like mint. I wanted to say yes to a lot of things lately. I felt as if I was turning into a whole other person. That I was losing myself to an unknown being. I just didn't know why or how.

"I sense the attraction between us, Chloe. I know you do, too. Otherwise, you would not have stormed out on me that first night."

I didn't know what to say. I would have a double dose of trouble if I dated Drake. Both Josephine and Erik would not be happy.

I wanted to say to hell with it all--and with what other people wanted. This was my life. If I wanted to date Erik or Drake, then why shouldn't I? In this day and age, why couldn't I have both? But, as much as I wanted to believe that, I couldn't. It would make me something I didn't want to be. They were making it hard to choose.

All I had to do was raise my head a few inches and I could plant my lips on Drake's. My eyes trailed down his lean body until I reached the place where his hips met mine. The muscles in his arms were taut from pressing down. The desire to have him spread through my loins, causing an ache deep inside. He looked so good and tempting right now.

I shook my head. "I can't do this. I don't know what I'm doing. I have so many emotions running through me."

"Like what? Tell me what you are feeling." Drake leaned closer to my ear. "As I lay on top of you, I can tell exactly what you want. The heat from your body has increased. Your breathing and pulse are rapid. Your pupils are dilated, which means you're sexually attracted to me. I can definitely shift for you now."

I opened my mouth to argue the fact, but he was right. He was good at reading body language. I read an article once about how pupils dilate when you're attracted to someone. I never thought it was true until now.

"Do you honestly want someone like Erik? Think about it, baby." He rolled off the bed, went over to the dresser, and scribbled on a piece of paper. "Here is my number. Give me a call sometime."

I lay there for a moment before running after

him. I stopped at the top of the stairs and watched as Drake closed the front door. I leaned on the wall and slid to the floor, resting my head in my hands. What was I going to do?

I must have sat there for hours, staring at nothing. My mind was blank. I felt empty inside. I wished my mother were here to talk to me about relationship issues. It saddened me that we'd never gotten that chance. My only option was Aunt Helen, and since Erik and Drake were not entirely human, that wasn't going to happen. I was on my own on this one.

I began to cry. I felt lonely inside. I wanted to be in love--not just in lust for someone. But, I couldn't stop thinking about them. What was I missing out on? What was I afraid of? Was I afraid at all? For my peace of mind and my life, I knew I should stay away from the club and never go back.

I should move on and continue to ignore the world as it evolved around me. I had kept myself sheltered this long and hadn't even known other beings existed. Maybe in the back of my mind, I did know and I refused to see it.

CHAPTER
9

I needed a distraction. I grabbed my laptop and turned on Pandora before sitting on the couch to do some writing. It worked for a while until a song came on that had been playing at the club. Again, visions of Drake popped into my head.

I turned off the music and saved my work. Next, I tried watching TV, but I couldn't find anything decent on. As I was about to turn it off, I saw news of another murder that had taken place. This time, it was in a home three blocks away from the club. There were always homicides, but the last two were not your normal killings, and the police weren't releasing a whole lot of information on either of them. No picture of the victims. No names. Nothing.

I needed to know more so I researched the web for any new material. There was a brief article on the latest murder. The police found DNA, but it had been thrown out as evidence because it was contaminated with an unknown substance.

"Contaminated? There has to be more."

I kept searching, but I came up empty. There

was only one person to ask—Uncle Bob. I knew he wouldn't be able to talk about the case. I didn't even know for sure if he was assigned to it. But, it wouldn't hurt to find out. I grabbed my purse and headed out the door.

Aunt Helen's ranch home sat at the end of the complex where the road circled back to the main road. It wasn't like I'd remembered. Uncle Bob had recently painted the house from blue to white. The roof was now black instead of brown. The porch had been expanded and a swing added on the end. Multi-colored pansies outlined the walkway.

I pulled in the driveway behind a red Dodge Caravan and Aunt Helen poked her head out the front door.

I smiled and waved. "Hi, Aunt Helen. How are you?"

Aunt Helen held out her arms as I approached and gave me a big hug. "Good to see you, sweetie. How are you doing?"

"I'm good."

Aunt Helen was a beautiful woman for her age. She was in her mid-fifties, and not one grey hair had popped out on her naturally blonde hair. She kept in shape by jogging in the evening or the morning with her friends.

"I was about to eat some pizza. Would you like some?"

"Oh, thank you. I haven't had lunch yet today." I rubbed my belly. "Where is Uncle Bob?"

"He's in the office, working on a case. What would you like to drink?"

"A diet soda would be fine." I followed Aunt Helen to the kitchen and sat at the breakfast bar. "It's good to see that he finally fixed up the house."

Aunt Helen laughed. "Oh, no, honey." She

waved her hand. "You should have seen him. He didn't know what he was doing. I had to call his buddy John to come over and help. Do you want ice?"

"Yes, please."

Aunt Helen held the glass under the ice dispenser. The motor clicked on with a hum and four ice cubes fell into the glass with a *clink*. She opened the can and poured the soda over the ice. It fizzed to the top before the bubbles finally settled.

Uncle Bob yawned as he strolled into the kitchen in his usual lounge attire—khaki shorts and a white t-shirt. Sometimes he wore sneakers, but today he had on flip-flops. His brown hair looked tousled, and I could see the stubble forming around his mouth. Dark circles outlined his bloodshot eyes.

"I thought I heard voices in here." Uncle Bob kissed the top of my head. "How are you doing, sweetheart?"

"I'm good. Looks like you could use some sleep."

Uncle Bob opened the cabinet and pulled out his coffee cup. "Yeah. What I need is a vacation. This case I'm on is killing me." He poured a cup of coffee and took a sip, trying to ingest some fuel into his system.

I sat up straight, leaning slightly forward. "What case are you working on?"

"I'm investigating the recent murders near Soulard. A couple of them are on the outskirts of the city." Uncle Bob took a slice of pizza, folded it, and shoved half of it into his mouth. The rest went into the trash. He always ate pizza that way.

He wiped his mouth with a napkin and finished his cup of coffee. "Now, I'm going to take a quick shower and go to the country club to work on my putting skills. I've got a tournament coming up next month."

Aunt Helen shooed her husband out of the

kitchen.

"So, what have you been up to?" She bit into a slice of pizza, causing two pieces of sausage to roll off onto the plate.

"Not too much. I'm sorry for not coming around more. I've been busy." I picked up a slice of pizza. The cheese was strung all the way to the paper plate and I pulled it apart with my fingers. One by one, I ate the pepperoni before consuming the rest of the pizza.

"I'm on vacation this week and made some new friends."

Helen dabbed her mouth with a napkin. "That's good. You need to get out more."

A fly buzzed around her and she swiped the air with her hand. "Do any of these new friends happen to be male?" She winked.

"Yes. Three guys and one girl."

"And where did you meet them?"

"At a club I went to."

"By yourself?"

"Only once. Hannah was with me the second time."

"You need to be careful out there."

"I know."

Uncle Bob limped in, carrying his golf clubs. "Well, I'm off. See you this evening."

"Why are you limping?" asked Helen.

"I hit my toe getting out of the shower." He kissed her on the cheek and waved to me.

"Good luck, Uncle Bob."

Helen finished her slice, and she was taking a quick sip of soda to wash it down when her phone rang. "I'm expecting this call. Excuse me for a few minutes."

"Sure. Take your time."

With Helen occupied with the call and Uncle Bob out of the way, I sneaked down the hall and to the

CHAPTER
10

I sprawled out on the couch, staring at the piece of paper and flipping through the pictures on my phone. I enlarged the area around the women's wrists to get a better look at the markings. The bruises were larger than normal hands. Fingers were elongated. No matter what, I had to be careful. I didn't want to end up behind bars--or worse…dead.

I came up with two possibilities.

One, the killer lived at the club. But, why would he or she jeopardize the club? Maybe the killer wanted to get into the public eye? I let that thought go. The evidence said there were no puncture wounds. Therefore, a vampire couldn't have done this. Neither could a wolf. And, what was up with that black ooze?

I was going with possibility two. The killer liked to scope out his victims before striking, and he was using the club as a cover to pin it on someone there.

I sighed, wanting to remove the pictures from the phone. My finger lingered on the delete button. Instead, I took a picture of the note, grabbed a box of matches, and went out to the patio. Placing the paper on the grill, I struck a match and held it under the corner. The white parchment turned grey to black before the flame ignited it entirely. In a matter of seconds, flamed consumed it.

Wiping my hands together, I went back inside. I had to do something to stop the killer and protect any more women in the club who may be in danger. I thought about my dream and the part that Cyrus had played. What was he trying to tell me? What betrayal?

Maybe I should contact Cyrus? But, how? This was Sunday and the club wasn't even open. Maybe I could call Drake.

I ran upstairs to get Drake's number. My hands shook as I stared at it. I pressed each number slowly and waited for him to answer.

After three rings, Drake picked up. The sound of loud music was playing in the background. "Hello?"

I opened my mouth to speak but froze.

"Chloe? Is that you?"

I cleared my throat. "Yes. Yes, I'm here. Sorry."

"Hold on a second. I can barely hear you."

I heard a door close and the music became faint.

"Hey, Chloe, What's up?"

"I don't mean to bother you, but I have some questions."

"Yes, I will go out with you. What time should I pick you up?"

I laughed. "That's not one of my questions."

"It isn't? Well, damn. What do you want to know?"

"How well do you know Cyrus? I mean…have you known him long?"

"I've known him for about seven years. Why do you ask?"

"I need to speak to him about a situation."

"Is this about last night?"

"No. It's a completely different subject." I paced back and forth around the bedroom, chewing on my lower lip. "Do you trust him?"

Drake laughed. "Where is this coming from?"

"Please, Drake. Between you and me, just answer the question."

"Of course I trust him. He is an honorable kind of guy. If it wasn't for him, we wouldn't have this club."

"And, how long has the club been there?"

"He opened this one about fifteen years ago. He travels back and forth between the two. Most of us, including me, transferred from the other club."

"He has two?"

"Yes."

I'd heard all I needed to know. If Drake trusted Cyrus, so did I.

"I need to speak to him. Where can I find him?"

"He's here. Chloe, what's this all about?"

"I can't say just yet. Can I speak to him please?"

I heard Drake let out a huff of air. "Yeah. Hold on."

There was a lot of shuffling and then loud music again. Once the music died down, there was a muffled knock and then Drake's voice.

After a moment of silence, Cyrus answered. "This is Cyrus."

I stopped pacing and tried to figure out what to say. Sometimes, acting on impulse isn't a good idea.

"I know I don't know you very well, but…um, there is something I need to talk to you about. It concerns the club. I know you're not open but…"

"No, it's fine. Go to the back door. Someone will let you in."

I hung up and glanced quickly in the mirror. I needed some eyeliner and lip gloss to brighten my pale complexion. I carefully outlined my eyes with black liner and, for my lips, a dark wine. Nodding with satisfaction, I grabbed my purse and was out the door.

I parked next to the building, walked down the alley to the back door, and knocked. There was a *click* and the slide of the bolt before the metal door scraped open.

"I'm here to see Cyrus. He's expecting me."

The guy nodded and stepped to the side. "He's in his office. You need me to show you where?"

"No, thank you. I know where it is."

Music played through the club and some of the employees danced around the cages. I expected to see Drake, but he wasn't around.

Riley ran up to me, waving. "Hey! What are you doing here?"

"I'm here to speak with Cyrus."

"For a job?"

I laughed. "No. It's something else."

"Is it about Drake going home with you? Or, Erik, maybe? If so, I…"

"How do you know about that?"

"I saw you and Erik on the dance floor, and then you disappeared, only to reappear and leave with Drake. Everything okay?"

I glanced over her shoulder and my eyes widened as I admired Kyle's chiseled frame. The way his jeans hung on his hips showed the V-shaped muscles pointing south. He didn't belong here as a security guy. He was built for much more.

He waved from across the room and I waved back.

"Yes, everything is fine. Excuse me. Cyrus is waiting for me."

I hurried up the stairs, taking two steps at a time, and headed down the hall. The office door was open a crack and I lightly knocked.

"Come in."

I pushed the door open enough to squeeze through and shut it. I noticed him wearing the same shirt as in my dream and I froze. I could almost taste his blood on my tongue again.

Cyrus leaned forward on the desk, interlocking his fingers. "What can I help you with?"

My eyes darted around the room, trying to avoid eye contact. I didn't know why I was nervous.

"Chloe, come and have a seat." His voice was serene.

I sat across from him, looking at the edge of the desk. "I assume you've heard about the murders around here?"

Cyrus nodded once. "What about them?"

"I think someone is trying to frame the club."

"What makes you say that?"

I handed Cyrus my phone, showing him the evidence. "My uncle is on the case and I was curious. I've seen these women here and I don't think this is a vampire or wolf issue. It's only a matter of time before someone comes in asking questions—specifically, my uncle."

Cyrus rubbed his chin and sat back in his seat, looking through the pictures and notes. "And, exactly, how did you get this?"

I didn't say a word. I'd already committed a felony by stealing evidence.

Cyrus shook his head. "Oh, Chloe. Why?"

"For the safety of the women and the others here. What do you think will happen if the world knows that vampires and werewolves exist? They would burn this place down. I don't want to see that happen. And, if I can do something to stop it, I will."

Cyrus handed me the phone. "I appreciate you sharing the info, but you should stay out of it. No need to get yourself hurt over this."

I wanted to mention the dream I'd had of him, and I wanted to ask him if there was something he was trying to tell me. But, I barely knew the man and didn't want to come off as a psycho.

"Thanks for taking the time to speak with me."

"You're most welcome."

As I descended the stairs, I saw Riley and Kyle in one of the cages. Her legs were wrapped around him and her skirt pushed up to her waist. I heard moans with each thrust of his pelvis, the motions bouncing Riley up and down against the bars of the cage. The music failed to drown out their screams of passion.

I should've felt awkward, but knowing what they were and seeing them on sexual display piqued my curiosity even more. Did they shift into their animal form while having sex?

My feet moved in their direction, my eyes fixated on them. I felt my heartbeat pulsating through my body. My breathing came in short, panting breaths. The ache between my thighs warned me about my sexual appetite.

A sudden chill from behind enveloped me and I stopped. The hairs on my arms stood at attention. Static surrounded me. I knew the feeling, and I knew who it was coming from.

I turned to find Erik standing there with his shirt unbuttoned, looking appetizing. Now was not a good time to encounter him. Not with the way I was feeling.

Erik smiled. His exposed, pointed teeth showed me he was ready to feed. He strutted toward me. "I'm surprised to see you. I want to talk to you about what happened between us last night."

I wanted to move away from him, but my feet wouldn't budge. "I'm fine, Erik. Really."

Erik held out his hand. "Please, come hang out

with me. You can meet the rest of us."

I took his hand and the electricity flowed from his fingers and into me. My body jolted, igniting the flame deep within my core that was already burning from seeing Kyle and Riley acting out a porn scene.

"Come on. Don't be scared." Erik escorted me to the basement, and at the end of the hallway, he made a right turn.

More music lay ahead. It was muffled and coming from behind a closed door.

"Where are we going?"

When Erik didn't answer right away, I stopped following.

He approached a large wooden double door and turned around. "Is there a problem?"

"I don't know. Tell me what's behind the door."

"It's a room where we entertain ourselves…privately. I guess you could say it is our playroom."

I stepped back, shaking my head as I remembered the dream. "I don't want to go in there, Erik."

"Why not?"

"I had a dream you brought me here. I don't want to go in there."

Erik raised his eyebrows as he tilted his head. "Is that so? What are you afraid of?" He held out his hand. "Let me show you. If you don't want to stay, we can leave."

I felt him pulling me into his web. I stepped forward, letting Erik lead me toward the door.

He pushed it open and the music suddenly blared as if the volume on the stereo was cranked to the maximum. Deep bass sounds thumped off the black walls.

I stared blankly around the familiar room. It was

a bit dark and a hint of smoke lingered in the air from all the incense. Only small lights on or along the stage lit the room. It felt a sense of
déjà vu. My body began to tremble inside and out. I knew something was going to happen if I stayed.

CHAPTER 11

I watched a girl with long white hair swing around a stripper pole. She slid to the bottom and crawled to a guy in one of the chairs. My mouth gaped open when I realized it was Drake. She straddled his lap, grinding her hips into him as she pushed her breasts in his face.

Drake's hands slipped around her waist, grabbing her ass and giving it a brief spanking. She leaned in and kissed him before rolling back onto the stage.

There was no doubt in my mind that the club was full of sex, lust, and desire. I closed my eyes. The pain in my heart was like a knife twisting deep into my soul.

"This isn't happening," I mumbled.

Josephine sat sideways on the back of a chair, massaging Devin's shoulders. She glanced up, and her smile faded when she noticed me. Her nostrils flared as she let out a puff of air. Her eyes squinted and she pressed her mouth together to form wrinkles around her lips.

Josephine slid off the couch and glided toward us. "What is she doing here?"

Erik held up his hand, pointing at Josephine. “You…don’t start.”

“She doesn’t belong here.”

“As long as she’s with me, she does.”

“You’re dating her?”

“I’d like to.”

“Chloe!” Drake stumbled across the floor. His eyes were almost white and his facial features were distorted. He had a smaller nose, high cheekbones, and pointed teeth. By the time he reached me, his features were back to human-like. “What the hell are you doing here?”

“I came to see Cyrus.”

“I mean in here.” Drake glanced at Erik. “Are you trying to get into trouble?”

I saw Drake’s erection and knew if I weren’t there, he would have shifted and maybe even have had sex with the girl. The pressure around me caused by the three of them was too much to handle. I slipped to the side to get away.

“Enjoying yourself, Drake?” I stared into his animalistic eyes.

Drake took a deep breath and briefly hesitated. “This isn’t the place for you, Chloe.”

“But you asked me out earlier today. Did you change your mind? Do you not want me to see what goes on here? The sex. The blood drinking. The orgies. I dreamt about this place last night. Something happened to me in the dream and it scared the hell out of me.”

“Wait.” Erik held up his hand. “You asked her out?”

“Yes, this morning after breakfast. I spent the night with her. You didn’t notice me missing last night after I escorted her out?”

Erik hissed and darted forward, but I stepped in the middle. “We didn’t sleep together, Erik, so back off!

He wanted to make sure I was okay and, as of right now, I'm not dating either one of you."

Erik and Drake stared each other down – a face off. Snarling and hissing. Hands curling and eyes twitching.

My body began to vibrate. It wasn't from the loud bass over the speakers. It was from Erik's power as he tried to ward off Drake. It not only affected him but me, as well. It curled around me like a blanket. Tiny tentacles probing at my pores, trying to work their way inside. I backed away, nearly tripping over a chair.

"Stop!" Josephine pushed Erik. "Why do you need to fight over her?"

"I don't want to be with someone evil like you anymore."

Josephine let out a small grunt. "You think I'm evil? You don't seem to have a problem when you're thrusting inside me. You're as evil as I am. I know what you do with most of the customers you dance with."

Erik jerked his head in Josephine's direction. His brow furrowed as he took a step forward.

Josephine closed the space between them. "Oh, come on, Erik. I've secretly watched you get paid for having sex." She walked her fingers up his chest and slipped them under his unbuttoned shirt. "It's hard to break old habits, but a threesome does sound like fun." She turned to look at me. "Just not with her."

Erik shoved Josephine to the side. "Knock it off!"

"Why are you pretending to be different when she's around? You're never this way to me!"

Josephine's power roared over me. It was stronger than Erik's. "I don't understand what your infatuation is with her!" She turned in my direction and got in my face. "I think you should heed my advice and stay away."

I straightened my posture and leaned in. I was almost nose to nose with Josephine. "You're the one with the issue, Josephine. Not me."

"I would have thought with Erik sleeping around and Drake playing with his bitch whore that that would be a problem for you. But, since you don't seem to have an issue with that, I will give you one."

"I didn't even come here to see them, Josephine."

"Oh? So, who did you move on to?"

"That is enough!" Erik was between Josephine and me in a matter of seconds. "You are out of line. You are dismissed."

Josephine hissed, her fangs fully extended. "I'm not leaving! I belong here! Everything was fine until she showed up!"

"I said get out!"

Everyone in the room was watching us. The music had stopped and no one dared to interfere with Josephine's confrontation. You were either with her or against her. I pitied those who were with her.

Josephine crossed her arms. "I'm not going anywhere. You have no control over me, Erik."

"And you…" Erik put his finger under her chin. "…have no control over me."

Josephine smiled and walked over to Drake, planting a kiss on his lips.

This time, Drake didn't refuse. He stood there, letting her tongue explore the inside of his mouth. His hand slipped behind her head and he grasped her hair and pulled her head back, growling.

Josephine turned her head, grinning at me. "He tastes wonderful." She slipped past me, nudging my arm.

I couldn't resist the urge to comment with a lie. "Yes, I agree."

Josephine whirled around and, in the blink of an

eye, was on top of me with her hands around my neck. "You bitch! Stay away from my territory!"

Drake and Erik grabbed Josephine, trying to pry her hands off. "Let go of her!"

Even between the two of them, they couldn't pull Josephine off me. Her nails dug into my skin, causing little pools of blood to seep out. The power of all three of them was enough to make me dizzy. I thought I was going to pass out as I gasped for air. Falling into a state of panic wasn't helping.

There was a sudden burst of power in the room and the force of it flung Erik and Drake backward into far wall. Josephine's eyes looked as though they were bottomless pits and she opened her mouth to expose her fangs, ready to strike at any moment.

My nails dug into Josephine's wrists, causing her to bleed as well. Anger boiled inside me like lava rising to the top of a volcano, ready to explode. I found the strength to pry Josephine's hands off and managed to punch her in the nose with my right hand.

Josephine brought her hand to her face as blood oozed from her nostrils. Her eyes widened at first with shock. Then her pupils dilated, consuming all the color in her eyes. She raised her arm and swung at my face.

Devin appeared from behind Josephine, seizing her by the arms to hold her back before she could get another whack at me.

"Get her out of here!" Erik demanded.

Devin dragged Josephine out of the room, kicking and screaming like a child. "This isn't over! I will kill you!"

Erik's eyes widened as he stared at me. "What the hell?" He stepped forward, but Drake got in the way, blocking the sight of my wounds, but it was obvious that there wasn't anything to see.

"Jeez, Chloe. You're playing with fire when you

battle Josephine. Are you okay?" Drake wiped the blood from my cheek. "Chloe, your face!"

I brought my hand up, covering the wound. "What's wrong? Is it bad?"

Drake shook his head. "There isn't a mark on you. Just like last night when…"

I knew something was wrong with me. First, the cut on the finger, and then Erik's bite. Now, this. This must be the reason why Erik was interested in me. He had to have tasted it when he had my blood.

"I need to go." I headed for the door, but Erik blocked my way.

"Please don't leave. Let me help you."

"I don't want your help, Erik. Let me go."

"Don't you trust me? Is it because of what Josephine said?" Erik placed his hand under my chin, forcing me to look at him.

I stared into his eyes and watched them darken from brown to black. I leaned away. "You better keep the bitch away from me."

"I'm sorry for Josephine's outburst and her attack on you. She's not one to mess with!"

I circled around him, pointing to myself. "I didn't start anything." Then I pointed toward the door. "She's the one that came at me! Why do you put up with her? Why not kick her ass out if she is causing so much trouble? Get rid of her! Maybe you can't. Maybe you do care for her. If you knew she was going to be mad about me being here, why did you bring me? Was that your plan?"

I couldn't think straight with Erik close to me. But, something inside of me wasn't going to let me forget about the lycan. I became confused and didn't know what to do.

Erik blinked and stepped close enough to look down at me. "Are you done?"

My eyes trailed over his body and stopped on the one place I wanted the most--other than his bite. I shook my head, stepping back as I pushed him. “Stop!”

Erik held his arms out to the side. “Stop what?”

“Trying to get inside my head!” I noticed everyone still watching. “What the hell are you all staring at? I can’t believe you’re all afraid of Josephine! Am I the only one able to stand up to her?”

“Chloe, calm down.” Erik grabbed my arm and I jerked away.

“You expect me to calm down after that insanely jealous bitch tried to kill me? You have some nerve. Now, get out of my way!”

I shoved past Erik and ran out the door, down the hall, and up the stairs. When I rounded the corner, I ran into Cyrus. Literally.

“I’m sorry, Cyrus. I shouldn’t have been down there.” I nudged past him and hurried to the back door, throwing it open. It began raining and I stood for a moment, letting the small pellets sting my face and cool my skin. Flashes of light illuminated the sky as if it were taking pictures of the city. The wind picked up as a clap of thunder roared above.

I never thought I would be able to fight off a vampire—especially Josephine. She was powerful. I’m not sure how I’d managed to do it. I hoped she didn’t press charges, but she did attack me. I was only defending myself. I vowed never to go back again.

At least, that was the plan, but I didn’t want to go home. A part of me wanted to stay and play, but with whom? The urge made me walk to the car even faster. I hurried to open the door and got in.

CHAPTER 12

Once home and showered, I stepped out of the bathroom with my towel around me. I nearly jumped out of my skin when I heard a tapping at the balcony door. It was Erik.

"What are you doing here? How did you get on the balcony?"

"May I come in?"

I stepped to the side to let him pass. I saw my reflection in his dark eyes. His fangs were fully extended. His power enveloped me, causing the hairs on my body to stand on end. The humidity became thick and I could barely breathe.

"I want to be alone with you, Chloe. I'm tired of the interruptions." He stepped closer.

"I'm not paying you," I whispered. "I'm not like those women Josephine spoke of."

"Money isn't what I want from you, baby." His hand slid up my thigh until he reached the center. "This is what I want."

I gasped as his hand cupped me. His other hand reached behind my head, pulling me against him. His lips brushed against mine and then he stepped back, giving himself enough room to unbutton his shirt.

My heart was pounding in my ears. My nipples hardened, making the ache between my thighs grow with my desire. I studied his eyes and fell deeper into his gaze. I closed my eyes as he stroked my cheek. The towel loosened and fell behind me. I felt myself falling into darkness and, in that darkness, his hands cupped my breasts, and he teased my nipples with his fingers. I felt out of control as I fell under his spell.

"Erik," I whispered.

"Yes."

"I can't breathe."

"Here. Sit down." He guided me to the bed and knelt down in front of me.

Erik massaged my thighs, leaning in to kiss my knee. He placed small pecks up my leg as his hand made its way between my thighs. Pushing my legs apart, his fingers toyed with and teased my small mound of flesh. His fangs pierced my inner leg and my body jolted with pain as I yelped.

Erik's power stroked me yet again. It was like bugs crawling over me and I responded to his calling. My insides ignited like a flame.

"Stop!" I scooted out from under Erik.

"What's wrong?"

I was throbbing between the thighs and wanted him to put out the fire that burned deep inside my core, but I just couldn't go through with it. Not yet.

"Erik, is what Josephine said earlier true?"

Erik grabbed his shirt from the floor. "We are not discussing this!"

I reached for my robe and slipped it on, then sat on the edge of the bed. "Erik, why is it so hard for you to deal with situations? You can't handle Josephine. You won't talk to me about why you feel the need to have sex for money. Do you have to influence women to sleep with you?"

Erik blinked and, like a flip of a switch, his human eyes were two black marbles. "This is all I know. Take it or leave it. And fuck Josephine."

"It seems you already have many times."

Erik glared at me. "Josephine is three hundred years old and more powerful than I am. I can't control her."

"Well, I'm not going to be one of your toys and piss her off."

Erik took a deep breath. "Look, I've never wanted anyone as much as I wanted you. I haven't been intimate with a woman since you walked into my life. What more do you want from me?"

"I want to know the real Erik, and yes, you have been with Josephine. Don't lie."

He threw his hands in the air. "Fine. You want to know more about me? My name is Erik Von Amberg from Baltimore, Maryland. My life drastically changed in August of 1908 when I was thirty-one. That is all you are going to get from me. I don't like speaking about my past or how I became what I am."

Erik slipped his arms through the sleeves of the shirt, leaving it hanging open. "And, no, I haven't been with Josephine since you. That is why she is pissed."

He sat on the bed next to me. "You're scared. I get it. This is all new to you." His thumb trailed across my bottom lip. "I've tasted your sweet blood upon my lips. Would you consider tasting me?"

I flinched. "What do you mean? You want to turn me?"

Erik shook his head. "No. You can't be turned that quickly."

I remembered the first time I saw him feed from Josephine. I was hungry to taste, then. And, even when I tasted my own blood while scraping Erik's fangs with my tongue. What about the time I tasted Cyrus in my dream? What did all this mean?

Erik picked up my hand, brought it to his lips, and kissed me lightly. He stood and went to the balcony. He stared out the door for a moment. "I don't normally walk away from a situation without a resolution. But, this time…" He glanced over his shoulder. "I will. Think about it and let me know what you want."

Erik disappeared into the night. The room fell silent and the heaviness that weighed on me was gone, leaving an empty feeling inside. I crawled under the covers, tears stinging my eyes.

I didn't like being confused. My body wanted Erik. No. My body craved him.

I quickly sat up, staring at the French doors. I wanted to run outside and yell for him to come back. Instead, I curled into a ball. I didn't know what was holding me back from being with him. All I had to do was take that step off the edge and give myself to him. But, I couldn't. There were things going on with me that I had to figure out. Why did I have a hunger for sex, and why in the hell did I have an ability to heal?

CHAPTER 13

It was already past noon when I woke the next day. I lay there for a moment and got an idea for a story. I jumped out of bed and dressed. Most writers need quiet time. I, on the other hand, can do it while watching TV. My eyes are on the screen while my fingers type away. It amuses my aunt.

"It's a gift," I say.

When I write, I write for hours. I get lost in my world. This is where I am happy. This is where I let my imagination go. At times, I find myself arguing with my characters. They want to do one thing, but I try to make them go in a different direction. In the end, they usually win.

My stomach growled, letting me know it was time for dinner. I started into the kitchen when a knock came from the door. I peeked out and saw Drake standing there. I unlocked the door and cracked it open.

"Hey, Chloe. Can I come in? We need to talk."

I opened the door wider for him to step inside. He started to say something and then stopped. He stared at me, narrowed his eyes, and let out a small growl. "He was here. Wasn't he?"

I didn't reply right away. I didn't need to since he already knew the answer.

"Do you realize the danger you are putting yourself in? Even after what happened with Josephine?"

"And I wouldn't be with you? Seems like Josephine has you and Erik wrapped around her finger."

"Dating me isn't the same as dating Erik. Besides, you said you weren't dating either of us and yet you let Erik into your bed."

I crossed my arms. "What's her name?"

"Who?"

"Your bitch whore."

"Really, Chloe? You're going to go there? Did you sleep with Erik to get back at me?"

"No. I don't play those kinds of games."

He let out a sigh. "Her name is Taylor and she isn't my bitch whore."

"Well, not that it's any of your business, but I didn't sleep with Erik."

"Chloe, I smell sex."

"Of course you do. Pheromones are running high around here, but nothing happened."

I headed into the kitchen and took some hot dogs out of the fridge. "I was getting ready to have dinner. You hungry?" I tossed the buns at Drake.

He stared at me for a moment and then opened the back door. "Grab some marshmallows, if you have any."

I found a pack in the cabinet and followed him outside. "Are we grilling?"

"Nope." Drake tried to start a fire with some wood. He grunted as he bent down, fighting with the matches.

I tore a couple of branches off a Maple tree for the food and sat down in the lawn chair to put the hot dogs on the sticks. "Are you done playing around with that match?"

"Yep. I got it now."

The wood began to crackle and the flames flickered orange and yellow. Drake pulled a chair beside me and I handed him a hot dog while rotating mine over the fire. One of the logs rolled off and almost hit Drake's foot. He nudged it back into place and leaned on his elbows, cooking the meat.

I picked a piece of burnt skin off the hot dog and flicked it to the ground. "Have you been watching the news about the murders near the club?"

"Yeah. It's sad and disgusting."

"Well…my uncle is on the case." I took a bun from the package and slipped the hot dog between the folds. "I snooped around his office and saw pictures and notes and stuff. I took one of the notes and snapped pictures so I can examine them."

Drake turned in his seat, raising his eyebrows. "You what?" He sat back in the chair. "What the hell, Chloe? Are you trying to get arrested? I can't believe you took evidence."

"Aren't you curious as to what I found?" I squeezed mustard along the top of the hot dog.

Drake shook his head. "You better get rid of whatever it is you have before someone finds out."

I bit into the hotdog and felt something cold on the side of my mouth. Drake ran his thumb across my lip, rubbing away the mustard and wiping it on a napkin.

"Drake, hear me out."

"No. You're in way over your head, Chloe. Stay out of it and let the cops do their job before you get into trouble."

I shoved the rest of the hotdog into my mouth and added a marshmallow to the stick, thrusting it into the flames. "I told Cyrus what I found and showed him the evidence. That is why I was there yesterday. If I can pinpoint who is doing this, then…"

"No!" Drake jumped out of the chair, knocking it over. "You're not a detective, Chloe. Leave it alone!" He picked the chair up and set it down hard on the ground. "Be right back. Do you want another soda?"

"Yeah, thanks."

I stared at the stars, remembering the constellations Drake showed me a few days ago. I shouldn't have told Drake about the evidence. I didn't want too many people knowing, but I needed help. This was their club and home, and a killer was using it as his hunting grounds while he searched for victims. I couldn't understand why they didn't want to find out who was behind it.

Drake shut the sliding glass door and handed me an orange soda.

"So, you don't want to investigate with me?"

"No. I don't." He finished off the first hot dog and reached for a marshmallow.

"I'm sorry, Drake. Deep down I know you're right. I thought you would want to help protect the club."

"I know Cyrus probably appreciates you wanting to help, but for your safety…"

"What about the safety of those women? They deserve justice."

"True. But, if you keep going down this path, you could end up like them." Drake opened the soda with another *pop-fizz* and gulped a mouthful down before letting out a loud belch.

I laughed, pulling the black marshmallow off the stick. It clung like mozzarella cheese and I tossed the gooey substance into my mouth. I met Drake's gaze and licked my fingers. "I see the wheels turning in your head. What are you thinking about?" I asked.

Drake leaned forward. "I'm wondering how I

can get you to lick me like that."

My eyes widened and I tried looking away, but I couldn't. A stream of heat seemed to stroke my legs and encircle my body. At first, I thought it was the fire, but this wasn't a sudden heat flash. This was teasing and gentle. And, in it was the scent of a wolf. The warmth increased between my legs and, slowly, I began to open them. Something invisible stroked me. I gasped, jolting in my seat, bringing my knees together. I reached for another hot dog as if nothing had happened.

"What's the matter, Chloe?"

It took me a moment to speak after clearing my throat. "Nothing."

"Are you sure?"

I stared ahead and asked, "What the hell was that?"

"What was what?"

"You know what."

"That was my wolf, Chloe. He wants to play with you."

My head jerked in his direction. "Play with me how?"

"You know how."

"What is it with you and Erik using your powers on people?"

Drake laughed. "I don't have powers, Chloe. It's just my metaphysical being making contact with you."

"How is that different from Erik reaching out to me?"

"I don't draw you into a dark hole and force you to do anything." He turned his chair to face me and laid his hands on my knees. "Look, I care about you. I need you to be honest with me."

"Okay, about what?"

"How are you different from any other human?"

I held his gaze for a moment. "I don't know

what you mean."

"Yes, you do." Drake tossed his stick into the fire and reached for a soda. The can made a *popping* sound as he bent the tab back. "I've seen your marks heal. Quite honestly, I don't detect you as one of us."

Drake brought the can of soda to his lips and leaned his head back, finishing off the bubbly drink. He tossed the can behind him and it landed in the trashcan. He watched the orange and yellow flames die down, leaving the coals pulsing red as the wood turned to ash.

Drake stood and walked to the pool. He watched the small ripples in the water. "I want you to trust me and open up to me. Help me understand what is going on with you."

"Help *you* understand? I'm the one at a loss here, Drake!" I stood abruptly and walked around the table and chairs, hands clenched into fists. "Things are happening to me and I don't know why! Yes, I have the ability to heal. It all started a few days ago. I can't explain it. And now Erik, along with everyone else, has witnessed it. I don't know what you want me to say."

Drake ran his hand through his hair. "You should talk to Cyrus about your healing. I'm sure he could help you figure it out. Maybe even suggest a blood test."

I shook my head. "I don't know."

Drake's phone went off and he checked his message. "I need to go. If you need me—or if you need anything--call me."

"Do me a favor, Drake, and don't say a word to anyone about the investigation."

Drake nodded. "I promise. But, you need to let the cops do their job. You're no detective, Chloe. And, think about talking to Cyrus. You may think it's awkward since you don't know him well, but he's the type of person who goes out of his way to help everyone."

I didn't even show him to the door. I lay under the stars for hours. At times, my mind was blank. I didn't want to think or feel anything. Why was I feeling a change within me? Why the pains, the hunger, the lust? It didn't make any sense.

One thing was for sure. I couldn't let the murders go. I was still going to investigate on my own. Tomorrow I'd go to the club and only observe. I'd never really paid much attention to the people there. I knew there were regulars, but maybe one of them would stand out amongst them all.

Detective Chloe at your service. And, while I was at it, I may take Drake's advice and speak with Cyrus about my issue.

CHAPTER 14

I parked two buildings down from the club. There was a different guy managing the door. I strolled up to the front with a smile and the man waved a finger at me.

"I've seen you before. You're the one who punched Josephine." He laughed. "That was classic but ballsy."

"Yeah, thanks. May I go in?"

He unhooked the rope, nodding toward the door, and I pushed past him. He didn't give me much room to get through.

There was also a different girl at the window. "Hi, Chloe. I'm Gloria. Nice to meet you, finally." She held the stamp to mark my hand.

Apparently, after what happened in the playroom, everyone was aware of who I was. I didn't know if that was a good or bad thing.

The club was crowded but not packed for a Tuesday night. I was on a mission and forced myself not to look for Erik or Drake. They were here somewhere. I could feel them. Maybe it wasn't them in particular, but the whole club made me feel as if I was on alert.

I eased my way through the small crowd toward the stairs. I wanted to see if Cyrus was in his office.

There were two security guards at the hall entrance. As I neared, they both stepped in the hall, blocking the way. "You are not allowed in this area. Staff only."

I smiled. "I need to speak to Cyrus."

The two men looked at each other and then back at me.

"Please. Tell him Chloe is here."

"No need. Go ahead." They stepped aside and I thanked them as I passed.

The office door was closed, so I knocked.

"Come in!"

I opened the door a little, poking my head in. "Sorry to bother you. Do you have a moment?"

Cyrus nodded. "Of course. Please come in." He held his hand out to the chair by the desk. "Have a seat. Can I get you a drink?"

"No, not yet. Thank you."

"What can I do for you?"

"Well…I…" I bit my lower lip, looking at the floor. "Drake said you could help me with something."

Cyrus interlocked his fingers, leaning forward on the desk. "He mentioned you may be requesting my help. I'm at your service."

The longer I sat there in his presence, the more relaxed I became. I wasn't as nervous anymore. After the intimidation passed, calmness took its place. I took a deep breath and explained the encounters I'd had that had caused people to witness my healing ability. When I finished, Cyrus sat back in his chair, rubbing his chin.

He stood, pointing at me as he headed for the door. "Stay here."

My leg bounced up and down while I watched the clock on the wall. Ten minutes passed, then a petite woman with short, curly blonde hair walked in, carrying a black bag. She reached out to shake my hand.

"I'm Dr. Nadia Clements. Cyrus tells me you

need a DNA test. So, I'm here to offer my help." She set her bag on the side table and opened it, pulling out a pair of medical gloves and the instruments she needed to draw my blood.

I watched as she pulled a needle from the bag. I sank farther back into the chair. "Oh, God."

Dr. Clements grinned and slipped her hands into latex gloves, pulling them up as far as they would go. When she released one, it snapped against her wrist.

"Hold out your arm and make a fist." She tied a rubber strap around my upper arm and tapped two fingers near the bend of my elbow until she found a vein. Then, she swabbed my arm with an alcohol pad.

I looked away and concentrated on an abstract painting on the wall with swirls of red and black color. The more I stared at it, the easier it was to make out a pair of male and female figures having sex. I drew in a sharp breath as the needle punctured my skin.

She released the tight strap. "You can relax your hand now." She pressed on the spot with gauze, bending my arm. "Here, hold this for a second." She put the blood sample in a secure round container and disposed of the gloves. "I will let you know what I find out as soon as I get the results."

"Should I come back in a few days or will you call me?"

"You will be contacted." Nadia closed the bag and headed for the door.

Cyrus passed her on the way in and nodded.

"You could've told me you were going to do that." I stood and threw the gauze in the trash.

"But, it is why you came here, no? Would you have agreed, had I suggested you do so?"

"Probably not. I hate needles." I rubbed my arm. "I was hoping for an answer without getting poked."

A slight smile formed on his face. "Don't worry.

Nadia is the best in the field. If anyone can find an answer for you, it's her."

Cyrus's phone rang and I excused myself, heading down to the bar.

Riley wasn't working. Instead, it was the stripper girl, Taylor. She was wiping down glasses and placing them on the back shelf. I didn't know how to deal with her, knowing what she may or may not have done with Drake. Either way, it wasn't my business. What did it matter anyway?

I sat down and she saw me in the mirror. She smiled and turned around. "Hey! Chloe, right?"

I forced a smile and nodded. "Can I get a chocolate martini?"

Taylor scooped some ice into a metal container and began pouring a dark and light liquid into it. She placed the lid on and began shaking. "I'm impressed with what you did to Josephine. Not sure how Erik feels about it, though. He is one tough cookie to figure out. Josephine's been gone since Sunday. No one knows where she is."

"Great. She's probably planning her revenge on me."

Taylor smiled and poured the drink into a glass. Then, as she poured chocolate syrup, she slowly stirred with a small pick to make it swirl. She topped it with a cherry and placed the glass on the counter. "I doubt it. But I'm sure you can handle it."

I stared at my drink for a moment, wondering if I should ask her about Drake. It wasn't Drake's business what I did with anyone, and it shouldn't be mine with what he did with others. But, I had to know.

"Taylor, can I ask you a personal question?"

"Sure."

"Are you and Drake together?"

A smile crept across her red lips. "We are not

dating if that's what you're asking."

"But are you with him a lot?"

"Let's just say I give him what he needs for his animal's sake." She winked and went to the other end of the bar.

Glancing in the mirror, I saw Drake across the room at the private entrance. I wondered why he wasn't entertaining tonight. He looked amazing in the club's security shirt. But, I preferred him without one on. I closed my eyes and recalled the first time I saw him in his cage. The muscles contorting in his back and abs as he moved his hips in circles.

I opened my eyes and saw a blonde woman caressing the side of his face. He smiled, took her hand in his, and kissed her palm. I looked away, only to see Erik with the blue-haired girl. He was always with her. It made me think something was going on between them.

I couldn't handle it. I knew this was their job, but the way Erik was handling the ladies set me off. He let them be so clingy.

The girl slipped her hand under Erik's unbuttoned shirt, moving it to the side. Her tongue lapped at his nipple before biting it. Erik grabbed her hair, yanked her head back, and looked deep into her eyes. He said something to her and she let go.

"Which one are you thinking about, Chloe?"

I jumped at the sudden voice. Kyle had taken a seat next to me.

"What makes you think I'm thinking about anyone?"

"Cause you're blushing. Girls do that when a guy is involved. But, you looked pissed. Jealous?"

"I'd be lying if I said no."

"Do you like taking risks and living dangerously?"

I laughed. "That's what Drake asked. And, I'm

doing well, Kyle. Thanks for asking. How about you?" I gulped my drink until it was empty and pushed the glass away.

"At least Drake and I agree on something--and stop being sarcastic. I'm fine. Then again, I didn't punch Josephine." He smiled and nodded. "You want another?"

"Sure."

Kyle went behind the bar and mixed a different drink. It looked like red Kool-Aid. He topped it off with a slice of lime. "Try this." He placed it in front of me and sat back down. "It's a cosmo."

I sipped while looking into his eyes. I saw something within them moving and almost choked. He really did have beautiful eyes. "This is really good. Where is Riley?"

"She's off tonight."

"And you're not with her?"

"She has class on Tuesday nights." Kyle turned sideways, leaning his elbow on the bar.

"What is she going to school for?"

"She doesn't know what she wants to do yet. She thought about becoming a vet, then changed her mind." He shrugged. "I have no clue from one week to the next."

Kyle tilted his head in Drake's direction. "He doesn't stop talking about you, ya know. I've never seen him so…infatuated with anyone like he is with you."

"I guess he's finally over Riley." I grinned. "Why is he not entertaining tonight?"

"He asked if he could do security tonight."

"Oh. Well, I'm not here to see him anyway. I'm just here to enjoy myself."

"What's going on with you, Chloe? I can tell something is wrong."

"I'm just preoccupied with stuff."

"Like what?"

"The murders have me worried, for one thing. And, secondly, I have mixed feelings for Erik and Drake. I'm not sure what is real anymore."

"Sounds like you need a girlfriend to talk to. If you want, I'll give Riley your number. I'm sure she'd love to hang with you."

"That would be nice."

Kyle checked his phone, thumbing through his messages. "I need to go. Talk to ya later."

I watched Kyle walk away. He had a nice ass. I dropped my head into my hands. "Get a hold of yourself, Chloe."

A voice from behind startled me. "Who's your friend?"

I turned to see Uncle Bob standing there in a gray suit and tie. He was out of place.

I smiled. "My friend Kyle. I didn't think this was your kind of scene. Does Aunt Helen know about your secret life?" I laughed, trying to ignore the gut-wrenching feeling of why he could be here. I knew it wasn't for the entertainment.

"I'm here on business. Can I ask you a few questions?"

My heart skipped a beat. "About the gothic lifestyle? Sure. What would you like to know?" I tried to make a joke, thinking that by being a comedian it would calm my nerves.

Bob looked around the club. "Is there somewhere we could speak in private?"

"You could use my office." A voice from the side interrupted the conversation.

I jumped, unaware of anyone standing there. Cyrus who had appeared from…where?

Uncle Bob did the same thing, except he stared at Cyrus as if he was studying him. He tilted his head slightly. "You. Do I…?"

"Don't think so." Cyrus held out his hand. "My office?"

"That would be great, thank you," Bob still didn't move. I had to nudge him forward.

We followed Cyrus upstairs and he shut the door as soon as I entered. "My name is Cyrus. I own the club. What can I help you with?"

Bob pulled a picture out from his jacket. "Have either one of you seen this girl here before?"

I leaned forward, squinting at the picture. Of course, I had seen the girl before, but I wasn't going to tell Uncle Bob.

"Why?" I asked.

"She's one of the victims of a recent attack."

I glanced at Cyrus, waiting to see what he was going to say. He said nothing.

When I didn't answer, Bob cleared his throat and continued. "One of her friends said she was with one of the male workers here. He goes by the name…" He thumbed through his notebook. "…Erik. Is he here?"

"I will get him." Cyrus left the room.

I picked at my thumbnail, which I do when I'm nervous.

"Do you know Erik?" Bob asked.

Again, I didn't want to be put in this position. I didn't want to incriminate anyone yet. "I only know him from coming here a couple of times. Not personally, though."

If Uncle Bob knew what Erik was capable of, he would have had Erik down at the station in no time.

When Erik and Cyrus came through the door, Erik looked twice at me and smiled. I felt my face turn pink as I looked away.

Bob extended his hand to Erik, but he didn't reciprocate the gesture. Bob cleared his throat again and wiped his hand on his jacket.

I tried not to laugh at the fact that with Erik being a vampire, he was intimidating. Uncle Bob seemed a bit nervous as sweat formed on his forehead.

"You wanted to see me."

"Yes." Bob pulled out a white handkerchief, dabbed his head, and then slipped it back into his pocket. "Do you remember this woman?" He held up the picture.

"Yes. She has been here several times. Why do you ask? Who are you?"

"Oh, I'm sorry. I'm Detective Grady. I'm investigating the murder of this woman, among others."

Erik held his arms out to the side. "What does this have to do with me?"

"Well, the woman's friend said she saw her with you."

"And, I have stated, she's been here several times. I wasn't the only one with her. I was one of her many favorites."

"You did not leave with her at any given time?"

"No. I do not leave with anyone that comes to the club. I showed her around the place, but that is all." Erik glanced in my direction.

"Would you be willing to give a DNA sample?"

I clutched the side of the chair, trying not to show my fear of what was about to happen.

"Do you have a warrant, Mr. Grady?"

"I could come back with one, but I don't think you want to expose the club to the public eye right now."

Erik stepped forward, but Cyrus placed the back of his hand against Erik's chest. "He will cooperate anyway he can. Won't you, Erik?"

I stood behind Uncle Bob, shaking my head and mouthing the word "No."

"Erik, I will need you to come down to the station tomorrow." Uncle Bob handed him a card.

"Are you going to have everyone else here do

the same thing?" I asked.

Uncle Bob, Erik, and Cyrus turned their attention to me.

"I don't think it is fair to single him out. How is his DNA going to help, anyway? The evidence they collected was not even conclusive."

"How do you know that?" Uncle Bob raised his eyebrows.

"It said so on the Internet." I paused for a brief moment. "I researched it."

"I still need him to come to the station. I could easily have everyone line up to give a sample if it comes down to it. Right now, I'm starting with this. Now, if there is anything else you can tell me that will help, I would appreciate it." Bob smiled, patting my arm. "Be careful. Okay?"

Oncc thc coast was clcar, I blew up at Cyrus. "What the hell are you doing? You can't have Erik take a DNA test!"

"Chloe, I didn't kill those women." Erik took my hand in his. "I won't match whatever evidence they have found. Why were you here, anyway? Did you have something to do with this?"

"Don't be absurd."

Cyrus hung his head, staring at the floor as he rubbed the back of his neck. "Let me see the evidence. Do you still have it?"

"Wait!" Erik stepped back. "You have evidence? How the hell do you have evidence?"

I met Erik's eyes. He was angry. I could always tell when he was angry. The whites of his eyes went black.

"Yes." I pulled out my phone, opened the file and handed it to Cyrus.

He examined it and handed the phone back. "Don't mention this to anyone else. And, you…" He pointed to Erik. “Don’t speak of this, either.”

“Chloe, answer me. What kind of evidence do you have? Do you know that guy?”

“He is my uncle.”

“What! Oh, wonderful. What did you do? Steal the evidence?” Erik plopped down in a chair. When I didn’t answer, he knew I had. “Dear God. You’ve got to be joking.”

I scrolled through the phone and didn’t find the file. “What did you do?”

“Deleted it. I also gave you my cell number. It’s the best way to get in touch with me.” Cyrus picked up a stack of folders from the desk. “Now, if you will excuse me, I have some calls to make. Erik, you stay.”

“Why did you delete it?”

“You don’t want to be caught with evidence, Chloe. Now, go.”

CHAPTER 15

I stormed out of the office like a child who hadn't gotten her way. There was nothing I could do. It was up to Cyrus now. I was sure hc would take care of whatever needed to be done. I headed down the hall and stood at the rail, looking down at the dance floor. Drake appeared from behind the stage area. He leaned against the wall, arms crossed, and watched the small crowd.

"Would you care for a dance?"

I spun around to find Devin, the security guy, leaning against the rail.

"Why does everyone tend to sneak up on people?"

He laughed and shrugged. "You just need to stop zoning out and pay more attention to your surroundings." He took my hand and led me to the dance floor.

We began jumping with the beat, hands in the air. I went in circles around him, and when

I met his eyes and chills ran through me. It was the vampire thing. I was hit with a sudden abdominal pain. I gripped my side, turning around to hide my discomfort.

"You okay, Chloe?" He touched my arm and I

nodded.

"Are you sure?"

"No."

I glanced past Devin and saw Erik at the top of the stairs. In the blink of an eye, he was on the main floor. I watched as he approached the blue-haired girl. She smiled as she slid her hand around Erik's waist and down to his ass.

Erik snatched her by the wrist and went behind her, twisting her arm and holding it against the lower part of her back. The girl gasped and arched her back, pushing her ass against Erik. He whispered in her ear and shoved her away.

Devin turned to see what I was staring at. "Are you and Erik dating?"

I grinned as I watched Erik decline the girl's invitation. Then, a couple of thoughts occurred to me. Either he'd done it because she liked it or because he knew I was watching. My grin faded. "Not really."

Erik's eyes darted up at me. His lips parted and he licked his bottom lip. In a few strides, he was in front of me. Before I knew it, he was dragging me toward the basement stairs.

As we passed Drake, I saw him out of the corner of my eye. His arms slipped to his sides as he straightened his posture.

When we reached the bottom step leading to the hall, Erik placed one hand around my throat, walking me backward until I hit the wall. His lips crashed down onto mine and he shoved his tongue inside my mouth.

I didn't come here for this, but his aggression made me want him more. He pulled away and I stared into his eyes. I didn't feel his power around me. This was the real Erik standing in front of me. I reached up and caressed his face.

He closed his eyes for a brief moment. "It is

taking every ounce of my energy to not go all vamp on you right now. Do you want to go to my room or shall I fuck you here?"

Those words made me clench my thighs, and the pressure made the ache worse. Erik's hand slid up my thigh and under my skirt. He whispered, "Do you want me, Chloe?"

My brain shut down and the word escaped my mouth. "Yes."

Erik spun me around and pushed my skirt up past my hips. I felt a tug on my panties and heard the material rip. He unzipped his pants and thrust himself inside me. The cement wall was cool on my face. My nails dug into the hard surface as he pushed against me.

Erik wrapped my long hair around his fist, pulling my head back with such force, I gasped.

"Is this what you want?"

The loud music upstairs muffled the sounds of pleasure escaping my throat. I felt a twinge of pain as Erik's teeth pierced the side of my neck. My legs nearly gave out.

The sudden removal of my support caused me to collapse to the floor. I looked up to see Drake standing there.

"I told you to stay away from her!" Drake pointed at Erik.

When he reached down to help me up, I slapped his hand away. "Don't touch me!"

Drake flinched, stepping back. "Chloe, what the hell is wrong with you? This isn't you."

Erik straightened his clothes and helped me up from the floor. "Back off, Drake."

"No! No, don't do this, Chloe. Please, I'm begging you."

I didn't say a word to him. I ran up the stairs and out the back door.

As soon as I'd stepped into the alley, Erik caught me by the waist. The sting of his power caressed me, reaching deep within my soul. "I want to finish what we started." He picked me up, holding me against the wall. I wore no underwear now and his erection strained against his pants. "I need you, Chloe."

He unbuttoned his pants and pulled out his swollen shaft. I eased down and felt him push past my opening. There was a rush of air as Erik leaped to the top of the building, holding us together. There was no way to conceal our private moment from the people living in the apartments nearby.

There was an old couch under an awning. Erik laid me down and I watched as he moved in and out of me with such speed, I couldn't keep up. Every second that passed, my breath sharply escaped my lungs as he drilled into me. I could no longer see the whites of his eyes. He was in full vampire mode. He held my arms above my head, trapping me against the couch.

I felt the heat rise inside me with each stroke until I couldn't take anymore. The orgasm hit and I began to scream. This time, Erik covered my mouth with his hand and sank his teeth into my neck, making the orgasm last longer. The swollen walls of my pussy clenched around him as he exploded inside.

The longer Erik drank, the closer I came to losing myself. My lust for it all overcame my fear of him killing or turning me.

Erik licked the blood from my neck and let go of my arms. "Fascinating." He caressed my cheek. "What makes you special, Chloe?"

I moved my head side to side. "Don't know."

"I've never met anyone like you. Such a unique specimen."

"Specimen?"

Erik laughed and helped me up. "I need to get

back." Taking me in his arms, he told me to hold on.

I put my arms around his neck as he walked over to the ledge and jumped down. I expected a jolt when we landed, but Erik's landing was smooth and fluid. We were like a feather floating down, only in fast forward.

Erik kept his arms around my waist as he looked down at me. "Have dinner with me tomorrow."

I nodded.

"I'll call you." He kissed me and disappeared back inside the club.

I stood there in a drunken stupor of pure sexual bliss. My legs went all jelly on me and I began to sway. I sat on a crate to gather my thoughts. How could I let this happen? The least he could've done was walk me to my car. Now, I had to walk around the building by myself at a bad time of night.

I carefully stood and straightened my skirt. When I rounded the corner, I saw a figure standing on the balcony where Cyrus's office was. It jumped over the rail, landing in a squat.

The figure vanished, but a shadow appeared behind me. I turned to find Cyrus standing there.

"You shouldn't be out here by yourself," he said.

I looked at where the figure had been, and then back at Cyrus. "Wait. Did you…was that you? How the hell did you do that? What are you?"

"Another time. Where is your car?"

I pointed to the left. "Two blocks that way."

I stared after Cyrus as he walked past me. Once he was a few feet ahead, I jogged up behind him. "What's going to happen tomorrow with Erik?"

"Nothing incriminating."

"Do you know where Josephine is, by chance?"

"No, I do not. There's something you need to know about Erik. He has trouble dealing with being both vampire and human. It's why he is kindhearted one minute and the next…you never know what's going to happen. It's why Josephine dislikes you. You bring out the human in him."

I stopped walking and Cyrus kept going until he noticed I wasn't beside him. He turned to look at me. He waited for me to catch up. I took out my keys as we neared the car and clicked the unlock button.

"I had no idea Erik wasn't a full vampire."

"There are many kinds out there, Chloe. Some are dead during the day, while others walk around twenty-four-seven. Some have powers and some do not."

Cyrus opened the door and I got in. "Don't always assume anything when it comes to other beings. Be careful with Erik. People can turn on you." He shut my door and I turned on the car and rolled down the window.

"I could be good for him. He needs someone like me in his life."

"I'm sure he does, but, sometimes, when you think someone is a perfect fit, they have an ulterior motive you can't see until it is too late."

Cyrus walked across the street and then was gone. In my mirror, I saw a shadowy figure with red eyes watching me. Gasping, I turned around but saw it was gone. Stupid me got out of the car and scanned the area. What did this thing want from me? Why was it following me? Then it dawned on me. The killer.

I took out my phone and quickly called Cyrus.

"Yes, Chloe?"

"The killer. I think he's here. Something with red eyes keeps following me."

There was a click and then silence.

"Hello? Cyrus?"

"I'm right here."

I spun around and there he was again. “Would you stop doing that?”

“Where did you see it?”

“A block down that way. It went to the left.”

“Get in your car and wait for me.”

I did as instructed and, five minutes later, he returned.

“I didn’t see anyone. You want me to have someone escort you home?”

“No, I’ll be fine.”

“Text me when you get home.”

“I will.”

I was paranoid on the drive home. I texted Cyrus, as promised, and then went inside to go to bed.

CHAPTER 16

My phone kept going off. After it went to voicemail, it would ring again. I thought I was dreaming until I saw my phone screen light up. I looked at the clock. It was 3:00 a.m. Who the hell was calling at this hour? There were several messages and calls from Aunt Helen. Something was wrong.

I turned on the light and read the messages.

Chloe, your uncle was attacked. We are at Saint Anthony's. He's in bad shape.

Where are you?

Why aren't you answering the phone?

Please call me.

I flung myself out of bed and called Aunt Helen. Putting the phone on speaker, I dressed while waiting for my aunt to pick up. She answered in a shaky voice.

"Chloe, honey, I'm sorry to wake you."

I sat on the edge of the bed to put on my shoes. "Are you in the ER or in a room?"

"I'm in the ER." Aunt Helen sniffled.

"I'm on my way."

I hung up the phone and ran to the car. I was glad there wasn't traffic to deal with and used my flashers in case the police were roaming around. I don't recall even stopping at the intersections.

My tires squealed on the pavement as I whipped the car into the emergency parking lot. I hurried through the sliding doors. A lady dressed in a bold yellow, flowered shirt looked up from the computer when I came in. "Can I help you?"

I glanced around the waiting room and saw that there were three people there. My aunt wasn't one of them.

I hated hospitals. Then again, who doesn't? I'd spent a lot of my time here last year because of my mother. I didn't want to be back so soon. I hate the smell. Whatever chemical they use to clean with stinks to high heaven. It makes me nauseous.

"My uncle was brought in. Bob Grady."

The lady typed on her keyboard, shaking her head. "No one here by that name."

"Could you try Robert?"

She typed in the name again. "Yes. He is having some tests done. Have a seat over there."

I pulled out my phone and texted my aunt, asking where she was. She typed back, *Chapel.*

I headed to the front of the hospital where the chapel was and found her sitting in the front row. The dark wood gleamed in certain spots from the small lights on the wall.

Aunt Helen quietly sobbed as she prayed to the statue in front of the room. I sat next to her and she snapped her head up as if I'd startled her. She threw her arms around me and I held her. We sat there for a while until she was ready to talk.

"What happened?" I asked.

She wiped her nose and looked at me with red, puffy eyes. "He was working late, as usual. I got a call that he was attacked outside the office as he was walking to the car."

My heart sank. "Have you spoken to Uncle Bob?"

She shook her head. "No. Not yet. I've been in the waiting room since I arrived." She held out her trembling hands. "Who did this to him? Why would they want to hurt him?"

I had a feeling in the pit of my stomach. I prayed this had nothing to do with him being at the club earlier.

"We should get back in case they call us."

We headed to the waiting room and the nurse on duty stood, directing us to another room. I thought the worse. They only take you into a room when something bad has happened.

We took a seat in the tan leather chairs and waited for the doctor. Five minutes later, he came in and closed the door, sitting across from us. He looked rather young and very good looking. His dark, wavy hair was combed away from his face.

I didn't notice a ring. His hands seemed strong as he interlocked his fingers, resting his arms on his knees. My eyes strolled up to the top of his scrub shirt where his clavicle was exposed.

Here my uncle was fighting for his life and I was thinking sexy thoughts about this doctor. What the hell?

He caught me staring and smiled before acknowledging my aunt.

"Mrs. Grady, I'm Dr. Reeves. Your husband is going to be fine. We will keep him for a few days to make sure we covered all our bases and testing. His face wasn't as bad as we thought once we'd cleaned him up. Most of the blood was from the wounds on his arms and abdomen."

The doctor's eyes shifted back at me.

"Can we see him?" Helen asked.

"Sure." He stood and looked at my aunt. "We will have him in a room shortly."

"Thank you, Dr. Reeves."

"You're welcome." He glanced at me again with a nod before leaving the room.

I was able to breathe again. What the hell was that? Did I just have a moment with a sexy doctor?

We left the room and went back to the waiting area. The desire to be with someone was hitting me at the wrong time. It was like puberty all over again, only somehow different.

I saw the doctor come back out to speak with the nurse behind the counter. She was a pale lady. She looked as if she avoided the sun altogether. From the look on her face, she found him attractive, too, because her face turned a slight shade of red.

As he stood there, looking at a file, he glanced sideways at me. A crooked grin appeared on his face.

I looked away and grabbed my purse. "I need some coffee. Do you want anything?"

"No dear." She patted my hand. "You go ahead."

I got up and headed to the snack area where the coffee machine was. I put my change in, but nothing happened. I smacked the side of the machine, cursing under my breath.

"Don't waste your time. Besides, the coffee in there sucks."

I turned around to see the doctor standing there. When I looked into his eyes, it was as if something pushed me back into the coffee machine. I saw something in his eyes shift, but not like Drake's or Erik's. This was different. His green eyes had light shards of grey and specks of red.

"You okay?" He reached for my arm to steady me.

"Yeah, just a little dizzy."

"If you want real coffee, you'll have to go

somewhere else." He chuckled.

"Maybe I'll just get a candy bar."

He took a step forward. "You look a little pale. Are you sure you're okay?"

I couldn't break the hold this man had on me. I tried to look away. I cleared my throat and managed to say, "Very sure."

I spun around, placed my money in the vending machine, and chose a KitKat. The wire spun around and, wouldn't you know it, the darn thing got stuck.

Dr. Reeves laughed. "Here, let me help." He placed his hand at the top of the machine and gave it one big push. He tilted it back and then let it rock forward with a loud thud. The candy fell to the bottom. He reached in and handed me the bar. "Here ya go."

"Thank you. I should get back and check on my aunt." I hurried down the corridor to the waiting room. She was speaking with a different doctor.

"What's wrong?" I asked.

"Nothing is wrong, sweetheart. Bob's in a room now."

We went to the fourth floor, taking a right as soon as we got off the elevator. His was the fifth room on the right. Both of his arms and his stomach were bandaged, and gauze was taped to his forehead. He had a slight cut on his lip and a swollen eye.

Helen went to his bedside and held his hand. His eyes fluttered open.

"Am I in Heaven? You're the most beautiful angel I've ever seen."

Helen and I laughed. He still had his sense of humor. She leaned down to kiss his forehead. "You had me worried."

"I'm sorry." Uncle Bob turned his head enough to see me. "Hey, pumpkin."

"Hi, Uncle Bob." I took a seat next to the bed.

He tried to sit up, but his ribs wouldn't let him. He winced, grabbing his side. "You know, the cops are going to be in here, asking questions."

"What happencd? Did you see who did this?" Aunt Helen asked.

"No, it was dark. It happened so fast. My arms got the worst of it because I tried to protect my face. Then I felt a swipe on my stomach and a kick to my side."

"Did they say anything?"

"Nope. I'm wondering if it has to do with the investigation."

"Don't you have cameras in the parking lot?"

"Yes. I will mention it when I talk to my boss." He caressed Helen's cheek with the back of his hands. "You look tired. You should go homc and get some sleep."

"I'm not leaving you."

"I'm fine, sweetheart. I will be here when you get back."

Helen smiled and a tear ran down her cheek. "Still not leaving."

A low buzzing sound came from Aunt Helen's purse. She fished through it and pulled out her phone. "I'll take this outside. You get some rest." Helen answered the phone as she walked out of the room.

Uncle Bob turned his head to me. "Now that she is gone, I need to tell you something." He let out a small cough, holding his side. "I didn't want to say this in front of Helen, but the person who attacked me did whisper in my ear before I passed out. They said to stay away from Erik and the club."

I didn't know what to say. This was getting serious now that my uncle had been attacked. It wasn't just about the women any longer.

"I will find out what's going on, Uncle Bob. I

promise I will get to the bottom of this."

"Don't go getting yourself killed. This is a job for the police and detectives. Let them do their job."

"But, I have the resources on this. I can get the answers. Just let me try."

"If anything were to happen to you, your aunt wouldn't take it very well, and neither would I."

"Trust me." I got up and kissed my uncle on the cheek. "I'm glad you're okay. I need to go."

He grabbed my hand before I could leave. "Is there something going on between you and that Erik guy? I saw the way you two looked at each other. Your face turned many shades of red."

Should I let Uncle Bob know that Erik was my boyfriend? Should I even call him that? I mean, yeah, we'd had a quickie, but what was I to him?

"I…I don't know what we are."

Uncle Bob let go of my hand. "All I ask is that you be careful."

"I will." I left without another word. I couldn't stand to look into my uncle's eyes right now. I could tell he was overwhelmed with mixed emotions. Concern. Fear. Uncertainty.

I walked in a daze to the elevator. If the killer had, in fact, attacked my uncle, then why did he leave him alive? To me, this was a warning. Murderers didn't really do that. Did they? I think this was something completely different.

Maybe I should've followed in my uncle's footsteps and become an investigator.

I pressed the down button on the elevator and the door quickly opened. I stepped in, pushing the floor one button.

When I got off the elevator, I ran into Dr. Reeves. He was dressed in jeans and a dark blue t-shirt.

He smiled and held his hand out for me to pass.

"After you."

"Thanks"

The double doors slid open and we stepped out into the sweltering summer heat. The sun was on the verge of making its morning debut. I clicked the unlock button on my key fob and opened the door.

"Drive safe." Dr. Reeves walked past me to the doctor's parking area.

"You, too."

CHAPTER 17

I worried about Erik all day. I had no idea what time he was going to the station for the DNA sample. I kept telling myself that Cyrus had it under control. He wouldn't let Erik take the fall or reveal that he wasn't entirely human. At five o'clock, my phone rang.

"Hello?"

"Hello, beautiful."

"Erik?"

"Were you expecting someone else? I'm sorry if I seemed a little tense last night, but I hate being caught off guard. Ya know with being questioned and all."

"I understand. I'm sorry you had to go through all that."

"Are we still on for dinner tonight? I was thinking of dinner at my place at seven. It will give us a chance to talk."

"So, where is your place?"

"The Mansion House, top floor, apartment 1005."

"Seven it is."

I hung up, smiling. I didn't know what to wear. A dress? Jeans? I rummaged through my closet, tossing everything on the floor and bed. Nothing was perfect enough. Why did I have to dress up at all? We weren't going anywhere. I chose a black and red skirt with a black spaghetti-strap top. It would have to do. Light makeup. Nothing rash. Hair up or down? Let's keep it down.

On my way to Erik's, my phone rang. I pushed the green phone button on my steering wheel to answer. "Hello?"

"Hey, Chloe. It's me, Drake. I need to talk to you. Can I come by?"

"Actually, I'm on my way to Erik's for dinner."

There was silence on the other end of the line. I swore I heard growling. "You there?"

"Yeah, I'm here. Please don't go to Erik's. I'm begging you. I don't know what the hell happened last night with you, but this isn't right."

"Drake, I know you're upset that I'm seeing Erik and I'm sorry."

"You're in danger if you go. Please listen to me for once. It's not just Erik. It's Josephine."

"I'm not going to sit around, locked up in my house, as if I'm afraid of her. I'm not. Now, I'm going to Erik's for dinner. Please don't ruin this for me."

I hung up the phone. I knew how Drake felt about me. I could have called Erik to cancel, but I'd made plans with him first. Were our roles reversed, I would have told Erik the same thing. Drake would have to deal with it. Maybe he could enjoy his pet, Taylor.

When I arrived, I pulled into the garage area, parking two rows over from the back. A group of girls were mingling with some guys four cars down. They were talking about what bar to go to.

I headed to the lobby and pressed the elevator button. The elevator dinged and five people darted out, laughing, almost knocking me over. The security guy told them to settle down before they hurt someone. They apologized and walked out.

I pushed the button for Erik's floor and waited patiently. I hoped it didn't make any stops along the way because I didn't want to be in the elevator with anyone. The elevator dinged once more and the doors slid open. I stepped into the hall and looked at the numbers to figure out which direction I had to go in. Right. All the way to the end of the hall and on the left. I took a deep breath and knocked.

Erik opened the door and I already felt the power surrounding him as it stung my skin. He stepped to the side to let me pass. "You look lovely this evening."

"Thank you. You look good, as always." Caressing his face, I smiled.

Erik kissed my palm. He then shut the door and followed me into the living room. All the walls were a cream color except for the one behind the leather couch. That one was black and held paintings of Paris and London. A large screen TV hung on the wall opposite the couch.

I placed my purse on the side table and went straight for the balcony doors. "Oh, wow!" He had a view of the Mississippi River and the Arch. "You have a great view."

"I sure do."

Erik slipped his arms around me, pulling me in for a deep kiss. My lips parted as his tongue invaded my mouth. My hands slide under his shirt, caressing his lower back. His kiss alone ignited the heat between my thighs.

Erik pulled away, leaving me breathless. "Please have a seat. Dinner is ready."

He took my hand and led me to a small glass table. Two black plates and wine glasses were set. He held the chair out for me as I sat.

I watched as he opened the oven, pulling out a dish of lasagna. He kicked the door shut and placed the dish on the table.

"That looks delicious, but…do you eat?"

"I do, but not as much as the average human."

He placed a slice on both plates and then grabbed a bottle of wine and a corkscrew. He twisted the screw as far as it would go and bent the sides down. It opened with a loud *pop*. Bringing the bottle to his nose, he inhaled deeply.

"Ah, smells tasty." He poured me a glass and placed it, and the bottle, in front of me.

"Are you not having a glass?"

Erik raised a different bottle. "This one is mine." He winked.

"Oh, right." I smiled.

"What happened at the station today?" I asked and took a bite of food.

"Nothing. I showed up and asked to see your uncle, but he wasn't there."

Normally, I sip wine, but I gulped it down this time. I needed a quick way to relax. As soon as the glass was empty, I poured another.

"What's the matter?" Erik asked. "You seem distracted. What's on your mind?"

I took another gulp and stared at my plate. "My uncle was attacked last night. He's in the hospital."

Erik straightened his back and clenched his jaw. He took a quick sip of his drink, then asked if my uncle was all right.

"He's pretty messed up, but he's going to be fine."

"Do they know who did it?"

"No." I dabbed my mouth with the napkin and placed it back in my lap before leaning on the table.

"Have you heard from Josephine?"

Erik ignored my gaze as he chewed his food and sipped his drink. He relaxed into the chair, resting his arm over the back. "I don't wish to discuss her. Let's enjoy our evening."

I wasn't sure if he was hurt that Josephine left him or because it was my fault she was gone. It was a touchy subject, but there were things about Erik I wanted to know. But, I wasn't sure how open he would be with me.

It was worth a shot.

"How did you meet Josephine?" I finished my second glass of wine.

Erik shook his head and poured himself another drink. "I do not want to talk about it, Chloe."

"Why won't you let me in? What was your life like before you became a vampire? Were you in love? Did you have a wife?"

His brow furrowed and he pushed his chair away from the table. As he walked past me, I turned in my seat, following him as he walked to the balcony. He looked out at the city below, hands in his pockets. There was a moment of silence before he spoke.

"It's like I've said before. I've done things I'm not proud of." He kept staring out the window as he continued. "No, I did not have a wife, but I did fall in love. It was the reason my maker banished me from his home."

I took my drink into the living room and sat down. "Why did he banish you?"

Erik spun around. His eyes were on the verge of turning black. "I told you, I don't want to talk about it!"

"But talking about things can help you get through the pain, whatever it may be."

Erik took a deep breath. "Josephine found me while I was in a vulnerable state. She took me in and the rest is history."

"That can't be all."

"It is for now." Erik picked up his drink and gulped it down.

I did the same. When I finished, I stood and the room seemed to move. I lost my footing and almost fell, but Erik caught me.

"I…I think I drank the wine too fast."

"What am I to do with you?" he whispered. He picked me up, carrying me into the bedroom.

The bed had black satin sheets with red pillows, and there was a dresser next to the closet. My hands trembled and I felt weightless as I lay there.

Erik stood next to the bed, holding another glass of wine. He set it on the side table and climbed on the bed in his usual seductive manner so he could lie next to me. He propped himself up on his elbows. Leaning in, he concentrated on my eyes.

"Your eyes. They're like emeralds with silver shards. They were not like that before."

I couldn't explain to Erik what was happening to me. I didn't understand it myself.

"Let me taste you, Chloe. I love having you upon my lips."

Erik rolled over, holding my arms above my head, and nibbled the side of my neck. When he sank his teeth into me and drank, sounds of pleasure escaped my throat. I lay there, aroused by his seduction. My body tightened below, burning with desire. Within seconds, Erik released that longing as it rippled through me.

He reached for the glass and put it to my mouth. I took my time sipping it at first and then gulped it down. I was able to get the full taste of the wine. It didn't seem right. The texture and taste were off. It wasn't smooth. It had a slight thickness to it, and that is when it hit me.

I rolled away from Erik, screaming at the top of my lungs. My body felt like a thousand bees were stinging me on the inside and out. Something inside me was fighting to get out.

There was a coldness flowing through me, spreading to every organ, artery, and vein. I clutched my head while visions of Erik's life flashed before me. I saw it as if I was there many years ago. I saw how Erik became immortal. I saw the women he had been with, including Josephine. The last image I saw was of Erik and me. But, before that, it was the girl with blue hair.

I tugged at my hair and rubbed my eyes, trying to get the hallucinations out of my head, but nothing worked.

Erik held me down to keep me from hurting myself.

I was scared of what was happening. I lay there, panting as the burning sensation subsided inside. Finally, I was able to breathe.

Erik relaxed on top of me. His erection pushed against my sweet spot. "You're going to be okay, Chloe. Try and get some sleep."

I couldn't sleep. I wasn't tired enough to sleep. I was afraid to close my eyes, but I knew Erik's intentions weren't to kill me. Something else was going on.

CHAPTER 18

The sound of a phone woke me. I had trouble focusing on the room and realized I was still at Erik's.

He grabbed his cell from the bedside table. "What?"

Erik was silent for a moment as I tried to move. "She's resting. I'm not going to wake her." He hung up and rolled over, placing small kisses along my arm to the shoulder. "Are you thirsty?"

I squinted at Erik. "What time is it?"

"It's late."

Erik reached for the glass of wine and took a mouthful. Leaning forward, he placed his lips over mine. As he kissed me, the wine filled my mouth. He moaned, rolling on top of me. "Be with me, Chloe."

I felt his power cover me like a blanket. This time, there was something different. The pressure and the darkness weren't there. I could feel myself lying underneath him. My mind was my own. Whatever Erik was trying to accomplish wasn't working. I knew what he was doing.

"No!" I pushed Erik away and rolled off the bed. The room spun for a brief moment. I gained my composure and headed into the living room.

"Where are you going?"

"Home."

Erik jumped in front of me before I reached the end of the hall. "I can't let you go, Chloe. You've been drinking. You can't even walk straight."

"I'm not drunk, Erik." I tried stepping around him, but he moved into my way.

"What are you afraid of?" Erik curled his hands into balls, head down, but his eyes looking up at me. Taking a calm breath, he said, "I've told you how I feel about you. If you don't want to believe me, then…"

"You lie!" I managed to make it to the living room. I spun around and continued my accusations. "You told me you haven't been with anyone and yet you slept with that blue-haired girl from the club! I'm not going to be one of your whores!"

Erik's head jerked back and he blinked his eyes once. I had slapped him in the face with my words. I don't think he knew what to say or how I knew that.

"Are you denying it?"

His silence suggested he had nothing to say. No matter what came out of his mouth, it wouldn't be the truth. At least, not what I wanted to hear. Either way, he'd hurt me. Not only with lies but with what he'd done.

From the visions I'd had of Erik being turned, I knew he'd tried to do the same thing to me. I walked over to his bottle on the table and picked it up, hurling it across the room. Erik ducked, and the bottle barely missed him. The bottle crashed into the wall and pieces of glass shattered everywhere. The red contents looked like blood dripping down the wall.

"You son of a bitch!"

Erik held his hands up, taking a step forward. "Whoa! What the hell is wrong with you?"

"You tried to turn me! How could you? Was this your plan all along? Lure me here because the other night didn't go your way? Sweet talk me and tell me you want me. And when I decided that I didn't want to taste you, you automatically decided for me?"

"Let me explain."

"Save it, Erik. I'm tired of your lies! Nothing you say is true. You don't care about anyone." I snatched my pursed and headed for the door, but Erik grabbed my arm.

"You don't understand! Please, I need you to help me!"

I jerked my arm out of his grasp. "How can I help when you won't talk to me?"

"You're the only one I have true feelings for, Chloe. Ever since you walked into the club, I've felt it. I want us to be together. With you by my side, I can deal with anything."

I looked at him and a part of me felt compassion and sorrow. The other half didn't believe him and didn't care. He did need help, but I wasn't the person to give it to him. Whatever Erik had going on in his head, it would never resolve itself. If it were going to happen, it would have already done so.

"You haven't dealt with anything so far. You can't even deal with Josephine."

That is when I felt his anger swirl around me. It pushed me back a few steps.

"I don't deal with Josephine because I can't! If I were to harm her in any way, there would be consequences to pay. Believe me, I would have left her a long time ago, if I could."

Erik stepped forward, and his left eye twitched. "Your eyes. Why do they keep changing? They're like the eyes of a wolf." The corner of his lip curled. "Did Drake do something to you?"

I pushed him away. "I don't know what's happening to me, Erik. I've been dealing with strange things since I went to that damn club." I shook my head. "I don't want any part of this. I'm done."

I headed for the door and, this time, he didn't stop me. I hurried down the hall to the elevator. As I waited, I kept looking for him to come after me. He never came.

CHAPTER 19

On my way to the car, thunder broke the silence of the night and echoed through the parking garage. I was the only one there, or so I thought. In the next row over, I heard shuffling and movement. I thought of a rodent or a homeless person taking shelter from the storm that was brewing. But, a swift shadow moved from one end of the garage to the other.

"This isn't funny, Erik! Leave me alone!"

Lightning illuminated the garage for a brief moment and I saw someone standing at the front of the garage. My heart fluttered in my chest as I focused my attention.

Again, lightning, followed by a crack of thunder, shook the building. Nothing was there this time. When I turned around to get into the car, Josephine stood in front of me. She hissed and snatched me by the wrists, lifting me off my feet. Her shrill laughter broke through the thunder as we flew out of the garage and over Interstate 55 to several abandoned warehouses and buildings.

"Let go of me!"

"Let go?" Josephine laughed. "If you say so."

I fell through one of the skylights, falling two

stories to the concrete floor. I lay on my stomach for a brief moment, unable to breathe. I was afraid I'd broken a few bones. It didn't matter. They would heal.

I rolled over and looked up. Josephine stood on the roof, staring down. We glared at each other for a second before I leaped onto a scaffold, scurrying to the top.

"How are you able to…?" Josephine stopped mid-sentence. "Your eyes. Why are they glowing silver?"

Josephine jumped down and, with one swoop of her hand, hit the bottom pole of the scaffold. It tumbled over, crashing to the floor, but I reached for a pipe above her head and hung on.

"Did Erik change you?"

I smiled. "You'd like to think so."

Honestly, I had no idea what had happened to me when I'd consumed his blood. If I was a vampire, I couldn't do anything about it now. However, I was going to use whatever I could to my advantage.

Josephine jumped up and grabbed my ankles, swinging me into a stack of barrels. There was a chain hanging from a large crane. Josephine grabbed the loose end and wrapped it around my wrists.

The tips of my toes barely touched the floor as I dangled from the chain. I struggled to free myself, but the chain tightened each time I moved. I had to think of a way to get out of this.

Josephine circled around me a couple of times, grinning. "Like a fly in a web."

I wiggled as if I were a fish caught on a hook. I had to think of something and quick. Pain was shooting from my shoulders to my wrists. "I put you in your place last time, Josephine. I will do it again. Only, this time, one of us will remain standing, and it won't be you."

Josephine stepped close, stopping inches from

my face. “Mm, I like a challenge.”

She glanced down at a piece of glass from the broken skylight and picked it up. “What makes you so special, hmm?” She tilted her head. When I didn’t respond, she drew her hand back and then swung it forward, slicing my belly. Thank God the wound wasn’t deep. After a few seconds, the wound healed.

Josephine stepped back. “What the hell are you?” She licked my blood from the glass and stared at me. “You shared blood? No! No! You will not take him from me!” She trailed the pointed end of the glass down the side of my face and neck, pressing hard.

My heart was pounding twice as fast. The thumping in my ears was giving me a slight headache. If I didn’t find a way to get down soon, I was as good as dead. So, I kept talking about Erik. He’d used me and now I was going to use him.

“Erik loves me. He needs me to make him a better person. You bring out the evil in him. He doesn’t want that anymore. He hates you. He’s glad you’re gone. Now, he can create someone to be with him forever. And that someone is me.”

“You’re lying!” Josephine slashed at my arm with the glass. Blood trickled from my shoulder.

I bit my lip, trying not to give Josephine the satisfaction of hearing me cry out in pain.

“He would never leave me for you!”

“You’re right. He can’t. But I can make it so he can.”

As Josephine lunged at me, something passed us in a blur, tackling her from the side. It knocked her into a bulldozer and she fell to the floor.

When I was able to focus, I saw a brown wolf standing hunched over, its back to me. I immediately thought of Drake because he knew I was going to Erik’s. Maybe he saw what happened and followed us here.

It turned around. I expected to see the face of a wolf with a long snout, but the mouth was still human. Saliva dripped from his canine teeth as he snarled at me. His hairy arms hung down at his side, and he flexed his long, bony fingers. His pants were ripped out on the sides, exposing his massive thighs. He stalked toward me and I kept my eyes on his. He stopped in front of me, eyes narrowed.

"Drake?"

"This could've been avoided if you had listened to me."

I didn't think he would be able to speak after transforming into an animal. His voice was low and raspier than usual.

I looked past Drake's shoulder at Josephine. She had managed to make it to her feet and was dusting herself off. She had that evil look in her eyes as she darted toward Drake.

"Behind you," I whispered.

When he turned around, Josephine's fist connected with his jaw. He wasn't prepared for the attack. His head jerked to the left from the hard blow, but he stood his ground. He rubbed the side of his jaw and popped his neck a few times.

Drake's growl started in a low rumble and grew louder. "You promised to leave Chloe alone!"

Josephine hissed, showing her sharp fangs. "We had a deal!"

"What is she talking about, Drake? What deal?"

"Go ahead, Drake. Tell her."

"Shut up!" Drake swung his left arm, backhanding Josephine. She did a 180-degree turn before falling to the floor. He didn't give her time to pull herself together. He wrapped his hand around her throat, lifting her off the ground.

Josephine's fingernails sliced into his neck,

hitting the main artery. Crimson liquid splattered across their faces.

Drake howled, releasing his hold on her and covering the wound with his hand. He tried to back away to buy himself some time to heal, but Josephine wasn't going to let that happen. She drew back to hit him again, but he ducked and turned sideways, bringing his foot up to kick her in the stomach. He put enough distance between them that it allowed him to lunge forward, tackling her like a quarterback. He kept running until they hit a stack of steel rods.

Josephine had an opening and kneed him in the groin. She gripped his arm and swung him around twice before letting go. He went airborne for a brief moment. Neither one of them knew he was going to land on the bulldozer's rusted, mud-caked scooper until it was too late. Drake's back struck the machine's spikes and then he fell to the floor.

CHAPTER 20

"No!" I felt like my heart had been ripped from my chest. He wasn't moving. "Drake!"

Tears stung my eyes even as I tried holding them back. I couldn't fall apart now. I had to be strong.

Josephine turned and pointed. "You're next."

She flew at me, crashing into me hard enough to break the chain. We soared through the air and hit several wooden planks as we descended. The boards split in half, crashing around us on the floor.

Josephine yanked on my arm, tossing me aside. I managed to get to my feet and we circled each other. At this point, I was starting to feel weak from the loss of blood. My legs wanted to give out. I could barely stand.

The need to feed came to mind. I knew what I had to do to survive. My gums tingled. Running my tongue over my top teeth, I felt four—not two—sprouting into sharp points.

It made me smile at her, exposing the double fangs. She gasped as I leaped over her head, landing on her back. I got my second taste of vampire blood as I sank my teeth into her neck.

Josephine turned in circles, letting out an ear-piercing scream. She backed up, slamming me against the wall over and over. I pulled my head back, ripping a piece of flesh from her neck. Strands of tendons and muscles hung from the wound. I felt warm liquid drip from my mouth and spit the meat onto the floor.

She fell to her knees, covering the gaping wound with her hand. Blood spurted between her fingers from the torn artery.

Licking my mouth, I watched her struggle to survive, but that didn't last long. She immediately jumped from the floor and grasped my throat, holding me against the wall.

"This is where you die," Josephine gurgled.

I could feel ancient power swirling around, probing my skin. I didn't fight it. Instead, I absorbed it. A sensation of increased strength filled my veins until I could no longer contain it. It had to go somewhere. If it built up inside of me, I would explode. That wasn't going to happen.

I released the power by throwing my hand forward. A ball of white light escaped my fingers, straight into Josephine's chest. She went flying across the room and into a stack of galvanized pipes.

Josephine shook her head as she crawled from under the pipes. She made it up to her knees and then looked up to see me sprinting toward her with a piece of glass. When she stood, I thrust the glass into her heart. Blood exploded from the cavity. Her mouth gaped open and she rapidly blinked her eyes. She fell to the floor and I twisted the glass farther inside.

I took the heavy chain from the floor and slung it around Josephine's neck, dragging her to the crane. I jumped up to wrap it around the hook.

Josephine, as I had, struggled to free herself. I latched onto her back and sank my teeth into her once again. This time, I hit an erogenous zone, causing Josephine to calm down and become putty in my hand. When I had my fill, I jumped off her back and picked an ax up off the floor.

I faced my enemy one last time. "You underestimated me, Josephine. Game over."

Josephine's youthful beauty had aged with wrinkles. Her skin was no longer tan but the shade of a pale, lifeless corpse. Her thick, brown hair became thin strands of grey with streaks of eggshell white.

"My maker will avenge my death."

"I will be waiting." In one swift motion, I swung the ax at her head.

It toppled to the floor and her body instantly burst into flames. I watched as Josephine's life was slowly extinguished from this realm.

The ax felt like a heavy weight in my hand and I let it fall to the floor, making a *clinging* sound when it hit. My knees buckled and I went to the floor, exhausted. The rush of adrenaline was over.

The floor cooled my feverish body. I lay there, staring up at the broken skylight that I had fallen through moments ago. Puddles of water had gathered on the floor from the rain.

I crawled to Drake. He had changed back to his human form. There were four holes in his back from where he'd been stabbed. I rolled him over, tapping his face with my hand.

"Drake. Drake, wake up."

He lay limp in my arms and I broke down. My body shook and the tears trailed down my cheek, dripping onto his shoulder. I felt for a pulse but it was very weak. He was going to die if I didn't get help.

I saw his phone under the bulldozer and retrieved it. I scrolled through the numbers until I found Cyrus. When he answered, all I could say was, "Help."

The last thing I saw were two beady red eyes staring at me from the roof.

CHAPTER 21

I woke in a dark room. Startled, I gasped as I darted up. My eyes focused on my surroundings.

I was in my bedroom. I had no idea how I'd gotten home. For a moment, I thought everything was a bad dream until I noticed I was covered in dried blood.

I glanced at the clock. It was 9:00 p.m. I'd been out of it the whole day. A part of me never wanted to go back to the club. I wanted to forget everyone and everything that had happened, but I couldn't do that. There were unanswered questions and a murder to solve. No one knew I'd killed Josephine unless Cyrus figured it out. Then I thought of Drake.

"Drake! Oh, my God!"

I had to know if he was alive. My legs almost gave out when I stood. It took me a few minutes to get to the bathroom. I flipped on the light and peeled my clothes with their dried bloodstains from my skin. It was gross. I kicked them into the corner and turned on the hot water in the shower, letting the room fill with steam. I used very little cold as I stepped into the water's stream. I squeezed a massive amount of shampoo into my hand. Closing my eyes, I massaged my scalp. It was hard to get past the dried blood that stuck like glue to my hair. I let it sit for a moment while I washed my body. The final bits of whatever was left of Josephine swirled around my feet before disappearing down the drain.

I shut off the water and wrapped a towel around my hair. After I dressed and dried my hair, I grabbed my keys and put my license in my pocket. I didn't feel like carrying a purse tonight.

There wasn't much traffic on the way to the club during a weekday. Parking was easier and there were no crowds. It didn't matter to me, though. I managed to get in rather quickly.

When I approached the bouncer, he caught my eye and stood straighter. He nodded and unhooked the rope. I didn't even acknowledge him as I passed, and I didn't bother stopping at the window. I pushed the doors open and the static in the air enveloped me. The hair on my arms stood up.

While I surveyed the club, several male entertainers stared at me from different areas of the room. I didn't know why. Maybe because they'd heard what I had done and were pissed. But, the look on their faces wasn't a pissed-off look. They had a hunger in their eyes, and those eyes glowed several different colors—gold, bronze, green, blue, and silver.

I didn't see Drake, but, then again, I didn't expect to after what had happened.

I ran upstairs and headed straight for Cyrus's office. I didn't bother knocking. I flung the door open and called out to him.

"Cyrus! Cyrus, are you here?"

There was no answer and he didn't appear.

"Shit!"

I hurried back down to the main floor. I saw

Riley at the bar and headed in her direction. She smiled when she noticed me, but then her smile faded. She was in the middle of pouring a drink but overfilled it as her eyes focused on me. I cleared my throat and glanced down at her hands.

Riley followed my eyes and jumped. "Oh, shit!" She grabbed a towel and covered up the mess on the bar. Her eyes connected with mine.

"What's wrong?" I asked.

"You seem…different. You've changed." She looked over my shoulder and around the room. "You have the attention of all the lycan males. What the hell happened to you?"

I knew why she thought I seemed different. It was all thanks to Erik. But, I had no idea why the Lycans were staring at me. "I'll have to tell you later. Listen, I need to see Drake. Is he here?"

She stared at me, biting her lip. "Chloe, there's something you need to know."

My heart fell into my stomach. I didn't want to hear bad news. I closed my eyes and took a deep breath. "What's wrong, Riley? Where is he?"

"He's downstairs resting. He was in some sort of accident last night. He was badly injured, but Dr. Clements took care of him the best she could. He's going to be fine."

"What accident? Did he say?"

"No, he hasn't spoken to anyone except Cyrus. His room is downstairs. The fourth door on the right."

I was relieved to hear Drake was alive. I would never have forgiven myself if he had died because of me. I made my way through the crowd, and each time I passed an employee, he sniffed the air. Maybe they liked my body wash. It was still unnerving.

I hopped down the stone steps two at a time and counted the doors as I passed them. I knocked and waited until I heard him say, "Come in."

I opened the door and stepped in. Drake was on the bed, reading. His eyes widened when he saw me. "Oh, my God, Chloe!" He winced as he got up and met me halfway. He pulled me into him with one arm. "Jesus, you had me worried."

"You? I thought Josephine killed you."

I wrapped my arms around him, and when my fingers touched his left shoulder, he flinched. "Oh, I'm sorry."

I went behind him and saw the marks on his back from the metal that had pierced his once flawless skin. My finger traced the outline of the mark and Drake's muscles tightened under my touch. "Is this permanent?"

"Only time will tell, but probably."

I shook my head. Tears dripped from the tips of my lashes. "I'm sorry. So, so sorry."

"Hey, I'm fine." He rubbed his thumb over my cheek. Leaning in, his lips brushed away the tear on the left side of my face. "I'd do anything to protect you, Chloe. It's why I…" He let out a long sigh. "…it's why I made a deal with Josephine. I promised to keep you away from Erik as long as she left you alone."

I stepped away from him and asked him when he'd made this deal.

"Sunday, after you left the club. Since no one had seen her the last few days, I thought she was staying true to her word, or at least giving me time to…"

"Time to what, Drake?"

He looked away, but I wasn't having it. I grasped his jaw in my hand and forced him to look at me. "Time to do what? Have sex with me? Is that why you came to the house?"

Drake pulled away from me. "No! I would never do that to you."

He stepped closer, backing me against the wall. His right hand rested on the wall beside my face and he leaned in. His breath warmed my skin. “When I stayed with you Saturday night, you don’t realize how difficult it was to stay in that room alone. And, when you came to me, I fought the urge to ravish you right there against the wall.”

My heart was pounding. The words he was using made me clench my thighs. The pressure alone almost made me orgasm right there.

“It was only a matter of time before you fell into Erik’s web of seduction. I knew I couldn’t save you after that.” He pushed me away, stepping to the center of the room. “But I tried.”

He held his hand out, then let it fall to his side. “I should have told you about the deal and I’m sorry. After I got off the phone with Erik last night, I knew something bad was going to happen. When I showed up at his apartment, I found your things in the garage and followed the scent of your blood to the warehouse.”

I didn’t know what to say. He’d made a deal with my enemy and yet not once had he broken and make me his. But, then again, I’d had many chances to be with him and, like a scared little girl, I’d run. The thing is, as I’d mentioned before, I liked and cared about Drake. I did love him, but I wasn’t in love with him. I only wanted to feel him inside me like I’d wanted Erik. I was getting the feeling of needing him now. The throbbing between my legs was getting worse. I felt the wetness soaking my panties.

Drake stayed across the room, staring me down. His eyes shifted to ice blue. “I smell the lust, Chloe. It’s all over you. But, that’s not all I smell.” He closed his eyes, leaned his head back, and took a long, deep breath. “Wolf.”

My eyes went wide. Why were Erik and Drake

mentioning wolf when I had vampire blood? It didn't make any sense.

"I don't understand, Drake. How can you smell wolf?"

"I don't know. But, right now, if you don't leave, I will rip off your clothes and take you where you stand."

I drew in a sharp breath. I wanted him to. I wanted to feel his hands on me. I wanted his lips kissing and licking every inch of my body. The need to have him fill me made me ache. My nipples hardened under my bra. I wanted his tongue lapping at them, sucking them between his teeth.

I managed one step. "I'm not with Erik. He…" I looked down at the floor. "He did something to me. Something bad."

"Let me guess. He cheated on you already. I told you he was no good. He'd say and do anything to get you to sleep with him."

My eyes darted up. That wasn't what I was referring to. Should I let Drake know what Erik did? No. No. In time, it would come out.

He was starting to sprout hair on his arms and he stepped back until he hit the wall.

I stared into his eyes and knew what was happening. It was the same as when we were in the cage. Only, this time, it was worse.

"Drake?" I reached for him, but he turned away.

"You need to go, Chloe. If you stay…" Drake hunched over and his back muscles began moving in ways I didn't know were possible.

"Let me help you," I said softly.

"Chloe, please, just go."

I was frozen. My body didn't want to move. I knew what he needed. His animal wanted sex. He, as a human, wanted sex. I wanted to give in and let him have me. My skin felt like it was on fire and I'd started sweating. But, I had to fight it. What would things be like between us the following day? Would he consider me his? Or would he just use me for his needs as Erik had?

Drake spun around. His face had begun transforming. *"Leave! Now!"* He pointed to the door.

His words were harsh but erotic. It brought me out of my trance.

I turned and ran out of the room, slamming the door behind me.

CHAPTER 22

I ran into Kyle at the top of the stairs. "Whoa there! Oh, hey, Chloe. How are…?" He stared at me for a moment, then stepped away.

I didn't understand why I was attracting the lycan males. I knew they could tell when a female was in heat, but why me?

"Come here." Kyle pulled me into his arms. His warmth and tenderness made my stiff body relax. Something about the way he held me made me feel safe. He walked me to the back door, propping it open with a crate. We went outside for some fresh air, only it wasn't so fresh.

I quickly covered my nose and mouth. "Eww! What the hell is that smell?"

We heard a buzzing sound coming from the dumpster. Kyle lifted the lid and the stench of something dead surrounded us. He jumped back, letting the lid slam shut.

"What is it?" I asked.

"I didn't get a good look. Smells so bad." He lifted it again and peeked in. "Oh…my…God."

I laid my hand on Kyle's shoulder. "What! What is it?"

Kyle shut the lid and took my arm, leading me to the door. "I need to get Cyrus."

I pulled away from his grasp. "I don't want to go back in."

"Well, I'm not leaving you here by yourself."

"I'll wait right here by the door."

Kyle nodded. "I'll be right back."

As soon as Kyle was inside, I went to peek in the dumpster. I used my shirt to help cover the smell and tried breathing through my mouth. When I lifted the lid, I was horrified. The one thing that stood out was blue hair. My heart felt like it had stopped. My stomach churned as bile rose into my throat. I gagged, slamming the lid. I stepped backward, my back hitting something. I turned to see Erik standing there.

"I didn't expect to see you here tonight. Does this mean you forgive me?"

I backed away, my arm outstretched. "Stay away from me! You…you killed her!"

"Who? Chloe, I didn't kill anyone." He peeked inside the dumpster and then slowly closed the lid. "I had nothing to do with that."

"You were the last one with her!"

"Was I? Look, I don't go around killing women, Chloe. Even if I did, I certainly wouldn't put the body here."

"When was the last time you saw her alive?"

"Tuesday, as did you."

"And, what exactly did you two do after I left?"

Erik smiled. "I didn't do anything with her. I've kept my promise that I haven't been with anyone since you arrived. I don't know why you think I have. I did sleep with her twice. The last time was a week ago today, to be exact."

"But when you gave me your blood, I had visions. I saw everything."

"Is that why you asked about it and are so pissed at me?"

"That and giving me your blood."

Erik chuckled. "Your visions aren't timestamped, are they?"

"That's not funny, Erik. And, if what you're saying is true, why was it so hard for you to say so when I asked?"

"Chloe, you didn't give me time to explain before you threw a bottle at me. You attacked me with all these allegations and stormed out. You didn't want to hear it, remember?"

Erik had a point. Even though Josephine was gone, my life was still in jeopardy. Not only did I have to worry about Josephine's maker, but I also had to make sure I wasn't the next victim on the killer's list.

He started to say something when Kyle came back with Cyrus. He looked inside the dumpster. "This does not go beyond the four of us. Do you understand?"

"Cyrus, we have to call the police."

"No! Are you nuts?" Kyle said. "We can't have cops here, Chloe. It will ruin us. No one will want to come back."

"But her family. Someone will be looking for her."

Erik shook his head. "I wouldn't count on it."

My eyes narrowed as I stared at him. "Why?"

"Julia's been a runaway since she was sixteen."

I crossed my arms. "Wow, you know a lot about her."

"Enough with the bickering." Cyrus held his arms out between Erik and me. "I'll take care of the body. Erik, go home. Take the night off. It's slow tonight, anyway."

"Are you sure?"

Cyrus nodded.

I could feel Erik's eyes on me as I ignored his stare.

Erik stepped up beside me and spoke in a baritone voice. "Our conversation isn't over, Chloe."

I kept my head down as I answered. "Yes, it is. We are done and I have nothing more to say." I felt a light breeze and glanced up to find him gone.

"Chloe." Cyrus brushed his fingers along my arm. "I don't want you being alone. Drake has some time off so he could stay…"

I whirled around, pushing Cyrus's arm away. "*No!* Absolutely not. I can't handle him right now."

Kyle raised his hand. "I'll do it."

"What's Riley going to say?" I asked.

"Don't worry about her. I'll let her know what's going on." He turned on his heel and went inside.

I didn't know if it was a good time to tell Cyrus about Erik, but after what had happened, I had to. I took a seat on a stack of crates. "Now that we are alone, I need to speak to you about something."

Cyrus sat next to me. "I saw Josephine's remains, Chloe. I can only imagine what you went through."

"You don't know the half of it, Cyrus. It's not just about killing Josephine. It's the murders. As far as I know, I could be next. I've been spending time with Erik and…" I let out a breath. "Standing up to Josephine twice was a bit scary, but I'm afraid of this killer. I don't know who or what to expect. And then there is Erik. Is there a punishment for overstepping certain bounds?"

Cyrus turned sideways to look at me. "What did he do?"

I dropped my head into my hands, pressing my palms against my eyes. I felt the sting as I held back the tears. I raised my head, staring across the alley. "Last night…he…he turned me."

My chin began to tremble and the damn broke, letting the tears trail down my cheeks. At the time, I'd been pissed, but thinking about it now, it infuriated me. I didn't know where to go from here and who to go to for help. I sure as hell didn't want Erik. Then I thought about what happened with Josephine. Without his blood, I don't think I would've been able to defeat her.

Cyrus placed his hand on my lower back. "What makes you say this?"

I took in a slow breath and let it out. "At first, what he gave me was normal red wine." I turned my head to look at Cyrus. "Then, he switched bottles and gave me his. I could taste the thickness and the metallic flavor."

Cyrus pinched the bridge of his nose and shook his head.

"That's not all that is wrong. After my uncle left the club, he went to the office to do some late-night work. When he left, he was attacked. Whoever it was told him to stay away."

"Jesus, Chloe. Why are you telling me this now?" He sat there for a moment, then stood. "I will look into the situation. Let Kyle stay with you until this gets resolved. I suggest telling him everything that's going on. And I mean everything. I'll have your car home early in the morning."

"So, you're going to ignore what Erik did to me?"

"No, but with that healing ability you said you have, I doubt you have anything to worry about."

"What does my ability have to do with this? When I fought Josephine, I sprouted fangs, Cyrus! Fangs! I ripped out her throat and drank her blood! I'd say that's vampirism!"

Cyrus squeezed my shoulder. "Do you trust me, Chloe?"

I let out a puff of air. “For some strange reason, I do.”

“Then believe me when I tell you that you were not turned.” He held out his hand. “Keys.”

I tossed them to him and Kyle came back with a small gym bag.

“I’m ready.”

I followed Kyle to the employee parking lot. He clicked the button on his keys and the headlights on his car lit up. It was neon green with a black top and two black stripes on the hood.

“Oh, wow! What kind of car is this?”

“A ’74 Dodge Charger.”

“Badass.”

Kyle chuckled. “Thanks. Leo helped me rebuild it. He’s another bouncer here, but he’s been in London at the other club for a few weeks.” He opened the door for me. The scent of leather and wax hit my nose. The black leather seats squeaked as I slid in. I’ve never known a man’s car to be clean.

“If you don’t mind, I’d like to stop by Saint Anthony’s Hospital to see my uncle.”

“What’s wrong with your uncle?”

I took Cyrus’s advice and told him everything I knew regarding the murders.

“Gee, Chloe, you’re turning out to be quite the detective. You want some help?”

I turned in my seat to look at Kyle. I was surprised by his response. It was the total opposite of what Drake had stated. Which made me like Kyle even more. “You don’t think I should stay out of this?”

“I think you should be cautious, but if you can do this secretly, then why not? I’d love to investigate with you.”

I smiled and stared out the window. It was weird how Kyle understood me better than anyone except

Hannah. If it wasn't for him and Riley, I didn't know how I would get through this.

CHAPTER 23

We went through the ER doors. The nurse behind the counter had her back to us and didn't see us come in. Kyle and I sneaked down to the elevators at the main entrance and pressed the button for my uncle's floor.

The elevator doors opened and we tiptoed to the nurses' station. No one was there. It reminded me of a horror movie where no one was around and a killer was stalking the halls. Good thing this wasn't Halloween.

"You want me to come with you or wait in the waiting room?"

"You better wait here. Not sure how my uncle will handle someone from the club being there."

"Yeah. Good idea."

I took in a deep breath and puffed it out before entering my uncle's room. My aunt must have gone home, for she wasn't there. I tiptoed to the bed, trying not to wake my uncle. His bandages had been changed. At least they were not blood-soaked as they had been before. The gauze on his forehead was off. A small red line, an indication of where he'd been sliced, was almost healed. It must not have been that deep.

I started to leave and heard him stir. His eyes fluttered for a few seconds before he squinted.

"I didn't mean to wake you. I know it's late."

"Hey, peanut. Is everything all right?" He reached for my hand.

"Yeah, everything is fine. Did Aunt Helen go home?"

"Yes. One of her friends is staying over." Bob stretched his neck to look over my shoulder at the door. "Tell me you are not roaming around alone at this hour."

"I'm not roaming around alone at this hour. My friend Kyle is with me." I took a seat beside his bed.

"Good." Bob clicked the button on his bed, raising his head a few inches. "I spoke with my boss today. They are viewing the video footage. I want you to take a look at it, too. They're going to send it to my email. I get to go home tomorrow. Can you swing by the house?"

"That's good news. Of course I'll come by. I spoke with Cyrus and told him what happened to you."

Uncle Bob's eye twitched. "How well do you know him?"

I pondered the question for a moment. To be honest, I didn't know what Cyrus was. I knew I trusted him with my life, and I let my uncle know that.

He gave me a slight smile. "I just want you to be careful."

"I am." I rose from the chair and leaned over the rail to kiss his forehead. "I'll let you get some rest. See you tomorrow."

I headed back to the elevator. Kyle was in a tan chair, looking at his phone. When I approached, he looked up and smiled. "Ready?"

"Yep. Let's go."

It was a quiet ride to the house. I fell asleep along the way. Kyle lightly shook me when he pulled into the driveway. "Hey, you're home. Wake up, sleepyhead."

I yawned, trying to straighten my arms and legs. As I got my bearings, my car door opened and I screamed.

"Why are you so jumpy?"

"You're like a silent ninja. I didn't even see you get out of the car."

He laughed and I practically fell out of the car. My legs were numb from the ride home.

As I attempted to put the key in the door, Kyle grabbed my hand. I jumped at his sudden movement. "What the…?"

Kyle placed his hand over my mouth and a finger over his lips. He whispered, "Give me the keys and don't make a sound."

"What is it?" I whispered back.

"I've picked up a scent."

"You mean someone's inside?"

"Don't know."

Kyle unlocked the door and eased it open. My hands clung to the back of his shirt as we searched the main floor. When he reached the bottom of the stairs, he let out a low growl. "Josephine."

He sprinted up the stairs and it didn't register with me, at first. I ran after him. "Kyle, no! She's not here!"

When I got to the bathroom, Kyle was standing in the middle of the room.

"Why do I smell blood in here? I smell her and…you?"

I poked my head around Kyle and saw that the clothes were gone. I panicked. I stepped backward, hitting the sink, and shook my head. "No. No. No. No."

Kyle placed his hands on my shoulders. "Chloe, what is it? What's wrong?"

I couldn't meet his eyes. I didn't know if I should tell him what had happened or call Cyrus. I walked out of the bathroom. My body was trembling. "I need Cyrus."

"Okay. You want to tell me why? What's going on here?"

"Kyle, I'm really scared. Josephine attacked me last night when I left Erik's apartment. That is how Drake got hurt. He tried to help me. It's my blood, too."

"And where is she now?"

I didn't say a word. I locked eyes with Kyle and he ran his hand through his hair. "This is bad. This is very, very bad. Does Erik know?"

I shook my head. "Nope." I stood there, arms across my chest. I'd held it together this long, but I knew what was coming. This wasn't over.

"My bloody clothes are missing from the bathroom. Whoever was here took them. Can you sense who it was?"

Kyle shook his head. "No. The blood is covering up anyone else's scent."

He wrapped his arms around me. The heat from his body warmed the chill inside me.

"I have a bad feeling that I am next on the killer's list." I pulled away and sat on the edge of the bed. "This isn't just about the Josephine situation. It's the murders."

"What about them?" Kyle knelt in front of me.

"I was with Erik after Julia. She's dead, which means I'm next." I felt the tears. I couldn't hold them back.

Kyle sat next to me and wiped the wet streaks on my cheeks with his thumb. "I won't let anything happen to you, Chloe. Neither will Cyrus. Do you want some water?"

"No, thanks. We need to call Cyrus. I have to tell him about the clothes."

Kyle stood and pulled out his phone. "I'll call

him."

I drew my knees up under my chin and sat there, watching Kyle pace around the bedroom as he told Cyrus what happened. He hung up the phone and shrugged.

"There isn't much Cyrus can do at this point. But, he asked that I be responsible for you."

I let my legs fall back down and shook my head. "I can't ask that of you."

Kyle held out his hand, pulling me up. "Too late. I've already volunteered for the job. You want to watch a movie or something? It will help keep your mind off of things."

I nodded. "Sure. I'll make some popcorn."

We headed downstairs and Kyle waited in the living room until I came back with the bowl and two sodas. We flipped to the Syfy Channel and watched a few cheesy horror movies. We couldn't help but laugh at the bad acting and terrible monsters. It calmed my nerves as we sat together until three in the morning. By then, I was ready for bed.

I showed Kyle the guest room before heading to mine. I peeked out of the balcony doors and two red, glowing dots in the woods caught my attention. I shut the curtain and ran to Kyle's room.

When I flung the door open, Kyle was about to get into bed. He was wearing dark blue Nike short and nothing else. The sight of him caused me to catch my breath and I almost forgot what I'd gone in there for.

"What's wrong?"

"There's something in the woods. I saw two red eyes."

"It's probably an animal, Chloe."

I shook my head. "No. I've seen it several times already. Whatever it is, it's been following me. It's no animal."

He nodded. "Okay, I'll go check."

Kyle slipped his shoes on and went outside to search the premises. He came back ten minutes later to find me huddled under the covers.

"I didn't find anything or anyone out there. Whatever it was, it's gone."

I wanted to stay in the room with Kyle. I felt safe around him, but I didn't want to make him feel awkward by lying next to him. If I accidentally made a move on him while sleeping, it would embarrass me and jeopardize my friendship with Riley. Instead, I put on my big girl pants and went back to my room.

Why didn't Kyle, with his animal senses, detect any odor? He would have picked up on it. Wouldn't he? Maybe this thing-- or person--had no scent, and that was why it was hard to follow.

CHAPTER 24

The next morning, I found Kyle asleep on the floor of my room. I could see the top of his shorts peeking out from under the blanket draped over his hip. A beam of sunlight streamed across Kyle's arm, giving his skin a golden hue.

I took one of my pillows and threw it at his head. He startled awake and I laughed. "Wake up, sleepyhead."

Kyle rolled over, flinging the pillow back at me.

"What are you doing on my floor, anyway? Did you get scared last night being all by yourself?"

"I didn't feel comfortable leaving you alone. So, I came in here."

"That was nice of you. I hope you weren't uncomfortable."

Kyle chuckled as he pushed himself off the floor and folded the blanket. "You'd be surprised by how well I sleep in weird places."

I got up and made the bed. Kyle helped with the other side. "Thanks."

"No problem. I'm going to go get dressed."

I watched as he strutted out of the room.

Shaking my head, I changed into a pair of shorts and a red tank top and put my hair in a ponytail. It was going to be another hot day. It was already getting warm. Maybe it was me. My phone beeped, letting me know I'd received a message. My car had been delivered and the keys were in the flower pot by the door.

I went downstairs to retrieve the keys and put them in my purse. I wanted to make Kyle breakfast so I went to the fridge and pulled out the eggs and sausage. I placed them on the counter and opened the oven to get a skillet.

I heard Kyle come into the kitchen, but even without turning around, I recognized him by his scent.

"May I help with something?"

I turned on the stove and sprayed the skillet with olive non-stick cooking spray. "Sure. You can make some toast if you like. How do you like your eggs?"

Kyle opened the bread and placed two slices in the toaster. "Over easy."

I covered the skillet to let the outer egg yolks cook and put the sausage in the microwave. "Do you want coffee, juice, or milk?"

"Juice is fine."

I took two cups out of the dishwasher and placed them on the table with the juice.

The toaster clicked and Kyle buttered the toast, putting each piece on a paper plate. He set the breakfast nook and watched as I slipped two eggs onto his plate with the sausage.

"Ah, smells great." He cut a piece of sausage and took a bite. "Mmm, this is good." He swirled a piece of sausage in the egg yolk and took another bite. "Didn't you make some for yourself?"

I shook my head. "I'm having cereal." I took the Cocoa Puffs from the cabinet and pulled a bowl and spoon from the dishwasher.

"I could have had cereal, too. You didn't need to go through all this trouble."

"No trouble at all." I took a seat next to Kyle and poured the round chocolate pieces into the bowl. When I added the milk, the contents almost spilled over the edge.

"I hope Riley doesn't get angry with me or you."

"Why would she? She's a compassionate and caring person. That's why I love her."

"You going to marry her?"

Kyle shrugged and shoved a forkful into his mouth, followed by a bite of toast.

I picked up my bowl and drank the leftover chocolate milk. Then I wiped my mouth with my left arm.

Kyle looked at me and let out a small chuckle. "I thought I was the only one who did that." His phone beeped and he read a message and typed someone back.

I put my dishes in the sink and leaned against the counter, watching him smile. From the look on his face, he was talking to Riley. I looked at the clock. It was almost noon.

Kyle put his phone down and got up to throw away the trash. He stood there for a moment, looking down. "I should get going. I have errands to run before work tonight."

The way he stood there before turning around gave me chills. His eyes were a vibrant teal and his animal's scent took over the room. "Before I go, is there something you need to tell me, Chloe? Anything at all?"

My breath caught as my heart began to pound harder. I didn't know what he was referring to. I shrugged, shaking my head. "I don't know. About what?"

Kyle leaned on the counter next to me, crossing

his arms. "I know you are upset about something. I hope you can find it in your heart to give me the courtesy of opening up and telling me what's going on with you."

I knew right away what he was asking. "What did Drake say to you?"

"Drake hasn't said anything to me. But, now…" Kyle stepped in front of me, placing his hand under my chin. "To know that he knows something about you makes me sad. I feel like you think you can't trust me enough to tell me. And I thought we were becoming great friends."

I valued Kyle's friendship and thought about what Cyrus said. He'd told me to tell Kyle everything. Maybe I should. There was no reason not to.

I walked into the living room and Kyle followed me. I didn't know where to begin. I guessed that from the time I went to the club would be the best place to start. I let it all out, and I mean everything. From Erik to Drake and how I felt around them. What Erik did to me and what happened when I killed Josephine. Even my healing ability. It felt good to let the burden of all that had happened to me off my shoulders.

Kyle sat next to me, placing his hand on my cheek. "Thank you, Chloe. You do realize that I can sense things within a person? And, you…I've started to get the scent of wolf. I've just never mentioned it because I was waiting for you to say something."

"That's the thing, Kyle. I don't know what the hell is going on. That is why I had the blood test."

Kyle pulled me into a hug and whispered in my ear, "You'll get the answers you've been searching for soon. I promise."

As I slowly pulled away, I stared into his eyes. For a moment, it felt as if we were going to kiss, but he cleared his throat and stepped back.

Kyle picked up his bag and opened the door.

"Despite the circumstances, I enjoyed myself last night. You know, watching movies and stuff."

"Me, too."

Was there something happening between us? No. No, I couldn't let that happen. I liked Riley too much to do that to her. I knew she was very much in love with Kyle. I'm sure it was all in my head.

I waved to Kyle as he pulled away and then went to the kitchen to clean the dishes. As I was throwing some clothes into the washing machine, my uncle called, asking me to come over and view the video.

He was covered in hair like a wolf. When the woman wouldn't stop screaming, he tore out her throat. His mouth…"

Uncle Bob shut his eyes, shaking his head. "It didn't seem real. I drew my gun, firing shots. The creature took off and I thought I'd lost him, but there was blood on the floor and I knew I had hit him. The trail led up a few floors to a naked man lying there unconscious. When I started to call for an ambulance, a man appeared from the shadows, yanking the phone from my hand. He said he would take care of the situation and I was not to mention what I'd seen to anyone. He took the body and was gone before I could ask any questions."

I immediately thought of Cyrus. He had the appearing and disappearing act down well. "Did you get a good look at the man's face—the one who took the body?"

"No, but I'll never forget his voice."

Uncle Bob and I stared at each other for a moment as if we were on the same page. I remembered how he'd acted the other night at the club when he'd heard Cyrus speak.

"I know there are other beings out there, Chloe. I assume the woman you spoke of is one of them. Is she not?"

I nearly choked on my water as I took a drink. Here I was walking on eggshells, trying not to give information out on the "not so human species," when all this time Uncle Bob had had an experience before me. It must have been difficult for him to not tell anyone about it. How it must have eaten him up inside.

I knew how it felt. I was there not so long ago. It was time to be there for him and tell him the truth. No sense in lying about it.

"Very much so."

"And the club is full of them. Isn't it?"

"Yes." I leaned forward, putting my hand on his forearm. "Uncle Bob, you can't say anything."

He laughed. "You actually think I would go around blurting this out loud? I'd be put in a mental institute just like..."

"Robert!"

Uncle Bob jumped in his chair as Helen's shrill voice cut through the room. His eyes widened.

"What's the matter, Aunt Helen? Is everything all right? Who was in a mental hospital?"

"No one you know, honey. Just a co-worker of Bob's. Isn't that right, honey?"

Uncle Bob looked away, ignoring Aunt Helen.

"What's going on?" I asked.

"Tell her the truth, Helen. She has every right to know." He raised his head and stood facing his wife. "She's an adult, not a child. Either you tell her or I will." Uncle Bob shoved passed Helen, heading for the office.

CHAPTER 26

I walked around the counter and laid my hand on Aunt Helen's shoulder. Her lower lip trembled and a tear trickled down her cheek. "Aunt Helen?"

She blinked a couple of times as if she was coming out of a trance and then turned to go into the living room.

I followed, stopping inside the doorway.

Aunt Helen stood next to the sofa, staring down. Her shoulders were slumped forward. "This is going to be hard for you to hear. It's just as hard for me to tell you."

"Tell me what?"

Aunt Helen sat down. She fidgeted with the hem of the garden apron. I could tell she didn't want to have this conversation with me.

"Before your mother married David, she was with another man for many years. One night, she showed up on our doorstep, crying hysterically, saying she saw him change into a large, hairy monster. At the time, she found out she was pregnant and wanted an abortion."

I found the nearest chair and lowered myself carefully into the plush seat.

"When I talked her out of it, she tried to commit suicide. Your uncle and I had no choice but to commit her to the hospital to save her life and yours."

My stomach tightened and I felt the bile rise in my throat. I closed my eyes, swallowing the burn back down into the pit of my soul. My heart raced. What Aunt Helen and my mother thought was insanity was reality for me.

"What happened to Mom? How did she get out of the hospital?"

Aunt Helen shrugged. "After a few months, she was released. She had no memory of why she was there."

"She was brainwashed?"

"I don't know, Chloe." Helen jumped up and walked around the sofa. "She just changed all of a sudden."

"What about the man? What did you tell him?"

"I told him Katherine didn't want to see him anymore. When he demanded to know why I threatened him with a restraining order."

"What? How could you do that?"

"What was I supposed to do, Chloe, hmmm? I didn't know what was going on or why your mother was upset that night. He could've hurt her, for all I knew."

"You should've told him the truth. Maybe hear his side of the story. What if there was a logical explanation?"

"I'm sorry, Chloe. It was for the best."

"Best for who?"

"For Katherine, of course."

I abruptly stood, hands clenched into fists. "You didn't even give him a chance?"

"Chloe, I'm sorry. I'm so, so sorry. I didn't…"

"What's his name?"

Helen shook her head. "Don't."

CHAPTER 27

When I got home, I didn't have much of an appetite, but I had to eat. I microwaved a quick meal and sat down at the nook. Looking around the kitchen, I remembered how my mother was always baking in here. I could hear her voice and laughter echoing off the walls. A vision of her appeared at the stove in her apron. I saw right through her. When she turned her head and smiled, I inhaled sharply.

I carefully stood, afraid of making the vision disappear. "Mom?"

She rippled into a blurry vision and then she was gone. I reached out my hand. "*No! No!* Come back!" All my hatred and sorrow erupted. Falling to my knees, I sobbed to the point where I couldn't breathe. Every breath was a hard gasp for air. My lungs hurt. I curled into a ball and stayed there until I had nothing left in me. I didn't know how long I'd lain there, but I woke up on the cold floor.

I moved the damp hair from my face. Making it to my knees, I sat there a moment to get my bearings. A knock on the back door startled me. I looked up to see Cyrus standing there. I pulled myself up, straightened my clothes, and opened the door.

"Cyrus, why are you here?"

"You were not answering my calls. I was

worried, and then I saw you lying on the floor. What happened?"

"Nothing. I'm just at a breaking point." I stepped to the side. "Sorry, come in."

Cyrus nodded. "Thank you."

"Why were you trying to call?"

"Nadia has your test results if you want them."

At this point, I already knew the truth, but it wouldn't hurt to hear what Dr. Clements had to say. "Sure. I can stop by tomorrow." I threw away the leftover meal. "Can I get you something to drink?"

"No, thank you. I just wanted to check on you. I'll be going now."

Cyrus slid the door open but I stopped him. I didn't want to be alone and needed a friend to talk to.

"Don't go. Please, I…can you stay for a bit?"

"Of course." Cyrus shut the door.

"Let's go into the sitting room and get comfortable." I grabbed a couple of bottles of water and sat down on the couch.

"What's on your mind?" Cyrus leaned against the wall, arms crossed.

"Lots of things. First of all, did you intervene with my uncle's case twenty-five years ago? He said he never forgot your voice."

Cyrus arched his eyebrow. "What makes you ask?"

"It started off with me watching the video footage from his attack. It was Josephine. I swear, if I could bring her back, I would kill her all over again."

A smile crept over Cyrus's face. "I don't doubt that. How did that bring up the subject of me?"

"Uncle Bob knows about other beings. He told me about this case he worked and how a strange man appeared from nowhere and took the body. Was that you?"

Cyrus straightened his tie. “Indeed. I was sent to deal with the situation.”

He walked around to the back of the couch and I turned, watching him. “What did you do with that man’s body all those years ago?”

“I gave him back to his clan to deal with him as they saw fit.”

“But, why didn’t his leader come for him and put a stop to it?”

“He did, but when the pack leader never returned with the man, they contacted me.”

“What about Julia?” I insisted. “What did you do with her body?”

“Don’t worry. It’s been taken care of.”

“I get that. But what did you do with her?”

“Does it matter?”

“Yes, it matters. She was a human being. You can’t just dump her somewhere.”

“You think so little of me? I am a compassionate person, Chloe. She’s in another realm.”

“Another…what?”

“Realm. You do know what that is, right?”

“Of course I know what it is. But…how?”

Cyrus’s phone beeped and he checked his message. “There are many dimensions to this world, Chloe. You didn’t know about the existence of other beings until a week ago.”

“What are you, Cyrus? Please tell me.”

“Someday, Chloe, I will tell you. Not right now.”

“Is it that big of a secret?”

“No. I’m a private person. I don’t like discussing anything about myself.”

“Are you ashamed of what you are or something?”

Cyrus’s eyes narrowed. “No. My kind keeps to

themselves. That is all you need to know right now."

"I'm sorry. I just want to know everything I can about different beings."

Cyrus sat in the chair next to the sofa. "What else did you and your uncle talk about?"

"My aunt told me my mother was institutionalized for a few months due to a tragic experience. Apparently, the man I thought was my father…wasn't."

Cyrus sat back in the seat, crossing his leg and resting his arms on the sides of the chair. "And?"

"And…I'm starting to piece it all together. The problem is my aunt won't give me his name. She says my mother never told him she was pregnant. I'm hoping my uncle can shed some light on this. Because of him, my aunt was forced to tell me that much. I need to find my father. I need to tell him what happened."

I paused for a brief moment. "I guess the blood test isn't going to shock me now that I know the truth. My father's a lycan. I guess this explains why I acted the way I did with Josephine. You were right, Cyrus. Erik didn't turn me."

Cyrus's phone went off again and he checked it once again. "I need to go. Just so you know, I consider you a part of the club and I've made a room for you downstairs anytime you want to stay."

"Why would you do that?"

"Why would I not?"

"I don't work there, Cyrus. And I don't plan on it."

He laughed, heading for the door. "Oh, if your uncle decides to come back, he better get a new wardrobe. He stuck out like a sore thumb."

Sometimes, Cyrus can make me smile. He does have a sense of humor, but not often.

CHAPTER 28

I locked the door and went upstairs. My phoned beeped. It was Uncle Bob asking if I was all right and telling me that we needed to talk. I texted him back that I agreed and I would talk to him tomorrow. I got ready for bed and climbed under the sheets. I lay there thinking about Kyle and then sent a message to see if he was coming over to stay with me tonight.

Yes. On my way now.

A sharp clap of thunder rattled the windows. Small drops of rain tapped at the glass, and then the pellets turned into a heavy stream. It sounded like someone was throwing rocks at the house. Even with the loudness of the storm, I swore I heard a noise downstairs. I tilted my head, listening. Maybe I was imagining things.

I heard it again. *Clank, clank.*

I tiptoed all the way to the kitchen. I didn't hear the sound anymore.

When I flipped the kitchen light switch, nothing happened. I went to my junk drawer for a flashlight, and guess what? No batteries. There was a click and then the squeal of a door opening. I froze for a few seconds and then turned to see the outline of the basement door swinging open.

My breath caught and I was afraid to move, but I had to check it out. I paced toward the door and peered down the steps, listening. The only thing I heard, other than the rumbling outside, was my heart pounding and the ticking of the clock on the kitchen wall. The hair on my neck was standing straight up. I had a feeling I wasn't alone.

My pulse began to race and I quickly shut the door, putting my back against it. I didn't know what to do except to try to hide. I took one step and a noise from the other room caught my attention. I dropped to the floor and crawled over to the island. Pressing my body against the cabinet, I peeked around the corner. Lightning lit the room and I saw a silhouette standing in the kitchen doorway with glowing red eyes. I covered my mouth as I gasped, trying to stay still.

I had nowhere to go. If I went into the dining room, I'd be trapped. There was no way I could make it to the back door in time, either. Unlatching the door would leave me exposed.

There was movement on the other side of the island so I kept moving in the opposite direction, staying against the counter. As I reached the end of the island, a pair of dark dress shoes appeared in my way. My eyes trailed up the dark figure's legs.

I tried to scurry away in a crab-like movement but the figure seized my ankle and I let out a high-pitched shriek. I fell on my back and kicked the man in the face with my free foot.

The impact snapped his head back, forcing him to let go. Scrambling to my feet, I headed for the stairs. I only made it halfway when the man grabbed my shirt. I lost my footing and fell forward.

I reached for the railing, holding on as tight as I could. The man kept pulling and, after one hard yank, he freed me. I cried out as pain shot through my fingers all the way to my shoulders.

The man picked me up by the waist and I flailed my arms and legs, trying to get loose. Because of the struggle, the man lost his balance and we both fell backward down the stairs. My head hit the floor but the carpet softened the hard blow. For a brief moment, I lay there with the wind knocked out of me.

I scooted out from under the man and slithered across the floor toward the front door. I reached up to unlock it and, as soon as I had opened it, the man snatched me by the hair, pulling me back inside. I held onto his wrist to relieve his harsh tugging on my scalp.

I screamed as loudly as I could, but who was going to hear me? Even if I had neighbors close by, the storm would have drowned out my voice.

The man dragged me into the living room and tied my hands and feet. I lay face down on the floor, crying. I fought to free my hands from the rope, but it seemed to tighten with every move, pull, and tug.

The man left the room and I didn't waste any time. I moved my legs under me and rolled back on my heels and into a standing position. I hopped into the next room and didn't see the man anywhere. The door was ajar.

Taking my chances, I bounced to the door and opened it enough to get through. Once I reached the porch, I went to a sitting position and slid down to the last step. I slipped between the bushes and the house. The rain felt like small shards of glass stinging my face. I wasn't far from the drain and figured I could use the metal to cut the rope.

As I slithered inch by inch in the mud, my body sank into the soggy ground, making it difficult to move. I was careful not to draw attention to my whereabouts. The thorns from the surrounding bushes poked my arms and legs like tiny needles.

I reached the drain and started moving my hands back and forth as fast as I could. I tugged and pulled until the rope gave just enough for me to free myself. Then I started untying the rope around my ankles.

Once the rope was off, I peeked between the hedges to see if I had an all-clear. I crept around the corner and sprinted across the yard in the direction of the woods. I didn't know where I was going. I just knew I had to get away. I wasn't even halfway there when a set of hands grabbed me and I fell face first with the man on top of me. I elbowed him in the gut and eye.

The man covered his eye with one hand and held onto my shirt with the other, trying to keep me from getting up. He managed to get to his feet and pulled me up by the elastic in the top of my shorts, slinging me over his shoulder.

I slapped and clawed at his back, shredding his shirt. I didn't even break his skin. Not even a mark. What kind of creature was I dealing with?

I wiggled so much that I slipped out of his grasp and onto the ground. My knee twisted under me, causing pain to shoot up my leg. I was face first in the mud and the man was lying on top of me. For the first time since our encounter, he spoke.

"Don't fight me!"

The voice sounded familiar. I stopped struggling and he rolled me over and held my arms above my head. When lightning illuminated the sky, I was able to see the face of my captor. It was someone I never expected.

"Dr. Reeves?"

Still sitting on me, he smiled. "Please, call me Philip."

"Why are you here? Let me go." I wiggled under him.

He caressed my cheek. "You're not like the

others."

My eyes widened as I took in a sharp breath. "It's you! You killed those women! You're an evil monster!"

He trailed his finger down the underside of my arm to my cheek. "No, my dear. I'm just trying to survive and do my job." His finger continued down my neck and between my breasts. "I've watched you and waited for this moment to be with you. I saw you kill that vampire. Impressive. I could use someone like you to spawn a new generation. This city is in for a rude awakening."

I squirmed under him, but he was too heavy. What was I going to do? "You're insane! What kind of monster are you?"

Philip smiled. "I'm something from your worst nightmare. Now, open that pretty mouth of yours."

He forced my mouth open and his tongue rolled out from between his lips. I cringed, shutting my eyes tightly as I held my breath for a moment. My heart thumped against my chest. I had no way out. I was vulnerable and at his mercy. Something slid down my throat, trailing deep inside. It cut off my oxygen and I couldn't breathe. There was a twinge of pain in my chest and my body started to go numb.

I couldn't move. I was in a paralyzed state. Warm tears mixed with the cold rain on my face. I didn't know how to defend myself against this thing and there was no way I was going to take its blood into my mouth.

I was losing all hope of getting out of the situation when Philip's weight on me disappeared. I gasped for air, and when I coughed, warm metallic fluid coated my mouth. I tasted blood with a mixture of some sort of slime. I couldn't move my head, but from the corner of my eye, I could see Philip on his hands and knees, heaving. Then a loud shrilling cry broke through the night. He rolled onto his back, convulsing until he became silent. Black ooze coated his mouth and some seeped out of his eyes and ears.

CHAPTER 29

I heard someone calling my name in the distance. Footsteps sloshed heavily through the mud as they raced toward me.

Kyle dropped to his knees at my side. "Chloe, you're bleeding!" He rolled me over so I wouldn't choke on my own blood.

He glanced at the body a few feet away. "What did he do to you? Oh, God!" He cradled me with one arm and pulled his phone from his pocket with his free hand. "Just hold on, Chloe! I'm calling Cyrus."

The numbness was starting to wear off, but I was losing consciousness. I knew I needed to be replenished, but was afraid to take any blood.

"Cyrus, Chloe's been attacked! Please hurry!"

Kyle ignored the body next to us. He picked me up and ran into the house, laying me on the bed. It wasn't long before Cyrus came through the balcony doors. He didn't say a word as he headed straight for me, taking my hand in both of his. His body jolted--a move that brought him to his knees. He shut his eyes tight. His grip tightened, then he let go. He sat back on his heels, controlling his breathing. When he looked at me, his eyes were not green but silver.

"I shouldn't have left you until Kyle got here."

Cyrus shook his head. “I should have sensed danger. Why didn’t I?”

“It’s not your fault, Cyrus.” Kyle placed his hand on Cyrus’s shoulder.

He shrugged it off and stood up so quickly he stumbled back, hitting the wall. Cyrus and I stared at each other. I saw the regret in his eyes, but there was something else. Something I had never seen before. A longing. A need.

The moment was quickly interrupted by Kyle.

“We should have Dr. Clements check her over. She could have internal issues.” Kyle paced the room. “I mean…shit! He’s still out there on the ground.”

Cyrus pinched the bridge of his nose, shutting his eyes for a brief moment. “I will get the body and let Nadia know to expect you. Get her cleaned up and make it quick. She’s as pale as a corpse.”

Kyle helped me from the bed and took me to the bathroom. I sat on the toilet in a daze while he filled the tub. I could barely speak. He shut off the water and knelt in front of me. “You’re going to be okay. Let’s hurry and get cleaned up.”

I stared into his eyes at my reflection. I didn’t recognize myself. “Kyle…” *Cough, cough.*

He rubbed his thumbs along my cheeks. “Don’t try and talk.” He leaned in and kissed my forehead. “Come on now. Don’t be embarrassed about being naked in front of me.”

I wasn’t so much embarrassed as I was uncomfortable to have him see me this way. But, I let him take care of me. Holding onto his shoulders, I stepped out of my shorts and lifted my arms for him to pull the muddy shirt over my head. He held my hand as I stepped into the hot water. I sank down until it was to my chin.

“I’ll give you some privacy.”

I didn't let go of his hand as he turned away. He sat on the side of the tub. "You're safe now. I won't leave the bedroom. I will be right outside the door."

I let my hand slide out of his and into the water. I couldn't bathe myself. I had no energy to move.

Kyle slid to the floor next to the tub. "You want me to help?"

I nodded and he took the sponge off the rack and poured Dove soap on it. Leaning forward, he washed my back in small, slow circles, and then my shoulders. He held my arm out, running the sponge back and forth.

I laid back and he lifted my leg out of the water. I closed my eyes. The sensation of his touch was overwhelming. I'd never had anyone bathe me like this before. When his hand went under the water and up my thigh, I inhaled, arching my back. I felt the air hit my hard nipples and knew I was exposed.

I bolted up, sloshing water over the edge of the tub.

Kyle put the sponge back and took out the stopper to drain the water. He helped me out of the tub and held a robe open as I slipped my arms through. He waited in the bedroom while I brushed my teeth and rinsed my mouth. The horrible taste of blood and Phil still lingered.

My body began to shake as if I had a chill. I held onto the side of the sink. Going from almost dying to an intimate moment with Kyle was too much. It took me a moment for me to catch my breath.

When I came out of the bathroom, Kyle was on his phone. He slipped it into his pocket and came over to me. "You feeling better?"

I shook my head. "Weak."

"Well, get dressed and let's get you to the club. I will be in the hall."

Kyle shut the door and I sat there for a moment.

Even though he was outside the door, I felt alone and scared. I managed to close and lock the French doors before dressing and throwing some things in an overnight bag.

Even if Kyle stayed here with me tonight, I didn't want him in another room and I didn't want him on the floor. I wanted him next to me. It was the only way I'd feel safe. But, that wasn't going to happen because of his relationship with Riley.

I opened the door and saw Kyle was leaning on the wall.

"You ready?" he asked.

I only nodded.

On the way to the club, Kyle held my hand. Most of the time, I stared out the window. Otherwise, I tried to sleep. One thing was for sure--Kyle's car was not comfortable to nap in.

CHAPTER 30

When we arrived, Cyrus was waiting for us and we followed him downstairs. He stopped at the door across from Drake's room. "This can be your room whenever you want to stay. It's furnished with everything you need. But, if you need something, just ask. Put your things away and meet me at the end of the hall."

"Where are Erik and Drake?" I asked.

"They are not here. You don't have to worry about them." He tugged on each coat sleeve and walked down the hall.

I entered the room and there was a huge four-poster bed with a white down comforter and black silk sheets. A white leather love seat was angled in the corner with a glass table. The carpet was a cream color. It was a "pure" room. I went to the bathroom and the shower was like a room of its own.

I tossed my bag on the love seat and met Kyle at the door. We headed down the hall. *Dr. Nadia Clements* was written in black script on a door. Kyle knocked and went in. It wasn't a bedroom. It was a lab with testing tubes, a gurney, a medicine cabinet, and machines.

I guess it was an all-in-one office and lab for their kind.

Dr. Nadia Clements turned around and smiled.

"Hi, Chloe."

She took me by the arm, leading me to a table. "Cyrus filled me in on his visions, but I need more information from you."

"Visions?" I glanced at Cyrus, who ignored my stare.

"Come here and lie down." Nadia patted the table.

I hopped up on the gurney and lay down. While I told her what Phil did to me and what I'd experienced, she put on the overhead fluorescent lights over my head and moved the machines around.

"Sounds like your body expelled the toxin after the creature removed his tongue from your throat. Now, I need to take a look down your throat. Swallow this."

She handed me a large white pill.

"Swallow it without water. It will numb your throat and you won't feel a thing."

"No offense, but I've had enough of numbing and things going down my throat for one night."

Kyle and Nadia laughed. Cyrus tried hiding a smile.

"This could get uncomfortable for you if you don't."

I let out a heavy sigh. "Fine." I took the pill and swallowed it the best I could without water. After a few seconds, I didn't feel anything.

Nadia held up a scope. "This is going to let me see if there is anything going on in there. Can you pinpoint where the tongue may have stopped or where the pain was?"

I tapped at my chest where my heart was.

She nodded once. "Open wide."

I reached for Kyle and he came to the table to hold my hand. Cyrus slid a stool over to Kyle for him to sit on.

I opened my mouth as far as I could and shut my eyes. I didn't want to see what was happening. I may not be able to feel the tube, but as long as I knew it was in there, it was going to freak me out. I heard my pulse in my ears. My skin began to feel like it was burning and I became dizzy. To top it off, I was having shortness of breath. I waved my hand in the air and Dr. Clements saw the distress on my face. She pulled the tube out and I gasped, my hands shaking.

"Chloe, what's wrong?" Kyle asked.

I sat up on my elbows, breathing heavily. Dr. Clements placed her fingers on my neck for a pulse. "She's having a panic attack. Have you experience this before?"

I shook my head.

"I'll give you a moment. I didn't see anything in the esophagus, but I do want to perform a bronchoscopy. Do you know what that is?"

I nodded and squeezed Kyle's hand. "Don't…want…to." I barely got the words out.

"Chloe, since you mentioned you were not able to breathe, this creature may have punctured a part of your lung to get to your heart. I have to check."

Kyle rubbed my arm. "Just relax."

I lay back down and opened my mouth. I didn't like this. I was afraid that at any moment I was going to feel the tube. As she inserted it, I did feel a bit of pressure as it entered my lungs. It was making me nauseous. I kept my eyes shut and squeezed Kyle's hand harder.

He stroked my head and whispered. "You're doing fine, baby. I'm right here."

To hear Kyle call me baby made my heart flutter. Tears streaked down from the corner of my eye. He wiped them with his thumb.

"It'll be over soon. Don't cry."

There were a few moments of silence while Nadia found what she was looking for. “There is a discoloration around this area where it entered through the walls. When it removed its tongue, it automatically healed, giving you the ability to breathe again.”

The pressure was gone and I rolled over to my side, gagging.

“Can we get her a cold rag?” Kyle asked.

Cyrus went to a cabinet and took out a white cloth. He let it run under the water for a moment and then brought it to Kyle. He placed the cool cloth on my forehead, dabbed a few times, and then placed it on the back of my neck.

“I would like to check her heart as well with an echocardiogram.”

I shook my head and whispered, “Tired. I’m fine.”

Nadia patted my leg. “If you’re sure.” She raised my head and looked at me. “I’m concerned about anemia. You lost a lot of blood.”

“Must…sleep,” I mumbled.

“I’ll take her to her room.” Kyle picked me up and carried me down the hall. He sat me on the end of the bed and pulled the covers down.

I continued to stare at the floor.

Kyle knelt in front of me, moving the hair away from my face. “Jesus, Chloe. Your lips are blue! Fuck this! I’m not letting you die.”

He ran to the door, calling for Cyrus.

My vision became hazy and I couldn’t focus on anything. I swayed back and forth and almost fell forward as Kyle caught me and put me down on the bed. At this point, I couldn’t open my eyes. I was being dragged into a darkness from which I might never return. I was beginning to realize I was dying from lack of blood.

I heard Nadia's voice. It was faint like it was far away, but there was also the sound of metal clicking in the background. "She needs blood, and fast."

Someone extended my arm to the side and tied the top of my arm off.

"I'll give her blood," I heard Kyle say.

Another man's voice filled the room. A voice I didn't recognize. "No, it should be me."

I wished I could see who the man was and what was going on, but I couldn't. I felt the poke of a needle and the strap coming off my arm. Warm blood filtered into my veins, sending my body into shock. My heartbeat became louder, moment by moment, with the invasion. Letting out a scream, my body shook violently and my back arched up off the bed.

Hands held me down. The voices in the room were muffled. This was different from when I'd consumed Erik's blood. I didn't have visions and not much pain. Moments passed and then there was silence.

CHAPTER 31

My eyes fluttered open and I realized I was tucked under the comforter. I yawned and gave a slight cough. A stir from behind caught my attention. I turned my head and saw that Kyle was asleep on the sofa. He opened his eyes, and when he saw me staring, he hopped up and came over to the bed. He pulled me into a hug.

"You had us all worried last night. If anything were to have happened…" Kyle pulled away. "But, you're safe now. You're going to be fine."

"For how long?" I scooted up into a sitting position. "Josephine's maker is still out there."

"Yeah, but we will deal with that if the time comes. You're a strong woman, Chloe. You overcame a lot of shit this past week."

"Besides the transfusion, what happened to me?"

Kyle slid a piece of hair behind my ear. "To answer that question, you need to go to the office."

There was another knock on the door and Riley came in. The last thing I needed was for her to find me sitting in bed in my underwear with Kyle. Her smile faded when she saw us together. Her lip curled and she let out a low, rumbling growl. She glanced back and forth between us. Before Kyle or I could explain, she hunched back and leaped in the air.

Kyle jumped in front of Riley and grabbed her in mid-air. "Riley! No!"

"What the hell is going on?" She struggled against Kyle but he pinned her to the wall. "How could you do this to me?" She looked over his shoulder at me. Her eyes glared with hatred. "And, you! I thought you were my friend!"

"You need to calm down. Look at me." Kyle moved his head so she could see him. "This isn't what you think, Riley. Chloe was attacked last night."

"I know. I heard. I come to check on her but find her practically naked, and you're not far from it!"

"I'm in gym shorts, Riley." He let her go but still kept close. "We need to talk. I'll explain everything." Kyle looked back at me as he led Riley to the door. "You okay?"

"Yeah, go on," I waved.

Once they left, I changed into a pair of jeans and a red t-shirt. When I stepped into the hall, I stopped to stare at Drake's door. There was a twinge of sorrow in my heart. It had been two days since I'd seen him.

I noticed it was quiet in the building. Too quiet. I didn't even hear music upstairs or in the playroom. It was odd for this time of day. Maybe Cyrus gave them something to do. As I reached the steps to the main floor, I heard someone calling my name. It wasn't in a bright, cheery tone. It was deep and harsh like when a father scolds a child for doing something wrong.

Erik stalked toward me with long, swift strides. He had something in his right hand. He shoved it in my face, causing me to flinch at his sudden movement. I didn't understand what it was until I blinked a few times and focused on the fabric covered in a black, sticky substance.

"Why is Josephine's blood on your clothes?" His right eye and the corner of his mouth twitched. He kept his head down but his eyes on me.

My words caught in my throat. Was he the one who took the clothes? There could be no other explanation. My heart was pounding. Not because I was afraid of Erik. I wasn't. It was because there were others here who would be pissed to find out I had killed one of their own. They would probably kill me and take the satisfaction away from Josephine's maker.

I met Erik's eyes. They were dark and empty. I wanted to step back, but my feet seemed to be glued to the floor. I couldn't move. I let my eyes break away long enough to examine the room. I wanted to make sure there wasn't an audience. I caught movement just beyond Erik's shoulder and saw Drake appear from the stage.

Erik's voice became louder as he snapped me back to attention. My body jolted at his sudden outburst. "Answer me!"

From behind, I heard movement, but I dared not turn to see who it was. Erik's eyes darted in that direction, causing me to stop. Then he fixed his glare back on me.

I swallowed the lump in my throat. It was the moment of truth and I didn't know why Erik should be so upset in the first place. I'd done him a favor, after all.

"When I left your apartment, Josephine attacked me."

Erik was a few inches away from my face. I could feel the warmth of his breath on my lips.

"What did you do?" he said between clenched teeth.

I was done playing nice. I was tired of being the victim and Erik acting like I was the one who did something wrong.

"The bitch tried to kill me and she attacked my uncle! But, you already knew that, didn't you?" I shoved him in the shoulders with both hands.

Erik grasped my neck with one hand. It was a move I never saw coming. I saw the evil vampire in his eyes. Flames of hatred flickered in the sockets. He tightened his grasp and the scent of my wolf surrounded me. I gave Erik an unsuspecting surprise. I opened my mouth and hissed at him. My long nails ripped his shirt open and I kicked out, making contact with his stomach.

Erik dropped me and Cyrus appeared out of nowhere, pulling him away from me. "What the hell is wrong with you?"

Erik held up the bloodstained shirt. "She killed Josephine!"

"Give me the shirt, Erik. *Now!* And keep your voice down."

Erik handed the items over and Cyrus snatched them from him. He tossed the clothes on the floor and, with a flick of his hand, they went up in flames. "Don't you ever threaten her again or you're done here."

"Why are you pissed at me, Erik? I had to defend myself. You told me you would get rid of her if you could. Why the sudden change of heart?"

"I wanted her gone, Chloe, not dead! There was a reason for that!" Erik ran his hand through his hair, grunting. "You don't know what you have done by killing Josephine. You will pay for it."

"Are you threatening me?"

"No, but I'm sure her maker will see to it that you suffer a long, agonizing death. Trust me; they will come looking for her now that she is off the radar. Not only did you put your life in jeopardy, but you also put mine on the line, as well."

I held my arms out to the side. "I'm not afraid. Let them come for me. They'll be sorry."

Erik shook his head. “My blood may have helped you fight Josephine, but you don’t stand a chance against someone who is centuries old.”

He paced in circles like a predator eyeing his prey. His face was blank. No expression. “My responsibility as your maker is to protect you, Chloe, but it won’t be enough. No amount of protection can save you from someone like that.” He leaned in, lowering his voice. “For your sake, I hope it is.”

“You’re not my maker, Erik.”

“How can you say that? I just saw your fangs.”

I started to walk away when he grabbed my arm. “You *are* mine! We are bound by blood! I created you!”

“Let go of me!” I slapped Erik in the face. “I’m a lycan, Erik! You’ve sensed it just as everyone else has. Your plan of trying to convert me isn’t going to happen!”

Erik took one step and Cyrus grabbed him by the shoulder. “I think you should take some time off and cool down. I don’t need you around the customers in this kind of state.”

“How can you be calm in a situation like this? She put our lives in danger!”

“If anyone put our lives in danger, Erik, it was you, because you couldn’t put Josephine in her place. You are the coward,” I said.

Erik’s eyes shifted from brown to black and Cyrus stepped in the middle of us with his hand up. “Don’t even think about it, Erik.”

He pointed over Cyrus’s shoulder at me. “You are mine, Chloe. We are not over.”

“That is enough!” a voice called from above.

Erik took a step back. “Detective. I was just…”

“Harassing my niece? Yes, I can see that. I should take you down to the station for assault.”

A man dressed in a grey button-down shirt and

slacks was standing next to my uncle. His dark brown hair was cut short along the back and sides. The top was combed in an upward slant—not slicked back, but wavy. I assumed they were here because of the investigation.

The man patted my uncle's shoulder. His voice sounded like the one I'd heard last night in my room. "No need for that. We all know Chloe is able to take care of herself."

"Who the hell are you?" Erik asked.

"Who am I?" The man laughed as he descended the stairs. "I own half this club."

Erik glanced at Cyrus, and so did I.

The man stopped next to me and I looked up into his sharp green eyes. Dark stubble outlined his square jawline.

"My name is Stephen. I'm also Chloe's father."

CHAPTER 32

My head jerked back and my mouth gaped open, but I had no words. A heaviness weighed on my chest as I blinked several times. I looked around the room for answers and saw everyone's eyes on me.

Stephen gave my shoulder a light squeeze. "The missing piece to the puzzle is complete. You've done well, Chloe."

"Let's go to the office for some privacy." Cyrus headed up the stairs.

Stephen and I followed.

I looked over my shoulder at Erik. His hands were balled into fists, but then he relaxed them. He pointed at me before walking away.

"Come on, sweetheart." Uncle Bob laid his arm over my shoulders.

Cyrus shut the office door behind us.

"Before we get started, I want to say that I'm glad you're okay. Cyrus told me what happened last night," Uncle Bob said.

I glanced at Cyrus and he gave a slight nod.

"Come have a seat, Chloe. We need to talk." Stephen patted the chair next to the couch.

I leaned against the wall, crossing my arms. "I'll stand, thank you."

Uncle Bob took my hand, leading me to a bar stool, and then took a seat. "You remember when I told you about the case I worked before you were born and how it was hard for me to process the things I'd seen?"

"Yes."

"Well, it was then I knew your mother was telling the truth. I couldn't let her waste away in that hellhole. So, I went behind Helen's back and told Stephen the truth and asked for his help. It was then that I learned what he was."

"Yeah." Stephen scratched his head. "I feel horrible about what she saw. She wasn't supposed to come to my house that night and I was out back shifting. We wanted Katherine to be able to raise her child without any regrets, and I knew of only one person who could help."

I glanced at Cyrus. He raised an eyebrow. "What? You think I had something to do with it?"

"Didn't you? You seem to be the link to everyone here."

Cyrus leaned back in his seat, resting his arm on the side of the chair. I'd noticed he did this when he was pondering a thought. Next, he would interlock his fingers. I watched. Waiting. Waiting. And, there it was. I was right.

"I know when you have something to say, Cyrus. So, spill it."

His eyes narrowed. "You're beginning to know me well."

"Call it an observation. You have to do that when you don't know what you're dealing with."

We continued to stare at each other.

"Very well." He sat up straight. "I met with Stephen and he explained what happened. I made some calls and someone—not sure who—went to the facility and worked their magic."

"So you had her memory erased?" I asked.

"The person did what they had to do to give your mom some peace of mind. Would you have rather her wilt away in a mental hospital the rest of her life instead of raising you?"

Uncle Bob reached for my hand. "She did live a happy life."

I pulled my hand away from Uncle Bob. "So you knew what I was all these years? Why tell me now?"

"Would you have believed us a long time ago if we had told you?"

"Probably not. If you knew the club was full of vampires and lycans, why did you act surprised when I told you?"

"I didn't know, Chloe. I didn't know Stephen owned half the club until today."

"I sent the invite without Bob's knowledge." Stephen paced in my direction. "I had to wait until your twenty-fifth birthday because that is the age at which your animal starts to develop. It was the only way. You had to find out on your own."

"What would my mother think about my ability if she were still alive, hmm? Did anyone stop to think about that? Would you all still have told me? This all seems so easy since she is out of the picture."

No one was able to answer the question right away.

"We would have told you, but it would still have had to be kept a secret for your mother's sake. There is no hiding what you are about to become, Chloe." Stephen handed me a picture of him and my mother together.

The room began to spin and I slumped to my knees. "This is too much. I…I can't process. I have so office. It was locked, but I knew where Uncle Bob hid the key. I retrieved it from a black antique vase by the door. When I opened the door, I was shocked. I didn't know how Uncle Bob could find anything in the messy room.

Papers were scattered across a dark mahogany desk. Some had spilled to the floor and the leather swivel chair. A large bulletin board sat beside the desk on a tripod, displaying pictures of the victims. Next to each photo was their name, age, weight, height, and hair and eye color. There was also dates and times of death.

I stared at one picture and then moved to the next one. I covered my mouth with my hand. "Oh, my God! I can't believe this." I recognized the girls from the club. They had been with Erik and Drake.

Right away, I knew I had to be careful around Erik and Drake or anyone else from the club. I didn't want to gawk at the pictures, but I studied them closely. The women lay naked and sprawled out on a bed in all the same positions, their arms above their head. It looked like they were posing for pictures. The only difference was that there was no emotion in their faces. Their eyes looked like glassy white marbles as they stared off to the side. Their mouth gaped open, but from what? Was it shock or had something been forced inside?

I shivered as a chill ran through me. I turned away with a tear lingering in the corner of my eye.

Those poor women hadn't deserved to be put on display like this. What could they have possibly done to get the attention of a killer? Maybe they hadn't done anything at all.

I took out my phone and took a few snapshots to take home and study. What the hell would I do with the information if I did find something? I could get into big trouble going through evidence. Would I get a thank you for breaking the case? Hell no. Arrested, maybe.

I didn't want to be in here too much longer. I only had minutes to spare. Careful not to move things around too much, I browsed through the papers on the desk and found some notes with DNA details underneath a pile. Uncle Bob's writing was sloppy, but I could make most of it out.

There is no forced entry into the homes. Bruises on the wrists showed signs of forced containment. Fingerprints are unclear, as well. Reports indicate the victims died from suffocation. There are no puncture wounds on the victims, yet their blood was drained and replaced with an unknown specimen—a black liquid substance—that was collected from the victims' mouths.

I folded the paper and put it in my back pocket. It wasn't like me to steal, but I needed to do something. Every one of the victims had been at the club at some point in time. It was up to me to figure this out since I had access to the club.

I made sure everything was in place when I left the office. I locked the door and placed the key back in the vase before hurrying down the hall to the kitchen. As soon as I picked up my trash, Aunt Helen came back into the room.

"I need to get going. Thank you for lunch."

"You are welcome, sweetie. Oh, by the way…" Helen ran out of the room and came back, holding out an envelope. "Here. Happy belated birthday."

"Aunt Helen, you didn't have to."

"No, but you are our only niece and we celebrate family every chance we get. I'm sorry we were out of town on your birthday. Maybe we could do a BBQ or something."

"That would be nice."

Aunt Helen walked me to the door and hugged me goodbye.

many questions."

Stephen knelt beside me. "But, at least you know the truth. And, now we can get through this together. And, there is one more thing."

I turned my head and met his gaze. Pulling away from Stephen, I used the chair to stand. Once I was on my feet, someone flung the door open and Riley stormed in, heading in my direction. She threw her arms around me. I couldn't move because my arms were being squished between us.

"I'm so sorry for almost attacking you." She let go and smiled. "It's so exciting that you're Kyle's sister. Well, stepsister. This is so overwhelming."

I pushed her away, glaring at Kyle, who stood near the door. "Are you kidding me? Is this some sort of joke?"

Kyle glanced at Stephen. "You didn't tell her?"

He shook his head. "I was about to get to that part."

I backed away from everyone. "Tell me, were Drake and Erik in on it, too?"

Stephen took one step and stopped when I shot him a look. He held up his hands. "No. They knew nothing about this."

I could barely meet Kyle's eyes. My feelings of adoration and attraction turned into embarrassment and rage. I thought I could trust him. He didn't want secrets between us yet he hid the biggest one. I should have known something was off when he told me I would get all the answers soon. I felt betrayed by everyone except for Riley. She was my only friend. If she had known like everyone else, it would've crushed me.

"I can't believe this! You all lied to me!"

Uncle Bob reached for my arm and I pulled away, hand up to warn him. "Don't. I need some time alone."

I hurried out of the office. I couldn't leave, for I didn't have my car. The only place I could go to was either my room or the rooftop. Since it was ninety degrees out, my room it was.

I thought I was going to be happy when I found my father and, for a brief moment, I was. Until I learned he knew about me all this time. Stephen, Cyrus, Uncle Bob, Kyle. How could they keep this from me? They saw me struggling and yet they stood by and let me drown. They let me put the puzzle together on my own. Alone. Right now, that was how I felt.

CHAPTER 33

Drake was sitting on the stage, legs dangling over the edge. He jumped down when he saw me coming down the stairs. I wasn't in the mood for any more confrontation, but he wasn't going to let me get by without a word.

"Hey. Are you all right?"

"Not really. I'd like to be alone right now."

"I, ah…heard everything. So, Erik gave you his blood?"

"That's what I was trying to tell you the other night in your room. It had nothing to do with him cheating on me."

"I'm so sorry. I just assumed."

"Yeah. Well, it's over. I'm done here. At least, for now."

I walked past Drake and his hand caught my wrist. "Wait. I thought you said your dad died."

"The man I knew as my father did. All this time, they knew the truth and never told me."

"Kyle? How did he know?"

"Don't ask."

"I just did. So, it's true? That man is your dad?"

"Yes."

"Geez, Chloe. I don't know what to say. At least you know, right? No more wondering why we sense lycan."

"Yeah, sure. Look, I just want to be alone." I passed Drake as he called after me.

I ignored him and headed down to my room. When I shut the door, the silence made the drumming in my ears louder. I flopped down on the bed, curling into a ball.

I lay there trying to process everything. Finding out the truth about myself was a relief, but it hurt that others had kept it a secret from me. My poor mother went through a horrible ordeal and they made it out as if it wasn't a big deal. Was I happy that she was able to live a good life? Of course. I just think there could have been a better way to go about it all. I'm not sure I would have believed any of them had they told me sooner. I would've laughed in their faces.

My phone beeped with a message from Hannah. She wanted to know if I could come to the club with her tonight. I laughed. If only she knew.

Chloe: *Sorry, I can't make it tonight.*

Hannah: *Oh, come on. Work this past week has been hell without you. Let's have some fun. Please. I don't think I can get in without you and I really want to go. What is so important? A Netflix binge? LOL.*

Chloe: *No. nothing like that. I just have some personal things going on. My uncle was in the hospital recently.*

I hated to use him as an excuse, but what else could I say? At least it wasn't a lie.

Hannah: *Oh no! Sorry to hear. Well, I hope he gets well soon. Maybe next weekend then? See you on Monday.*

Chloe: *Yeah, see ya.*

As I tossed my phone aside, there was a knock on the door. Riley called from the other side to see if I was in here. If it were anyone else, I would've kept quiet.

"It's open!"

Riley opened the door, poking her head in. "Are you okay?"

I wiped my face and forced a smile. "As good as I can be, I guess. You can come in."

I sat up against the headboard and Riley flopped down on the bed next to me. "I knew something seemed different about you every time you came to the club. I started to sense it."

"Yeah, I gathered that." I pulled one of my pillows close to my chest, hugging it for comfort.

"You still upset with everyone?"

"No. I get why they did it. It was just hard to hear. What all did Kyle tell you?"

"Everything."

I sat up straight, turning toward Riley. "You know I wouldn't do anything to jeopardize my friendship with you, right?"

She smiled, placing her hand on my arm. "Yes. I know. I'm not mad at you Chloe. None of this mess is your fault."

My body relaxed and I slouched against the headboard. "All of this is new to me. I know nothing about how to be a lycan."

"Well…" Riley pulled her legs under her, turning toward me. "…I can give you advice on some stuff."

"Like what?"

"For starters, I now know why all the male lycans were eyeing you up like candy. With you blossoming into a new wolf, they were responding to you. They were testing you to see if you were their mate. But, you are not responding to them."

"What do you mean 'testing me?' How do I know if any of them is my mate?"

"When you find the right one, your animal lets you know. It moves around inside, aching to make contact with that person. Marking is a commitment and a promise to protect one another. Kind of like a pre-marriage thing. Jealousy plays a huge role. If another person tries to intervene, be prepared for a fight. Which is why I almost attacked you. And, again, I'm sorry about that. When I saw you and Kyle together, I lost it."

"And, how do you mark someone?"

Riley slid off the bed and started pacing around the room. My eyes followed her back and forth.

She stopped and leaned on the bedpost. "You shift into animal form and the male mounts you from behind. Then, he places his mouth over your neck and bites." She closed her eyes as if visualizing it. "The sensation is so powerful. Makes your body numb and limp and orgasmic."

She then looked at me. "At least, that is what I was told."

"Are you marked? You and Kyle?"

Riley's lips turned down. "No. But, I don't understand why we aren't if we're meant to be together. How are you and Drake? You two seem to have a connection."

I felt the emptiness in my heart. I wanted that feeling of a mate. What would it be like to have that connection? Now I knew why I was hesitant with Drake.

"Hey, what's wrong?" Riley sat on the bed, reaching for my hand.

"Drake isn't the one. I want him to be, but the feelings I have are not what you have described."

Riley pulled me into a hug. "I'm sorry, Chloe. You know, you can still be with Drake. Not everyone chooses to be with their mate. If you love him, then why not?"

I shook my head and slipped out of her arms. "I

"Who is my father, Aunt Helen? Tell me now!"

"Chloe, he doesn't even know about you. Katherine didn't have a chance to tell him."

I froze. The longer I stood there, processing the information, the quicker the boiling rage melted the cold within my veins. "What? I can't believe this! Why didn't she tell him?"

"I don't know. Maybe she was finding the right time."

I held my hand up. "Don't say another word. I've had enough." I spun around, heading for the door.

Aunt Helen called to me. "Chloe, please! I know it's hard to understand, but…"

I spun around so fast that Helen skidded to a stop. My finger was inches from her face. "Don't! Don't even tell me how hard it is to understand! You have no idea of the shit I've been through this past week. Open your eyes, Auntie, 'cause there are things in this world that are fucked up in ways you can't possibly imagine."

Aunt Helen's mouth dropped open as she gasped. "Young lady, don't you take that tone with me. You may be an adult but…"

"That's right! I am an adult. I should have been told this a long time ago, and so should have my father. You had no right to treat him that way! I will find out who he is."

I ran out of the house, slamming the door behind me. The drumming in my ears muffled Aunt Helen's voice as I got in the car and peeled out of the driveway. When I came to a stop sign, I closed my eyes and gripped the steering wheel.

This was worse than what Erik had done to me. It was worse than dealing with Josephine. My life was a lie. They had wiped my mother's memory clean. My real father did not even know of my existence.

Suddenly a light went on in my brain. Did Uncle

Bob believe my mother's story, since he'd had the same experience? Did he know I was different? Maybe he was the one who got my mom out of the hospital. I was going to let things cool down before speaking with them again.

If I were a normal human being, it would have been hard for me to believe what they were telling me. But, I was not human. I was nothing that I thought I was. I was turning into a different person. The old Chloe was about to be nonexistent. No more lies. I had to make this right. If not for me, then for my father—whoever he was.

At first, I couldn't speak. I didn't know what or how to tell him. I tried the easy way out. I scooted the seat back and stood. "Sorry, I can't help. I need to go."

I barely made it to the office door when he grabbed my arm. "Chloe, what is it? You know who it is, don't you?"

I stared into his eyes. They were filled with hope. I couldn't lie to him. I couldn't tell him the truth, either. This had been a bad idea.

"Just answer me this. Does this have to do with the murders?"

I shook my head. "Just someone protecting her lover."

Bob blinked several times. "Her? You mean you were able to see the person who did this?"

I leaned against the doorframe and stared at the floor.

Bob began pacing up and down the hall. "Who is she, Chloe? You said lover like…like she's involved with Erik. I thought you two were…?"

"She was his lover, but it doesn't matter now. She's gone."

"Gone? Gone where?"

"She attacked me, too, but I managed to get the upper hand." I really didn't mean for that to slip out. But, there was no turning back now.

Bob grasped my upper arm. "What is going on, Chloe? Please tell me. Did you kill her?"

I nodded.

Bob stumbled backward, hitting the wall. He ran his hand through his hair. "Where is the body?"

"There isn't one." I stalked off down the hall toward the kitchen. I needed a drink and took a bottle of water from the fridge.

Bob followed. "What do you mean there is no body?"

I twisted the cap off the bottle and took a long drink. I didn't want to have this conversation. Cyrus was going to kill me. "I could take you to where it happened and show you the charred remains."

If my uncle's eyes could have gotten any bigger, they would have popped out of his sockets. "You set her on fire?"

I managed a laugh. If he only knew, and he was about to get the story. He might have me committed after today. "Not personally. I chopped her head off and then she went up in flames on her own."

It was Bob's turn to laugh. He grabbed his side. "You got me, Chloe. You really had me there for a minute."

When I didn't smile or admit that I was joking, he stopped laughing. "Wait, you're serious?"

I took a seat at the table and Bob joined me. Slouching in the chair, he cleared his throat. "Chloe, I need to tell you something."

My uncle's face paled as he sat in silence. Beads of sweat seeped from his forehead.

I reached for his hand. "Uncle Bob, you okay? You want some water?"

Shaking his head, he replied, "No. I'm fine." He took a deep breath, letting it out slowly. "Before you were born, I was on a case. Women were being brutally raped and slaughtered. It was a horrible massacre. I thought it was some type of cult. I mean, no one person could be responsible for such a mess.

"But, one night, I couldn't sleep and went for a drive around the area where the victims were last seen. I was sitting in my car and saw a woman leave a bar. A man crept up behind her from an alley and grabbed her. Instead of calling for backup, I followed him to an abandoned building. I watched between a stack of crates as he converted to some…oh, I don't know…creature.

CHAPTER 25

I pulled into my aunt's driveway. She was on her knees, digging holes for purple and yellow tulips. She glanced up when she saw me. She had a smudge of dirt streaking her cheek.

"Hey, sweetheart. What brings you by?"

"I'm here to see Uncle Bob. How is he?"

"He's doing well. Go on in. I think he's watching baseball."

I let myself in but didn't see Uncle Bob in the living room. I knew he was in his office. I walked down the hall and poked my head in. He was sitting at his desk, looking through a stack of papers. "You look better. How are the wounds?"

Uncle Bob spun around in his chair and smiled, holding out his arms. "Not bad. I'll have scars, but at least I didn't need stitches."

"Aunt Helen babying you?"

Bob laughed. "Of course. It took all of my energy to get her to go outside."

He stood, waving me in. "Come in and shut the door. I hope she stays outside for a while. She doesn't know about this."

"Have you seen the video?"

"Yes." Bob booted up the laptop. "You know I could lose my job if the boss knew I was disclosing this to you. But since you are involved, I could use your help."

I took a seat at his desk and waited for the laptop to run its update. Holding his ribs, Uncle Bob pulled a chair next to me and sat down.

"I could have done that for you."

He smiled and patted my knee. "I'm fine. So, how's your friend Erik? I heard he showed up at the station Wednesday, asking for me."

"I'd rather not talk about him." I glanced at the screen. "It's ready."

Bob leaned forward, moved the mouse to his email file, and clicked on the video. "I can't make heads or tails of it. Too blurry. Hopefully, you can find something to give me some answers." He looked at me. "You ready?"

I nodded once and hit play. I thought with it being a black and white video, it would be hard to make out, but everything came together for me like an old silent movie. To me, it wasn't pixilated.

Bob was heading to his car, and while in the process of unlocking the door, a blur whipped by him, knocking the briefcase in his hands to the ground. He whirled around in time for his face to meet his attacker's hands. He raised his arms to protect his face as he fell to the ground. The attacker slashed at him several times and kicked him once in the ribs. Then the attacker leaned down, saying something to Bob, and, in a fraction of a second, the figure was gone.

I sat back in the chair, my heart beating in my ears. I wished I hadn't seen the video. It was horrifying to see my uncle lying helpless on the ground.

"Well?" Uncle Bob took the laptop and closed the file. "Were you able to identify them?"

don't know. I have this gut feeling. I just need to be patient."

I lay back on the bed and rubbed my eyes. "Ugh, my life has changed so much this week. I have a lot to think about and learn."

"Well, anytime you want to talk, I'm here."

"Thanks, Riley."

"I need to get going. I have to work in a few hours. Are you hanging out at the club tonight?"

I shrugged. "I don't know. I may go home and try to relax. I have to go back to work in two days and I've spent my entire vacation fighting vampires, chasing down a killer, and learning my life was a lie. It's been exhausting."

"Don't forget two males fighting for your affection."

"Right. That is the cherry on the top."

We laughed and she waved goodbye as she closed the door. I sat there thinking about Stephen—my dad. I could spend some time and get to know him a little better. I knew he had to stay out of my life because of my mother, but I felt we could have somehow made it work.

I decided to head back to the office in the hopes that he was still here. When I stepped out of the room, I saw Drake coming down the stairs. His strides increased when he saw me.

"Why didn't you tell me you were attacked last night? Jesus, Chloe, you could've died!"

"I take it you spoke with Kyle?"

"Not just Kyle, but Cyrus and the other two men in the office. They filled me in on everything." Drake pulled me into his arms. Embraced me to the point where I almost couldn't breathe.

"You drive me crazy, Chloe," he whispered into my hair. "Now that Erik's out of the picture, be with me."

I shook my head. "What I feel for you is not love but lust."

Drake placed my hand on his bare chest. The heat from his body warmed my palm. "I don't think you are allowing yourself to love. You've shut down that part for some reason. I know what you want, Chloe. Since we first met, I could see it in your eyes. I've fallen in love with you." He placed his palms on my cheeks, leaning in. "I want to kiss you."

I stood there breathless. My heart pounding in my ears. Knees weak. Stomach fluttering. I waited for the darkness to surround me and for the heaviness to weigh me down, but nothing happened. No forced emotions. No drowning in the depths of someone else's power. This was real, but still too much to handle.

I stepped away, cheeks flushed. "I need time, Drake. Please."

Drake closed his eyes. His jaw clenched and unclenched several times. I could hear the air going in and out of his nose with each heavy breath. He came at me, pinning me against the wall. My heart raced as he leaned close. His hands rested on the wall near the side of my head. His nostrils flared and his chest rose and fell with each breath.

"Do you have any idea what you do to me?"

I shook my head.

He took my hand and placed it on his erection. "This is how hard you make me, Chloe."

My eyes widened and I felt the heat flare between my thighs. I ached to feel him inside me. I closed my eyes and whispered his name. "Drake, please."

"Please what? What are you afraid of, Chloe? Why is it so easy for you to give yourself to Erik but not me?" Drake grasped my jaw in his hand. "Look at me!"

I opened my eyes and stared into his ice-blue eyes with slivers of white that looked like shiny crystals.

"I'll tell you why, Chloe. Because what you had with Erik was not real. He made you do those things. That is the difference between him and me. This…" He pointed back and forth between us. "…this is the real deal. I'm not a fake. Erik doesn't know how to love. He never will."

We stared at each other, and I wanted him. I wanted him in the worst way, but I just couldn't do it. There is a difference between what the heart wants and what the body wants. I wasn't going to give in. I had already done that with Erik.

"Do you want me to be like Erik and just take you right here? Did that turn you on?"

I still couldn't answer him. The right words weren't forming. He took me by surprise when he leaned down and placed his lips on mine. I gasped when I felt his tongue lick my lips as if pleading to let him in. I parted them enough for him to break through, finding my tongue.

One of his hands slipped behind my head and the other went around my waist. The kiss was soft at first but became harder and full of longing as if he needed more. I felt the burning desire between my legs. I fought the urge to touch him. I knew if I did, I would be lost. If I slept with Drake, it would be a mistake. Sleeping with Erik had been a mistake, but I knew how Drake felt and I didn't want to hurt him.

He pulled away, still holding me in his arms. "Tell me you didn't feel anything from that kiss. Tell me and I will walk away."

I tried to speak his name. My voice was lost at first.

"Drake…" I cleared my throat. "After everything that has happened, I need time to myself. I need time to process what I am. I've been lied to my whole life. My father was never my real dad. I killed, for God's sake, and now I may have to face another enemy. I'm not ready for all of this."

Drake let his arms fall to the side. "And, you won't let me be there for you? Fine. I will give you space if that is what you want. I would like to say that I will be waiting for when you are ready, but…I am done."

Drake turned away, but I quickly grabbed his arm. "My life has suddenly been disrupted and is changing. I don't know how to handle this. I'm sorry if I hurt you. I didn't mean to. I'm not going to sleep with you just because my body wants to. It's not fair to you or me."

"Chloe, we don't have to have sex right away." Drake shook his head, letting out a sharp breath. "I know I may have scared you the other night in my room, but my animal was about to break through to get to you. That is why I was so harsh. If you hadn't left, I would have done something that I would have hated myself for. It scared the shit out of me because I'm not like that."

He rubbed my bottom lip with his thumb. "You won't even give me a chance to show you how much I love you."

"We are not meant to be together, Drake."

"Oh, come on!" Drake pushed himself away from me, taking a few steps down the hall. "Tell me you don't believe in that mating bullshit."

"Yes, I do. Riley told me."

Drake shuffled his way back, placing his hands on my cheeks. "Chloe, I believe we make our own choices in life. If two people love and care for each other, it is all that should matter."

"I just can't right now. I'm sorry."

He let his arms fall to the side. "So am I." He

there and blitzed Army with two touchdowns in the second half to record a stunning 12–6 upset.

Legend also has it that when running-back Jack Chevigny crossed the goal line for the first Irish touchdown he cried, 'That's one for the Gipper!'

A plaque with Rockne's speech on it stands on the dressing room door of Notre Dame's football team to this day. How much is legend and how much strictly true?

At least let the record show that after long research, the American magazine *Sports Illustrated* established that enough of it is true for us to safely dip our lids to its essential veracity—though the question is moot as to whether Rockne was simply a motivator of genius who pulled the deathbed scene out of his imagination.

There are two postscripts to the story, one well-known, the other fairly obscure. The well-known story is that three decades later, a B-movie actor by the name of Ronald Reagan would play the part of George Gipp in a movie that would be endlessly replayed when he later went into politics.

The lesser known story is that some thirty years after the famous Notre Dame victory, Michigan State were preparing to play Notre Dame in what was their own biggest game of the year.

Just prior to the game, the Michigan State coach, Duffy Daugherty, approached one of his players, Clarence Peaks, and said to him, 'Clarence, you going to let the Gipper beat you this afternoon?'

'If the Gipper shows up,' Peaks replied, 'exit 15 is mine.'

Sexual Horror Stories

THINK FOR A MOMENT on the enormous grip that the whole Lorena and John Bobbit/severed penis saga has had on the world's imagination for the last year or so. There have been plenty of worse physical assaults going on around the world, and literally millions of violent domestic disputes, but none has gripped us anywhere near like that one.

Why is it so, Julius? Why are we all so incredibly fascinated?

Perhaps because we can all think, even as we tightly cross our legs, 'Well, hey, things might be bad, I might only have got second place in the marmalade jam competition, I might even be looking a bit shaky in my job, but they're not *that* bad.'

For many men, having your penis cut off is quite genuinely a fate worse than death—because however bad death might be, at least you don't have to live with it.

It was essentially the *sexual* horror of it all that most got to us, and for what it's worth, what follows is a collection of other sexual horror stories. They are drawn from a variety of differ-

pulled away, taking two steps back. “I hope you find the answers you need to start the next chapter of your life.” Drake disappeared into his room, slamming the door. The sudden thud echoed off the walls.

I stood there, staring at nothing. I wasn’t sure if I had made the right decision in letting him go. I had to learn more about myself before I could commit to anyone. What I really wanted was his friendship, but he couldn’t give me the support I needed right now. His feelings for me were too much.

CHAPTER 34

I headed up to the office. The door was open, so I let myself in. Stephen was the only one there. He stood next to the bar, holding a tiny glass containing a brown liquid. He gulped the contents and then set the glass down, staring at me. We both froze at that moment, waiting to see who was going to break first.

I don't know what came over me, but I found myself heading straight for him. I wrapped my arms around his waist. At first, he didn't respond. His arms hung at his sides, and then he embraced me. We held each other for a few minutes. I felt loved and safe. In my heart, I knew he was my father.

"I'm sorry for running out."

"I'm sorry for waiting so long. But, I had to."

"I know. It's okay." I pulled away, wiping the tears from my cheeks. "Where did everyone go?"

"Bob stepped out to call Helen. He took a big risk, ya know. She isn't happy with him right now. Cyrus took a business call, and Kyle is getting ready for work."

I shuffled to the couch and plopped down. "Kyle," I mumbled.

Stephen sat next to me, setting his hand on my knee. "Sweetheart, I'm sorry I involved Kyle in all this.

But, I wanted him to get to know you and look out for you until it was time."

"Great. Makes me feel better knowing I was put in an intimate situation with my brother."

Stephen laughed. "Stepbrother, Chloe. There is no blood relation, so you're fine."

I sat up straight, remembering my conversation with Riley. "I'm not one to break up a relationship. Riley told me about mating."

He smiled, bobbing his head a few times. "Ah, yes. She's a firecracker." Stephen stood, smoothing his pant legs.

"Does your wife know about me?"

He grew quiet for a moment, then walked over to the bar, snatching a handful of peanuts from a bowl. "Yes. I told her about you as soon as she and I met. She's anxious to meet you. She's always wanted a daughter."

"Why didn't you two have kids together?"

"She's unable to." Stephen sat on a barstool. "After Kyle was born, his father became abusive and hurt her real bad. She lost her uterus."

"Was he arrested?"

Stephen took a bottle off the shelf, twisted the lid, and poured the liquid into a glass. "Lycans deal with their own. Let's just say that she hasn't seen or heard from him since." He gulped the drink and put the bottle back.

"Did he ever hurt Kyle?"

"No. From what Suzanne told me, he loved his son."

"Does Kyle know about this?"

"Nope. He knows his father left, but not the reason why."

"More secrets in the family, huh?"

"It's not a secret that's mine to tell. If she wants

Kyle to know, she'll tell him."

I opened my mouth to comment when Uncle Bob walked in. His shoulders slumped forward and his mouth turned down in a frown.

"What's wrong, Uncle Bob?"

"Your aunt is impossible to get through. She's upset that I went behind her back and that Stephen knew all this time about you. I don't know why she's dead set against you knowing. It's not like Katherine or David can do or say anything about it." Bob held his hand up. "No disrespect to them, Chloe."

"It's fine, Uncle Bob. She's probably scared because she still believes he somehow hurt mom."

"I suppose. How are you holding up? I know it was a lot to lay on you all at once."

"I'm all right. But, it's going to take some time."

He hugged me and kissed the top of my head. "Good to hear, sweetheart."

Cyrus strolled into the office, carrying a folder. Kyle filed in behind him. When Kyle and I met each other's gaze, I quickly turned to avoid him.

"We need to talk about the guy who attacked Chloe last night." Cyrus tossed the file onto the desk.

Bob turned to acknowledge Cyrus. "Why? The bastard's dead. Case closed."

"Not quite. The worst is yet to come."

"What do you mean?" Bob asked.

"I had my contacts research the creature's body. We are dealing with an embalmer. As they feed on blood, they inject a black substance into the body. For centuries, they've been extinct. We're not sure how they resurfaced. The women he killed are going to come back as those beings, and then more are going to be created. We need to get the victims' bodies and put them in a confined chamber until we can figure out what to do."

I took a step toward Cyrus. "Did you get Julia's

body?"

"No. She's gone."

"Gone! What do you mean…gone?"

"Who's Julia?" Uncle Bob asked.

We ignored his question.

"That was the message I received last night. She somehow escaped."

"To come back here?"

"Possibly. I don't know." Cyrus rubbed his forehead.

"Can't you find her?"

Cyrus's eyes gained a silvery hue. "If I could track these creatures, I would have had this situation taken care of when it all started. As far as I'm concerned, no one can track an embalmer."

So, I was right. They had no scent. Explained why Kyle didn't find anything outside the house the other night.

Uncle Bob raised his hand. "Does someone want to fill me in here?"

I gave my uncle a brief explanation and he stared at me blankly.

My eyes locked with Cyrus's. "So, what do we do now? We can't just sit here and let whatever is about to happen happen."

Kyle reached for my hand, but I moved away. I began pacing. "We have to get into the morgue tonight to get the other bodies and kill them—if it isn't too late."

"Chloe, how did you kill this thing?" Stephen asked.

"It apparently didn't like my blood."

"I have a question," Kyle said. "Won't people wonder where the bodies are? It would be kind of odd for them to just disappear. That will draw attention."

"This is insane!" Bob threw his hands in the air. "I can't go to the coroner with this information."

"You don't have to," Cyrus said. "My people are stepping in."

"What people?" Bob asked.

Cyrus smiled. "Those who deal with this kind of thing."

"How did that work out for you with Julia?" I crossed my arms, tapping my foot.

Cyrus was suddenly in front of me. I saw the fire in his eyes. Actual flames flickering within his pupils. "Do you have a better idea?"

"Yeah. As a matter of fact, I do. I will be bait."

Stephen slammed his fist on the table before getting up and stomping over to me. "Absolutely not! That's out of the question."

"I agree," Bob said.

"I'll do it." Kyle raised his hand. "I'll be the bait. Chloe will inject them with her blood."

"That won't work, Kyle. When I fought that thing, its skin was like rubber. There is no way a needle is penetrating the outer surface."

"Then, how are we to get it in them?"

"Salt," Cyrus said. "Salt will eat through the epidermis. Then the blood can be administered, but…"

"But…what?"

Cyrus turned away and I yanked on his sleeve. "But what, Cyrus?"

"Your blood at the time was mixed with vampire blood."

Kyle stepped between Cyrus and me. "You mean to tell me vampire blood may have killed this thing?"

"It is a possibility--or it was the mixture."

"So, let's combine it in tubes and…"

Cyrus shook his head. "That may work to a point, but if at any given time she is attacked again…"

"So…what? We infect her with vampire blood

again?"

"No," a voice from the door answered.

We all shifted our gaze that way and saw Dr. Nadia Clements was standing there.

"She has no trace of vampire blood in her." Nadia strutted into the office. "I need to discuss your test results, Chloe."

"But, why? I already know what I am."

Nadia glanced at everyone in the room.

"Whatever it is you found, you can say it in front of them," I said.

"Very well." Nadia pulled a bar stool out and sat on the edge. She leaned her elbows on the counter. "Yes, it is confirmed. You are a lycan, but there is a small percent of something else. I ran several different tests and this is a DNA strand that I've never seen before."

The room became quiet. I felt nauseous and quickly sat in the nearest chair. "So, what is it about my blood that killed the embalmer? Was it the unknown strand?"

Nadia shook her head. "Not sure. I am still working on it. Until then…" Nadia slid off the stool and held out her hand. "I need more blood. Not for just what you have planned, but so I can keep researching."

"Wonderful. Can't wait."

CHAPTER 35

Cyrus and I followed Nadia to her office. Once there, she laid out several syringes on the table.

"Jesus! How much do you need?" I said.

Nadia laughed. "You'll be fine, Chloe. Now stop being a baby and sit down."

I rolled my eyes and did what she told me.

"I will be right back." Cyrus hurried out the door.

"He's a strange one." I cringed when Nadia stuck me with a needle. "What is he anyway?"

Nadia smiled. "I'm sure he will tell you when he is ready."

"I don't see what the big deal is."

"It is a big deal to him."

"Is…ah…he seeing anyone?"

Nadia stopped what she was doing and looked at me. She raised her left eyebrow. "Wow! No one has asked that before."

I shrugged. "Just seeing if there is someone out there who puts up with his weird sense of humor."

"Yeah, that he does have, but, no…he isn't attached to anyone. Not that I know of, anyway." She snapped off the gloves, tossing them in the trash. "There.

All done. That wasn't so bad, was it?"

I rubbed my arm. "Yeah, it hurt."

Nadia reached into her pocket and handed me a red lollipop. "Here. Will this make you feel better?"

"I like orange."

"Sure you do."

Before she could shove the candy back into her pocket, I snatched it from her hand and ripped off the wrapper. It was a small lollipop, so I bit it off the stick with one bite. I sat there crunching loudly with a grin.

Nadia laughed, put the syringes in a holder, and then closed it up before handing them to me. "You are a brave young woman."

"Yeah, well, I don't have a choice." I hopped off the table and left the room. What was I going to do now? Sit and wait in my room. Yep. That was exactly what I needed to do.

I stopped at my door and turned to look at Drake's. I took a deep breath and let it out in one hard puff. I needed to see him. Just in case something happened. I knocked and waited. No answer. I knocked again. "Drake? It's me, Chloe. Can we talk?"

Still no answer.

"He's not here."

A tall blonde man was coming down the hall. He held out his hand. "Name is Matt. You must be Chloe."

"Yes. Um…where is he?"

"He left to go visit his mother for a while. Not sure when he will be back. It was nice meeting you." He continued down the hall.

"Yeah, you, too."

Cyrus appeared from the stairwell, carrying a bag. He handed it to me. "Here. Put these on. I will be back to check on you."

Ever since Cyrus left my house after the attack, he'd been acting strange. It seemed as if he was trying to avoid me but couldn't. I would crack that shell of his, but, for now, I had a war to prepare for.

I put the contents on my bed. "What the hell, Cyrus?"

There were black boots, a trench coat, and a one-piece jumpsuit. From the look of it, it zipped only midway. I was sure my cleavage would be nice and exposed. I laughed. "This is not going to be comfortable in this hot weather."

There was a knock and Cyrus came in. "You're not dressed."

"Really, Cyrus? I can't wear this. Could we try for *Tomb Raider* instead of *Underworld* meets *Catwoman*?"

Cyrus shook his head. "Be right back."

I smiled, knowing I may have gotten my way. He was like a flower. Petal by petal, layer by layer, I would reveal the true person behind his façade.

After a few moments, Cyrus came in without knocking this time. "Here. But, the boots stay. And these…" He handed me two knives with curved blades. "…go in the sides of the boots. The handle blends in so it won't look out of place." He left without another word or for my approval.

I peeked in the bag. "Much better."

I changed into a pair of leather shorts and a vest. What was it with him and having my cleavage on display? If this were a movie, I could see it. I put on the boots and slipped the knives into the slots. Then I attached the thigh holster for six syringes and slipped the remaining ten in the vest pocket—five on each side. I pulled my hair into a ponytail and left the room.

Cyrus and Kyle stood in the hall, waiting. Their eyes grew when they saw me. Kyle tilted his head to the side to get a look at my ass.

Cyrus cleared his throat. "Let's go. I will fill you

in on the way."

I couldn't stop staring at Kyle's backside as he went up the stairs. What could I say? It was nice. Then I found myself checking Cyrus out for the first time. If I didn't find someone to mate with soon, I was going to end up doing just anyone, and I didn't want that to happen.

As soon as we were in the alley, Riley called after Kyle. She ran up to him and leaped into his arms. "Be safe. I love you."

I kept walking and yelled over my shoulder. "Time is ticking!" I headed for Kyle's car and waited. Cyrus took the backseat so I could sit up front with Kyle.

"So, here is what I found out. The bodies so far have not left the morgue. Philip Reeves picked his victims for a reason. He chose those who had no family or next of kin. No one will be claiming them."

"Where are we going?" Kyle asked.

"Oh, sorry. St. Anne's Mortuary. All the victims are there."

"So the plan is we walk in, pour salt on them, and shove a needle in the wound?" I asked.

"That is the plan."

"Sounds too easy. You know something is going to go wrong. Don't you watch horror movies?" Kyle said.

"Let's hope it doesn't come down to that." I sank down into the seat. "What are Stephen and my uncle going to be doing?"

"Staying put at the club for now."

Cyrus's phone beeped. "What ya got?"

Silence.

"Are you sure?"

Silence.

"We will be there in twenty minutes." Cyrus tapped Kyle on the shoulder. "Turn left two miles up."

"But this isn't the way. Is it a shortcut?"

"No. The bodies were moved to Westwood Pines Asylum."

I turned in my seat. "By who?"

"I assume by the embalmers."

"Wasn't that place shut down?" Kyle asked.

"Yes. Fifteen years ago. Turn right."

Kyle put on his blinker, looked over his shoulder, and pulled into the right lane to make his turn.

"How are we going to get in?" I asked.

"There is always a way," Cyrus replied. "We are here. Drive to the next block and park."

Kyle parked the car and we stood there for a moment.

"Did you bring the salt?" I asked Kyle.

"No, I thought you did."

"What? Are you kidding?"

Kyle laughed. "Calm down. I'm only joking." He patted his pockets. "I have it right here."

Cyrus held out his hand. "Shall we?"

The closer we got to the asylum, the creepier it became. Trees hovered over a tall iron fence surrounding a four-story building. Large vines had woven their way around the iron poles. Overgrown grass and shrubs hid the walkway and the front of the building. The red brick and cement of the asylum, covered in greenery, was worn, weathered, and discolored. The east and west wings had lookout towers. The arch-shaped windows sported iron bars. I could see using them to keep the insane from escaping, but they were bad for those who might need to get inside in the case of an emergency.

"Why would the embalmers bring the bodies here?" I asked.

"For privacy. For whatever they have planned." Cyrus replied. "When you get in there, head for the hydrotherapy room. These things need moisture and that would be the most logical place to find them."

"Psst, over here," Kyle whispered. "We can squeeze in through there."

"Or we can have Cyrus transport us." I playfully hit him in the arm, smiling. "Right?"

Cyrus shook his head, walking away.

"What? Oh, come on!" I held my hands out to the side.

Kyle tapped me on the shoulder. "Hey, let's go."

I sucked in my breath and slipped through the opening. By the time Kyle got through, Cyrus was waiting for us next to the building, grinning.

I flipped him off, and when Kyle walked by, he grabbed my finger, pulling me along. "Play nice."

We stood staring up at the building.

"This was built in 1842. Not so pleasant things happened here back then." Cyrus placed his hand on my shoulder. "Chloe?"

I kept staring up at a window as I answered. "Yeah?"

"This is where your mother was."

CHAPTER 36

I jerked my head in Cyrus's direction so fast that I became dizzy and almost fell.

Kyle caught me under the arms. "Whoa, you okay?"

"I…I guess I looked up too long." I bent over, hands on my knees.

"Can you handle this?" Cyrus asked.

"Yes. Are you sure this is where she was?"

Cyrus nodded.

"I could only imagine the things my mother went through here."

"Don't worry, Chloe. Things had changed by then. Your mother was in good hands. Nothing bad happened to her here." Kyle gave my shoulder a light squeeze.

I looked over my shoulder at him. "How can you be sure? Were you there?"

I jerked away from Kyle and headed along the side of the building. On one of the windows, the iron bars were missing. In its place was a piece of rotted wood. I gave it a hearty tug and it broke off into many pieces. The bottom half of the window was broken. I put my legs through the opening.

"Chloe, be careful. We don't know what's in

there." Kyle whispered.

My feet touched something solid and I carefully lowered myself down. "Hand me a flashlight."

"You really need one? You are a wolf, Chloe."

"Just give me a damn light, Kyle."

"Okay. Okay. Here. She's a feisty one."

"I heard that."

"Oh, you heard that, but you can't see in the dark?"

"Why don't you come down here and let me show you…?"

A noise caught my attention and I spun around, aiming the light in front of me. The room was full of metal shelves and boxes covered in thick dust and cobwebs. I walked down a row, shining the light on the boxes. They were labeled by numbers and letters.

"Chloe? Chloe, what's going on? You there? I'm coming in," Kyle said.

I continued to the end and opened one of the boxes. Inside was a pink sweater, a coloring book, a pair of brown penny loafers, and a photo of a little girl.

Kyle came up behind me. "We don't have time to go on a scavenger hunt. Well, at least not for this."

"Do you know what all this is, Kyle? These are the belongings of the people who were once committed here. The boxes are labeled with their corresponding room numbers. What if something of my mother's is here?"

"Chloe, this stuff belongs to those who were left here by relatives who probably didn't give a shit. No one came back to claim them, so their stuff went into storage. Your mother was well cared for. There's nothing here of hers."

I closed the lid on the box. "It's so sad."

"Yes, it is. Come on."Kyle pulled on my arm and we headed for the door.

I noticed Cyrus wasn't with us. "Where did Cyrus go?"

"I'm sure he will show up when you least expect it. Let's keep moving."

The door creaked as we moved it open enough to get by. A wheelchair and a gurney were in the hall. Wallpaper hung off the top part of the walls. Cracks splintered the walls from the ceiling to the floor and, in spots, there was black mold.

"I feel we should be wearing masks to protect us from this place." I covered my mouth.

"It won't harm us, Chloe. You know, at some point, you're going to have to turn off the light. We are trying to sneak up on these things, not attract them."

I switched it off and threw it down the hall. "There. Happy?"

"What the hell did you do that for?"

I swept my hand to the side. "You take the lead since you can see better than me. I'm not at my full potential yet, Kyle."

"I know. I'm sorry." He stepped around me and we continued down the hall. "So, are we going to talk about what happened between us and the fact--?"

"Nope," I said, cutting Kyle off.

"At least let me explain."

"No. Let's focus on our mission. Do you know where the hydrotherapy room is?"

"Not really."

"Shouldn't we check the morgue first for the ones they brought in?"

"Yeah, we can start there. Let's get to the main floor and see if we can find the office. There should be a map or something."

I clung to Kyle's arm as we continued down the hall. This wasn't going to work for me. "I wished I could see."

"You shouldn't have thrown the flashlight." He nudged me and I nudged him back.

"Good thing I have a spare." Kyle flipped on a mini flashlight.

I slapped his arm. "Asshole."

We headed toward a flight of stairs. The double doors were chained on the other side.

"Great. Now what do we do?" I asked.

Kyle shone the light along the wall. "Up there."

"The vent?"

"Yep." Kyle stuck his fingers into the grate of the metal cover and gave it one hard yank. It was so old that the screws came right out with it.

"Impressive."

"Thanks." He jumped up, grabbed the sides, and pulled himself up. His biceps flexed as he did. His shirt was so tight that I thought he was going to rip it. Not to mention his pants.

Kyle stuck his head and arms out. "Come on."

I jumped up and he caught my wrists, hoisting me inside. He pulled so hard, I fell on top of him. We lay there for a moment and he held me. I felt his breath close to my lips.

I rolled off and followed him through the air duct. He peeked through one of the vents, and then, with his foot, kicked it open. He hopped down and held out his arms. Instead of jumping, I slithered out until his hands grasped the back of my thighs. Why were we always getting into these situations?

We found ourselves in the main hall. Papers and trash lay all over the floor. Seats were overturned and graffiti covered the walls.

The reception area was lined with windows. There was a small opening above the counter where items, charts, or papers could be exchanged.

Kyle pushed the metal door open and we

squeezed through. He rummaged through drawers and filing cabinets until he found a huge binder. “Here. This is the directory and map to the building.” He ripped the map out.

“We need to take the left corridor and go down three flights to the morgue, or else we go right and head down to the hydrotherapy room.”

“I say the morgue first.”

Kyle nodded. “If you say so.”

The flashlight flickered and went out. Kyle laughed. “Guess I forgot to put new batteries in it.”

“Kyle, I can’t do this unless I can see.”

“I have an idea.”

A few seconds later, I smelled blood. “What are you doing?”

“Here.”

I reached out to find his wrist by my mouth. “Maybe if you take my blood, it will give you a boost. It will be temporary.”

“How do I know I won’t freak out like last time?”

“Because you’ve already had lycan blood. You’ll be used to it.”

I didn’t bite into him. Instead, I licked the blood and sucked as much as I could. I didn’t get a lot, but it helped. My eyes focused as though they were the lens on a camera. I saw the room more clearly.

“Did it help?”

“Yes, thanks.”

As we were exiting the reception area, a noise from the end of the hall caught our attention. We quickly dropped back behind the desk. Two naked women walked by, heading in the direction of the morgue. One had blue hair. I knew right away who it was. They stopped in the middle of the hall and said something to one another. The blue-haired girl nodded and turned to go down a different hall.

"Kyle, that's Julia. I'm going after her."

"That is out of the question, Chloe. We stick together. Each of us has what the other needs to make this happen."

"Give me some salt and I will give you some syringes."

"No. Now, let's go to the morgue." He took my hand and we scurried down the hall. Kyle peeked around the corner and continued down three flights of stairs. The door to the morgue was at the end. We stopped just before we reached the door.

Kyle whispered, "Are you ready?"

I felt my heart beat in my neck.

Kyle placed his hand on my cheek. "You can do this. I got your back."

"Kyle, if we don't make it…"

"Don't. We will. You're stronger than you think, Chloe. When the adrenaline hits, you won't have time to be scared. Your survival instincts will kick in and you will become aggressive. Whatever you feel going on in here…" He tapped my chest. "…let it out. Don't hold back. Okay?"

I nodded. "Yeah. I got it."

If I could kiss Kyle right now, I would. I wanted to ask why he and Riley were not marked. Was he holding out for someone else? Now wasn't the time, and it wasn't my business. I didn't want him to know that Riley had spoken about their relationship. I know she wanted more from Kyle but, for some reason, he couldn't commit.

I looked down at the floor and the words just flew out of my mouth without me even thinking. "I love you, Kyle."

I couldn't meet his eyes after I said that. But, he didn't take it the way I'd wanted him to. I know he thought I meant it as a friend or sister, but for me, it was much more.

He grasped my chin. “Love you, too, Chloe. Now let’s kick some embalmer ass.”

Kyle pushed the door open and we stepped into the room with our backs against the wall. “I don’t see her,” he whispered in my ear.

Clear plastic strips hung on the other side of the room, leading into another section. We heard movement. Kyle and I hurried behind a counter. The naked girl pushed the plastic aside, appearing in the archway. She walked over to the refrigeration unit where the corpses were kept and opened six small doors. She pulled out the metal slabs with the bodies on them. When she finished, she walked past us and left the morgue.

My skin became clammy and I scooted away, hitting the wall. I brought my legs up against my chest, wrapping my arms around them. I rocked back and forth to keep my muscles from tensing.

“Chloe, what’s wrong?”

“These are new victims.” I jumped up and went to the nearest table, pressing my finger against the side of the body’s neck. “She has a pulse and is still warm.”

Kyle came over and placed his finger on her wrist. “These are innocent people. Seems like they have been knocked out.”

“We have to do something. How are we going to get them out?”

Kyle shook his head. “I don’t know. We are too late for Plan A.”

“So, what is Plan B?”

“We inject these people with your blood, and when it comes time for the assholes to feed…” He held out his hands. “Well, there ya go. They won’t know what hit them.”

“Are you crazy? I can’t infect them with my

blood."

"These people are as good as dead anyway, Chloe. Your blood won't have time to affect them once that black shit is injected into them."

"I'm not going to kill innocent people."

"So, you're going to let them be their victims, instead? We could stop this…" Kyle quickly stopped talking and tilted his head, glancing at the door. "We have to hide. Quick."

"But, the bodies."

"Now, Chloe." He grabbed my hand and ran into the other room. He pushed a tall cabinet away from the wall just enough for us to hide behind. I reached for Kyle's hand, squeezing it for comfort. My heart was racing. I tried not to breathe so loudly. Kyle had to cover my mouth.

When I heard movement in the room, I held my breath. My body stilled. I prayed they couldn't hear my rapid heartbeat.

There were scraping and clanging sounds. Then six loud bangs. After a few minutes of silence, Kyle stepped out from behind the cabinet. He pulled his phone from his pocket and hit a button.

"Cyrus, we are in deep shit," he whispered. "There are new victims here. We are in way over our heads." Kyle paced in circles around me. "Well, your sources don't know shit. Figure something out and soon." He put the phone back and took my hand. "Come on."

"Where are we going?"

"To the hydrotherapy room. I'm sure that is where the rest are gathered. We can get a better picture of how many more we are dealing with."

"How are we to do that with only one way in and out? We can't hide."

Kyle pulled the floor plans from his back pocket.

"There is a room next to it. Looks like the shock therapy room. There is a metal vent in the wall. We can peek through it."

"I don't know about this. We should go and re-think this whole situation."

"Chloe, we have to find a way to stop this tonight."

"Fine. But, if I get killed, you're the first person I'm going to haunt for the rest of your life."

"And, if I get killed, we can haunt together." He laughed and I punched him in the arm.

"Not funny, Kyle."

I followed Kyle back into the other room. The bodies were now gone. Kyle opened the door and peeked out. We hurried down the hall and back up the three flights of stairs to the main level. A sign hung overhead in blue noting the West Wing. Arrows pointed down for electroconvulsive therapy, hydrotherapy, and lobotomy.

Luckily, we had a clear shot. But, as we neared our destination, we could hear moans and groaning coming from the room.

We slipped into a room labeled ECT ROOM 54B. I stopped just inside the door. A table with straps and one of the machines used for shock therapy had been left behind. The machine gave me the chills. "Kyle, this is creepy."

"Yep." Kyle moved the table over to the wall and placed it under the vent. "Come on."

"I don't want to get on that thing. People have probably died on there."

Kyle looked down at me. Even in the dark, his eyes gave off a green iridescent glow.

"Fine, just stop staring at me like that," I said.

I took a hold of his hand and he pulled me up. We peeked through the slender slats of the vent. On the far side of the room was a woman with six tentacles flowing behind her. Large, red, bulbous eyes sat high on her head, the bridge of her nose was almost flat against her face, and she had two small nostrils. Her lips and chin were like a human's.

"What the hell is that?" I asked.

"I have no idea."

"Well, this keeps getting better and better."

Six embalmers came in, pushing gurneys. There were three naked women and three naked men strapped down on their gurneys. A metal object kept their mouths open.

"Those are the bodies. Oh, this is bad, Kyle."

"No shit."

"No, I mean really, really bad. I only have sixteen vials. If they make six more of these creatures…I don't have enough, as it is."

"We have to split them up," Kyle said.

"No, we stick together. Remember?"

"There are too many to take on all at once. If an opportunity arises, we separate, Chloe. Promise me."

The woman's head turned in our direction. It looked like she was staring right at us. We quickly ducked down and waited a few minutes before looking again. The embalmers mounted their victims and began feeding.

I turned away and slid down the wall, shutting my eyes. "I can't do this, Kyle. I want to go. We need to get out of here. This was a dumb idea."

Kyle pulled me into his arms. "Sorry, Chloe."

The door flung open and two large men with glowing red eyes came into the room. The taller of the two smiled as he walked toward me. "Well, look who it is? Philip's choice for a mate."

"How do you know about me?"

The man laughed. "Philip told us all about you. Even showed us a picture and said you're off limits. Too bad he isn't here."

"That's because I killed him."

"Is that so? Good. Then I call dibs." The guy grabbed me and tossed me over his shoulder.

"Let go of her, asshole!" Kyle lunged toward my captor.

The other man jumped on Kyle and pinned him to the floor with Kyle's hands behind his back.

"Kyle! Kyle!" I kicked and screamed until we turned the corner and were out of sight.

CHAPTER 37

I reached into my vest pocket and pulled out a syringe. I rammed the syringe into his mouth and pushed the blood through.

He burst through the doors to the hydro room and we both dropped to the floor. The man's body flopped around as if he was a fish and black ooze seeped from his pores. Everyone in the room turned to watch him deteriorate.

The man who had been with my captor bolted into the room with Kyle in an armlock.

"What is this interruption?" The woman asked.

"Intruders, my queen. We found them snooping around in the other room." The man kicked me in the side. "This one here is the one Philip spoke of."

"And, where is he?"

"The slut claims to have killed him. From the looks of it, she just killed Garret. She brought one of her lycan boyfriends, too."

I quickly stood, dusted myself off, and turned to the man. "Hey, it's 'bitch' to you."

Kyle laughed and the man tightened his hold.

"Bring her to me." The woman said.

One of the guards grabbed me by the arms and pulled me forward. The woman leaned in, focusing on my eyes. "You have many suitors—Erik, Drake, and Kyle. I assume you're Kyle?" She looked over my shoulder at him.

"How do you know all this?" I asked.

The woman let out a cackle that echoed through the room. "Philip has kept a close watch on all of you, my dear. He says you have special abilities."

"I don't know what he's talking about. I'm no one special."

"But you killed a vampire. How could you withstand such ancient power?"

I shrugged. "Just lucky, I guess."

Another guard came up beside her and put something in her hand. She held it up and examined it. "What is this?"

"Oh, that." I laughed. "That is what I used to kill Garret. Oh, and Philip, too. I am known as the Executioner, and I'm here to put an end to you all."

"Chloe! What the fuck?" Kyle wriggled in the clutches of the embalmer.

I gave Kyle a sideways grin. I knew what I had to do to get my inner being to come out, and it wasn't going to happen by playing nice.

"Is that so?" The woman stepped forward. "You think you can destroy us? You are outnumbered."

"You want to test that theory?" I tilted my head.

The woman glanced down at my leg and ripped off the holster with the syringes in it. She could have them. I had other plans.

She pulled out the syringes and stared at me. "Let's see how well you react to these. Hold her down!"

I wanted to laugh in her face. She had no idea she was injecting me with my own blood. Kyle was in the background, struggling to get free as he yelled for them to stop. He was a good actor. Hell, I even believed him. But, I thought the award should go to me.

When they finished, they tossed the empty syringes on the floor and waited for something to happen. With only nine syringes left, I had to use them wisely.

I rolled over, clutching my stomach as if I was in pain. I used my violent movements to disguise the fact that I was preparing one of the syringes. I squirted a bit of blood into my mouth and then quieted down. I lay there motionless.

"Check on her," the woman ordered.

One of the men turned me onto my side. With the needle ready, I shoved it into his eye. He fell back with a high-pitched yelp, rubbing his eyes. Within seconds, his lifeless body was a black, sticky mess.

"How is this possible? Seize her!"

A howl rumbled through the room and I saw Kyle shifting into animal form, breaking the embalmer's hold. His tight leather pants were no longer and Kyle stood tall, naked, and proud.

The distraction was enough for me to lose focus. Two embalmers grabbed me and held me down while another positioned himself on me. I didn't want to go through this again, but this time I was prepared. When the embalmer neared, I spit my blood into his face. He clawed at his eyes but the damage was done.

There were twenty embalmers now down by three. With seven needles left, I wasn't sure how I was going to pull this off. Thank God I had the knives, and I prayed that Kyle could do some real damage.

The two men who were holding me down retreated. I didn't know what had upset them, but then I saw parts of their skin burning. I glanced up and saw Kyle standing there with the salt. I jumped up and ran to one of the men, stabbing him in the back with the sixth syringe, then the other with number five.

"This is monstrous!" The woman had nowhere

to hide. The remaining embalmers gathered around her, including the newbies. I met Julia's gaze.

"You!" Julia pointed.

I smiled. "Yes?"

"Because of you, Erik ditched me!"

"Well, I hear he is available now. It's sad that you won't get a second chance because you'll be dead. Oh, wait! You're dead to him anyway."

"Bitch!"

Julia lunged at me and I stepped to the side and spun around, kicking her in the back. She fell face first on the concrete floor. I pressed my knee into her spine and grabbed a handful of her hair, lifting her head. When her mouth opened, Kyle appeared in front of her and poured salt down her throat. She foamed at the mouth, gagged, and gasped for air. I took out a syringe and applied only half of it to her tongue. I let her head fall to the floor and stood up.

I'd thought there was going to be a bigger battle. But, these embalmers couldn't fight to save their lives. "Who's next?"

"Kill her, *Now!* And get those syringes!" The woman ordered.

"Oh? You want them? I'd be happy to give them to you. Come and get 'em, boys."

I took Kyle's suggestion of splitting up and raced out of the room, leaving Kyle behind. I was sure I would get an earful from Cyrus later.

Five embalmers came after me. There weren't many rooms on this floor to hide in. I had an idea to go to the boiler room. I remembered seeing it on the map. I had to go back to the main floor and then go to the basement. I had to buy myself some time to prepare for the next round. I had to plan my moves against five monsters. I couldn't lure them all into one spot. That was too many for me to handle. I had to take them out one by one somehow.

I made it to the main floor, and as I turned the corner, a shadow stood by the boarded-up front doors.

"Need some help?" Cyrus asked.

"Decided to finally join the party?" I jumped over a chair in my way.

"Throw me a syringe."

I did and kept moving. The shadow disintegrated and moved up the side of the wall. If I had time to stay and watch Cyrus in action, I would have.

I kept going toward the door to the basement. Behind me, I heard the creatures yelp as I descended into the bowels of the asylum. I wondered how many Cyrus had been able to take out.

The boiler room was straight ahead. I was expecting a regular room with massive metal ovens, but no. This was larger. I stopped immediately inside the door and shut it. I had to take the time to study my surroundings. There were three levels in the room. Each level had a metal walkway surrounding it. The lower level contained four large boilers on each side.

There was a loud bang on the other side of the door. Three creatures were trying to get in. I took the stairs to the third level. A small office was blocked off by its door, which had fallen off its hinges. I ducked down, crawled through the small hole and into the room, and prepared for my next attack.

I took the knives from my boots and used up the last of the syringe by coating the blades with blood. This would take care of two out of the three if the blades could slice through their skin. If not, then I don't know why Cyrus would have given them to me.

I crawled back out onto the catwalk. There was a loud bang and I saw the main door fly across the room. My vision blurred and I started to see double. Kyle's blood was wearing off and soon I wouldn't be able to see. I wondered when my ability to see in the dark would kick in.

I was lost in thought and didn't notice the three predators coming my way. One on each side and one in the middle. I kept my arms behind my back as I leaned against the wall.

"You think you can hide from us?"

"No, that wasn't my plan."

I let them get close to me and, when I swung my arms, they tilted backward out of the way and grabbed my wrists, pinning me to the wall. The knives fell to the floor.

"Nice try."

The embalmers trapped my legs against theirs and I couldn't move. The third embalmer stood in front, licking his lips. "A girl with your aggressiveness would make a great mate. What Philip didn't get to do, I will."

He reached up to caress my face, then trailed his finger down between my breasts. He started to slip his hand under my vest when a black shadow swooped down from above, knocking the middle guy backward. He lost his balance and fell over the rail to the lowest level. I'm sure the fall didn't hurt him, but it bought me some time with the remaining two.

"What the hell was that?" one of the men asked.

Each of the men looked over his shoulder, causing their grip to loosen around my wrists. I slid down to the floor, grabbed the knives, and sliced into their abdomens. As they bent over, I brought the butt of the knives up into their noses. They fell backward with their insides spilling onto the floor.

The embalmer who had fallen over the rail made his way back and grabbed me from behind, trapping my arms against me. I flung my head back, hitting him in the nose. I kicked him in his groin with the heel of my boot. He dropped me as he keeled over, wailing from the blow. My foot connected with his jaw, sending him backward. I took both blades and cut into my arms to get blood on the blades. While the wounds healed, the man scurried toward the back wall.

"What…what are you?"

"I'm your reaper." I crossed my arms in front of me and brought the blades down, cutting across his neck.

The man grasped his throat, making gurgling sounds as he coughed and spit up black ooze before falling silent.

I sensed a presence behind me and smiled. "Thank you for your help." I put my knives back in the slots on the boots. "I need to get back to Kyle, but I have a slight problem."

"What is it?"

"I can't see."

CHAPTER 38

Cyrus placed a small bottle in my hand. “Drink this.”

I drank the liquid with no questions as to what it was. When I opened my eyes, things were clear. They weren’t in color, though. More in shades of black and grey. “Is Kyle okay?”

“No. He needs your help, Chloe. We will speak of this later.”

“Hey, it was his idea to split up. Why didn’t you help him?” I followed him back to the main hall. I was jogging to keep up with him.

“Because I was busy helping you. I can’t be in two places at once. Believe me, I’ve tried.”

“But, you are fast. Aren’t you?”

“I am. But, I was not able to help Kyle. Besides, my loyalty is to you.”

“Me? Why me?”

He spun around so fast, I ran into him. “I made a promise. Now, we don’t have time for this. You must go to him now.”

I blinked a few times and Cyrus was gone.

I hurried down the corridor to Kyle. When I’d left, there were nine embalmers. Now, three remained, including the woman. Bodies lay in pieces all over the floor in pools of black goo and blood. Kyle was back to human form and coated in both liquids. He was hurt and I couldn't tell how bad it was.

He lay on the floor next to one of the remaining female embalmers. She snuggled against Kyle, caressing and licking his naked body.

"Kyle!" I wasn't going to cry. I was angry. Angry at myself for leaving him alone. If anything happened to him, I would never forgive myself. What I'd done was selfish, but I'd thought it was the right thing to do at the time. It was a stupid idea.

"Get your slimy hands off him!"

The girl's mouth curled down into a pout. "Aw, jealous are we?"

"If you so much as…" I darted forward and the women held up her hand.

"Not another step or he will die."

I halted a few feet away.

"Now, that's better. Since you have killed off most of my children, I want to negotiate. You come to me willingly with no weapons or syringes and I will let him go."

"Don't do it, Chloe," Kyle mumbled. "She'll kill me…" He winced. "…regardless."

I had two syringes left and my knives were back in the boots and camouflaged. I was willing to accept my fate if it meant saving Kyle. If it weren't for me, he wouldn't be in this position.

"But, I want him for myself," the female embalmer said. Her hands trailed over the muscles in his abs. "He's so strong and handsome."

"Get a hold of yourself, girl!" The woman snapped. She looked back at me. "Well? What's it going to be?"

I took the syringes out of my pocket and

dropped them on the floor. “There. That’s all I have left.” I held my hands out, palms up. “Now, let him go.”

The woman snapped her fingers. The last male embalmer carried Kyle out of the room. A few minutes later, the man came back and shut and latched the doors. He smiled as he strutted in my direction, rubbing his hands together.

“I want her. Please let me have her, my queen.”

“Request denied. You are a disgrace to our kind. You and Emily both.”

The man hurried to the woman and knelt in front of her, as did the female. “How have we disgraced you? We are the last two standing.”

“You’re weak. I saw you both hiding while the others were being slaughtered. You not once fought in my honor. But you will now.”

The man and the girl looked up at the woman. “What? You want us to fight each other?”

The woman smiled and caressed the man’s face. “No, darling. I want you to fight her.” She pointed in my direction.

“But, my queen…”

“You have no choice!”

I quickly searched the room to get a better feel for the setup. A set of shackles hung from one wall with a water hose lying on the floor. This place was evil back in the day. Tubs lined the wall opposite the shackles. By the door, Kyle’s pants lay tattered on the floor with one last bottle of salt. I was ready to finish them off so I could go home, take a hot bath, and sleep for a few days. At least until Monday.

“Are we going to do this or stand here and whine about it?” I asked.

The female embalmer was the first to lunge at me. I turned and ran toward the entryway. I dropped to the floor, grabbed the salt, and stood back up. I spun around in time to bring my foot up, kicking the girl in the face. Her head snapped back and she landed on the floor.

"Get up and fight, girl!" The man yelled.

The girl stood, eyeing me up and down. She swung at me and I ducked. As I came back up, my fist met her jaw. Again, she fell to the floor.

"I have such weaklings!" The woman roared.

I ran over to the shackles and waited for the girl to come at me. From what I had seen, she wasn't all that smart. She ran toward me and tried swinging at me again, but I caught her arm and swung her around until she hit the wall. Holding her arm in place, I locked the shackle around her wrist. She kept swinging at me with her free hand, but I captured it, as well. She tugged and pulled, screaming at me.

"You bitch! I'll kill you."

"I don't think you know how. Anyway, you're in no position." I took the lid off the salt, holding it up.

"What's that?"

"An antidote for your condition." I tossed the contents on her, causing blisters to form in several areas. The boils broke open and puss began to drip, making the lesions worse. She kicked and screamed, yanking on the shackles. I walked over to the syringes, picked up one, and inserted it into the sores. Her body blackened and became a puddle of goo.

I looked at the woman and shrugged. "I know you said no weapons, but…"

She held up her hand and glanced at the last man standing. As the man walked over to me, he picked up the last syringe and emptied the contents onto the floor.

"I'm not taking any chances."

I smiled. "Fine by me. I don't need it."

We stood staring at each other, closing the space between us.

"How can a beautiful woman like you be so fierce?"

"How can someone like you call yourself a man?"

The back of his hand met my cheek. It jolted my head to the side but didn't affect me. I half grinned and repaid him with the same gesture. We were toying with each other at this point.

He picked me up by the throat, my feet dangling. I kicked him between the legs and he dropped me. This was a common move if you wanted to bring a man to his knees. Once on the ground, I kneed him in the face. He fell back and used his leg to sweep mine out from under me. I must say, he was putting up a good fight. I finally had some kind of competition.

He grabbed my ponytail and pulled me to my feet. Holding onto me, he kicked me several times in the ribs and then slung me across the room. My back hit the edge of a tub. I cried out as pain shot through my spine.

The man stalked toward me, grasped my leg, and pulled me away from the tub. He climbed on top, putting his full weight on me, and held my arms above my head. It was the Philip scene all over again.

"I'm going to make you my slave." His mouth met mine and I opened to let him in. He tasted me as I tasted him. He worked his tongue toward the back of my throat.

I let all of my anger build up inside me. I thought about Kyle, and it pushed me over the edge. My canines finally decided to come out of hiding. I bit into my own tongue and cheek and then bit into him, coating our mouths with my blood.

The man's eyes widened. He coughed and scratched at his throat as he tried to crawl away. His weak body collapsed, and he heaved and gagged on the blood. Dark, thick matter seeped from his pores until he lay motionless, eyes staring off into the abyss of death.

The woman's red eyes lightened in color. A small black pupil formed in the middle of both. "How did you do that without any weapons?"

I lay there in pain, unable to move. It hurt even to breathe. I knew I had some broken ribs and that they would heal, but I needed blood for them to heal faster.

The woman came over to me. Two tentacles lifted me up by the wrists. Two held my legs open. "You may be able to kill my minions, but you can't kill me." A fifth tentacle wrapped around my neck and a sixth my waist.

She pulled on my limbs, stretching me as far as I could go. I let out an ear-piercing scream as pain shot through my joints. I was losing all hope of getting out of this one. I had nothing and no one to help me.

From the corner of my eye, a black mist filtered through one of the vents and floated up to the corner of the ceiling. A shadowy figure formed, staring at me with two white glowing orbs for eyes. I'd never seen anything like it before.

"Chloe! Chloe! You must fight!" Kyle banged on the door. "Think of what Erik and Josephine did to you! Think about your uncle's attack! Don't hold back, Chloe! Let it go! Remember what you are!"

Kyle's voice gave me the strength I needed. I closed my eyes and searched for whatever I had inside of me and tried to bring it forth. My animal retreated, but in its place was another vengeful force. Something that was there when I'd fought Josephine. I felt the power inside of me. When my eyes flew open, the woman gasped. I didn't know what she saw, but it scared the hell out her.

My body began to tremble and my hands tingled. White electric sparks formed on the tips of my fingers. I closed my hands and the energy grew in my palms. I opened my fists and two white orbs shot out at the woman, leaving two burn marks on her chest. This only seemed to piss her off more. Her grip tightened, pulling me farther apart.

I didn't want to give her the satisfaction by showing her the pain she was causing me, so I bit my lip. Time was running out and I didn't know what to do.

The pounding on the door became louder and louder as if something was trying to break through. The door flew open and a large, hairy beast sprinted toward the woman.

The tentacle around my waist whipped through the air, knocking the animal backward.

The shadow on the ceiling swooped down and swirled around the woman, causing dust to rise.

"What is this?" the woman yelled. "I can't see!"

The wolf attacked again. His mouth latched onto the woman's neck and she shrieked, loosening her hold on me. I fell to the floor and reached for a knife. As Kyle held her down, I sliced through her tentacles. One by one, they dropped to the floor. Blood spewed all over us.

Kyle jumped off the woman, leaving her thrashing back and forth on the floor. Her grey skin became ashen and withered like a thousand-year-old corpse. Blood pooled around her lifeless body.

I lay on the floor, looking around the room for the mist, but it was gone.

"Chloe! Chloe, are you okay?" Kyle crawled over to me, sweeping me into his arms.

I looked at him with a smile. "You're naked."

Kyle's grip tightened. "I figured since I saw you naked, I should…"

"I'm so sorry, Kyle. I shouldn't have left you. I could have gotten you killed." I finally broke down, sobbing into his shoulder.

"You did what I told you to do. Otherwise, it would have been too many for us to handle." Kyle held my head as he kissed my forehead and cheeks all the way to the side of my lips.

"You're a bloody mess." He wiped at my face with his thumb. "If anything were to have happened to you…"

I gaze up into his eyes. A hint of tears lingered in the corners.

Kyle let out a huff of air. "You are one hell of a fighter."

I managed a smile. "I took Tae Kwon Do classes a few years ago. Never thought I'd put my skills to use."

Kyle laughed and kissed my head again.

Cyrus appeared next to us. "I'm glad you're both safe." He handed Kyle a fresh pair of clothes and he quickly dressed.

"Let's get back to the club and get cleaned up. Your uncle and Stephen are waiting for you."

"Can you stand?" Kyle asked.

"I don't know. I feel like she tore some tendons. I'm surprised I was able to cut off her limbs."

Kyle stood with me in his arms and, together, we made our way out of the asylum.

CHAPTER 39

The sun was beginning to rise. Cyrus drove, giving Kyle and me time to rest in the backseat. Kyle had draped his arm around me, and his head rested on mine as I nestled against him. No one spoke on the drive back.

Uncle Bob and Stephen were waiting for us as we pulled into the parking lot. I managed to get out of the car on my own and Uncle Bob ran up to me, pulling me into a hug. "I'm so glad you're back. I was beginning to get worried." He stepped back, looking me over. "Are you okay? You're covered in all kinds of…stuff."

I drew back for some space. "I'm fine."

"I didn't doubt she could pull it off." Stephen gave me a one-arm hug across the shoulders.

"I almost didn't. It's a good thing Cyrus and Kyle were there."

"Well, go get cleaned up and get some rest. I'll drive you home later." Uncle Bob gave me one last hug.

"You stayed here all night?"

"Of course. I wasn't going anywhere with you out there fighting those things."

"How's Aunt Helen? Have you spoken to her?"

Uncle Bob hung his head and slipped his hands into his pockets. "Not since yesterday. I will see her later after I drop you off."

Kyle took my hand. "I'll walk you to your room."

We were silent on the way inside. Once we reached my door, Kyle took my other hand in his. "That was an eventful night. I've never had one that exciting before."

"I'm still pissed at you for keeping secrets from me."

"I know. I'm so sorry, but I couldn't tell you. I hope you can forgive me."

"I'll try." Letting go of his hand, I stepped away. "Riley will be happy to see you back in one piece. Don't keep her waiting."

I went inside to take a long hot bath and go straight to bed. I slept most of the day, waking a few times from nightmares.

The last dream I had was of me dying and turning into one of those creatures. After that, I couldn't go back to sleep. I dressed and headed upstairs to see if my uncle was there. I found him and Stephen sitting in the corner of the office, playing a game of chess.

"Checkmate!" Stephen called out with a laugh.

"One of these days, I'm going to win." Uncle Bob leaned back in his chair, stretching his arms above his head.

His eyes darted in my direction. "Ah! She has awakened." He stood and glided to me. "Did you sleep well?"

"Not too much. I had nightmares."

"Yeah, Cyrus and Kyle told us what happened."

I glanced around the room. "Where is he?"

"Who?"

"Cyrus."

"Business thing." Stephen placed the pieces on the chessboard back in their starting position and stood up. "I need to get home to Suzanne. I'd like you to meet her soon. Maybe we could all get together for dinner or something."

"I'd like that."

Uncle Bob and I walked out with him. We said our goodbyes and Uncle Bob drove me home. I laid my head back against the seat, eyes closed with my sunglasses on. My eyes had always been sensitive to the sun, but lately, that sensitivity had been more intense.

"Kyle seems smitten with you."

I jerked my head up. "What?"

Uncle Bob laughed. "It's okay, Chloe."

"No, it isn't. He belongs with Riley." I laid my head against the window.

"Are you sure?"

"Yes. Can we talk about something else?"

Uncle Bob looked over his shoulder, put on the blinker, and moved into the left lane. "Erik is…"

I didn't even give Uncle Bob a chance to finish the sentence. "Nope. Different subject."

"Okay, what do you want to talk about?"

I turned in my seat, placing my knee against the console. "What are you going to tell Aunt Helen?"

"About what?"

"She needs to know the whole truth. She needs to know that other things exist and what mom said was true."

Uncle Bob glanced at me twice and then busted out laughing. "I don't think so."

"Why? You don't think she could handle it?"

"Now isn't a good time, Chloe." He patted my knee and I spun back to face the front, crossing my arms.

"Fine. I'm just tired of secrets."

"We will tell her eventually." He reached over, squeezing my shoulder. "Together."

I gave a nod and pulled my phone out to check

my messages.

"I bet you're excited to get back to work. This has been some vacation for you."

"You could say that."

Uncle Bob pulled into the driveway and I asked if he wanted to come in for dinner.

"I would, but I should get home and face the wife."

I laughed and gave him a hug. "Love you, Uncle Bob."

"Love you, too."

I waved goodbye and went in to fix spaghetti for dinner. As I was finishing putting everything together and retrieving the garlic bread from the oven, the doorbell rang. For some reason, I thought it might be Kyle, but to my surprise, it wasn't.

"Cyrus, what are you doing here?"

"We need to talk."

"Whoa, the great Cyrus wants to talk." I giggled.

Usually, he would smile, but not this time.

I stepped aside, letting him in. "Would you like to have dinner with me? I made spaghetti."

"No, thank you."

I'd never seen him like this before. He always held his head up, standing with perfect posture and square shoulders. Now, he slouched as if he was relaxed and not so rigid. Only he wasn't relaxed. He seemed nervous, a trait I didn't know he even had.

I took the edge of his jacket sleeve and led him to the couch. "What's wrong? Has something bad happened?"

He shook his head. "I need to get a few things off my chest and discuss something with you." He took a deep breath and let it out slowly. "What you did with the white energy…" Cyrus pinched the bridge of his nose. "Where did that come from?"

"I don't know. It first happened with Josephine. I thought I just used her power against her. Why do you ask?"

"After witnessing that, and knowing you have an unknown DNA strand…" Cyrus placed his head in his hands.

"Cyrus, what is it?"

"Chloe, only my kind have powers like that."

"Cyrus, I don't even know what the hell you are. Are you saying I'm related to you?"

He shook his head. "I'm a mystic, Chloe. There are many different kinds out in the world and, no, you and I are not related. But how you can be even the smallest portion of one is the question."

I rubbed my temples with the tips of my fingers for a moment and then threw my hands up. "What is a mystic?"

"Mystics are of a spiritual nature and very secretive. I have studied every religion known to man and even some that are unknown. I can change form, and when I touch people, I see a part of their lives. This is to name only a few abilities. My mother was a witch."

"Do you cast spells and perform rituals?"

"My mother did. I, on the other hand, do not. I don't flaunt my abilities or take advantage of them. I use them when necessary."

"What do you change into?"

"Last night you witnessed my true form. I've never shown it to anyone outside of my kind."

"You mean the shadowy figure with the white eyes?"

"Yes. I have also changed into a raven." He winked.

It took a moment for that response to set it, and then I got it. "You were the bird on my balcony?"

He nodded. "Indeed."

"I thought I was nuts, talking to a bird. And you understood me?"

"Yes, I understood." He stood, placed his hands in his pockets, and went over to look at the family pictures on the wall. "It isn't in my nature to kill, Chloe. And, last night was my first time doing so. I wasn't supposed to help you in any way."

"Oh, my God!" I got up from the couch, my hand over my chest. "I'm so sorry if I…"

He held up his hand, still looking ahead. "It's been hard sticking to the rules around you. One by one, you're tearing down the brick wall around me. No one has been able to that for centuries."

I was a few steps away from him. He was focusing on a picture of me and my mother from two years ago. We were on the sandy beaches of Florida on vacation. It was before my mother started her chemotherapy. She wanted one last trip before her health went downhill.

"Is that why you've been acting so strange around me?"

"In a way."

This conversation was leading to the one question that had been weighing on my mind during the last few days. I had to ask. "Cyrus, are you…do you have feelings for me?"

He sighed, stepping away from the wall and walking around behind the couch. "My feelings for you are of a spiritual nature. Like a mentor. Mystics tend to live a very long life if they stay with their own kind. If not, their powers weaken and their life spans are shortened."

"Why? Is it a rule?"

"It isn't a rule. Some have strayed. I didn't believe it until I learned it the hard way." Cyrus pinched the bridge of his nose. "Anyway, in time I got my powers back."

I stood there dumbfounded. "What happened?"

"I'd rather not speak about it. This is the life I choose to live."

"So, do you not have anyone of your own kind?"

He shook his head. "No one of interest. But enough about me." He looked over his shoulder and toward the kitchen. "You want to have your dinner? I'm sure it's cold by now."

"Only if you join me."

He held out his arm and escorted me into the kitchen. We both made a plate and sat in the dining room. I handed Cyrus a bottle of red wine. He kindly opened it and poured us each a glass.

"This feels like a date."

Cyrus tiled his head and handed me a glass. "No. It isn't a date." He raised his glass to make a toast. "Here's to your newfound life." He took a sip.

"Here's to you finding love." I raised my glass and took a mouthful. I wasn't in a sipping mood. Not after the week I'd had.

"Not going to happen, Chloe."

"Yes, it can if you let it. So what if your powers weaken? You deserve to be happy. Sometimes it's a sacrifice we all have to make." I swirled the noodles around my fork and shoved them into my mouth.

"Like you did with Drake?"

I slurped up the dangling noodle and let out a cough. "Excuse me?"

"You didn't take a chance at happiness with Drake."

"I have a good reason."

"As do I."

I shook my head, wiping my mouth with a napkin. "Not the same thing."

"Explain to me how it isn't?" Cyrus rested his

elbows on the table, interlocking his fingers as he always did when he was serious.

I poured another glass of wine and gulped it down. "Do you know about lycan mates?"

He bowed his head in acknowledgment of what I was asking.

"Drake isn't the one for me, Cyrus. If I dated him, it would be a mistake. I find him extremely attractive, yes. But I'm not in love with him." I dipped my garlic bread in the sauce and took a bite.

Cyrus raised an eyebrow and picked up his fork, shoving it into a pile of noodles and slurping them into his mouth. A bit of sauce lingered on his lips.

I laughed and picked up a napkin. Reaching out, I dabbed the corner of his mouth.

I scooped up the last of the sauce on my plate with a slice of garlic bread and washed it down with one more glass of wine. At least this time I wasn't feeling the aftereffects from three glasses like I did last time.

"Cyrus, is my father part mystic?"

He finished off the last of his food and wine, wiped his mouth on the napkin, and sat back in the chair. "First of all, I never said you were a mystic. That's just your assumption. Stephen had his blood drawn to get verification, and he is a full-blooded lycan."

Cyrus reached out and touched my hand. "I don't know what is going on, but I'm going to do my best to find the answers. I just have to be careful."

"Why?"

"Because our kind does not crossbreed. If the council were to find out what you are…"

I waited for him to finish his sentence. He never did. But, I knew what he would have said. Chances were good this council would kill me or keep me prisoner somewhere.

"I'm concerned for you, Cyrus."

He glanced at me and let out a laugh. “Me? Why me?”

“Wouldn’t you be punished for protecting someone like me?”

He bowed his head. “Indeed. But, you are an innocent. You didn’t ask for this kind of life. It chose you and we need to figure out why.”

“Do you think I have a higher purpose? You know how certain things skip generations and then *boom* you have a lucky winner?”

“It’s possible. But, what about your mother?”

“What about her?”

Cyrus and I stared at each other. I let out a chuckle. “I highly doubt I inherited anything of the sort from my mother.”

“Are you sure?”

“Yes, I am sure.”

“Maybe you should look into it.”

“Maybe I will.”

Picking up the bottle of wine, I asked if he wanted a refill.

“No. I’ve had plenty.” He scooted the chair back and picked up his plate, taking it to the kitchen. “Thank you for dinner.”

“Thank you for finally telling me what you are. You know what this means, though?”

“No.”

“It means I can’t give you shit over it.”

I smiled and followed Cyrus outside. “Should you be traveling after drinking?”

Cyrus’s shoulders bounced a little as he gave a small chuckle. “You and your sense of humor.” He brought my hand to his lips. “See you soon, Chloe.”

I watched Cyrus disappear into the shadows of the night and thought about how I could be a threat to others. I certainly was for the embalmers. Maybe some of the creatures out there would see me as useful. But, would it be for the greater good or evil?

Only time would tell what fate had in store for me as I began the next chapter of my new life.

ABOUT THE AUTHOR

Christine Cofer lives in a rural area of Missouri with her husband and son, along with her dog, cat, and rabbit. She has an Associate Degree of Applied Science. She has channeled her love for the supernatural to create a world of self-driven characters. What started out as a short story--for fun--has grown into something more.

Visit her site at christinecofer.wordpress.com or follow on social media at

christinecofer.wordpress.com
facebook.com/christine.cofer

Made in the USA
Columbia, SC
12 November 2019

82932199R00169